FINE LINE

IRONS AND WORKS: KEY LARGO

E.M. LINDSEY

Fine Line
E.M. Lindsey

Editing: Sandra with One Love Editing
Cover: Ozark Witch Cover Design
Photographer: Wander Aguiar

Content warning: This book contains audism, ableism and ableist language, minor injuries, an HIV scare, HIV positive side character, and mentions of past childhood abuse and neglect.

EM LINDSEY LINKS

EM's Discord

EM's Patreon

EM Lindsey's Website

Free Short Stories

EM Lindsey's Amazon Account

EM Lindsey on Instagram

EM Lindsey on Bookbub

1

BEN BLAMED INSTAGRAM AND THE HIPSTER BULLSHIT OF THE OLDER GEN Z for making people think Key Largo was some tropical paradise that looked exactly like Bali. They drove in expecting overwater bungalows and the crisp, Instagram Blue Caribbean sea. Instead, they got mangroves, and water a sort of earthy green, thanks to everything growing beneath the surface, and vegetation so thick you couldn't see the water until you pushed through the trees and ended up on the waveless shores.

It was *technically* a tropical island. It was close enough to the equator that the temperature didn't change significantly throughout the year. He could wear shorts and sandals anytime he wanted. He spent the holidays on his boat with a little hibachi grill, and he spent most mornings chasing iguanas off the railings of his hotel rooms because the dumbass tourists always tried to fucking pet them and feed them pieces of their Starbucks croissants.

But it wasn't *paradise.*

It was humid, and the mosquitos were year-round little blood-sucking monsters that descended at sunset, leaving him with swollen, itchy ankles. And the *tourists.* Every day of every week of every goddamn month was tourist season. Not that he could complain about that one. Tourists were how he survived.

That was the curse of a crappy motel owner whose property overlooked one of the narrow, mangrove-lined canals that led to open water. He had to deal with people renting Jet Skis who pretended like they had any idea how to ride them, forcing him to perform at least half a dozen rescues a day, and kids who thought stand-up paddleboards looked easy, then realized it required actual balance.

Ben wasn't really built for that kind of life. He'd stumbled into hotel ownership after his older brother died and his parents abandoned the place they'd raised him and Levi. He'd been living in Orlando, dealing with the pain while drowning himself in his job for a certain theme park he was never allowed to talk about, thanks to the NDA he'd signed. He was actually at work, feeling more and more like a corporate zombie, when his mom sent him a FaceTime request.

"I think we're going to put the motel on the market and move to Brooklyn, but your dad doesn't want it to go to some stranger. He'd really like it if you'd take over so we don't lose what we have left of Levi's memories."

He knew it was mostly her grief talking.

His own had led him to do some wild things, like pierce his tongue and buy a drum set he never touched because even when he took his cochlear implants off, the loud noise fucked with his equilibrium. He also spent a few months drinking and crying and driving to Daytona Beach to scream at the ocean until he realized none of that shit would bring Levi back.

Levi had escaped the monotony of pandering to tourists the moment he turned eighteen, and while they'd spent a good portion of their childhood, it hadn't held the important memories Ben kept of Levi. That quiet, now-empty space in his head was reserved for the long weekends when Levi would ride his bike down to Orlando to visit him and his insistence he play wingman for Ben at the gay bars in spite of the fact that he was terrible at it. And the early mornings where neither one of them had slept, sitting on the sofa with ice cream and the TV on, and easy ASL conversations between them.

But his parents hadn't been part of that, so Ben understood why they were reluctant to let go, even if they couldn't stay at the motel any longer. His PR job no longer held interest for him, so when his parents made him the offer of taking over the motel, he turned in his two-week notice, then packed his things into a Pod and drove his happy ass across the bridge to the place he'd once called home.

He remembered when his parents had bought the motel. He and Levi were still in middle school, which meant they had to transfer and be new kids all over again. It was worse for Ben, being Deaf with his accent, which all the kids found fascinating until they didn't. Until they started pushing him around because he was small and looked smart, even though his raging inability to stay focused made sure he barely scraped by with a C average.

But his parents hadn't noticed any of that. They'd been too damned excited to start that little venture. His last grandfather had died and left their family an inheritance and a request that they do something meaningful with it. His parents used it to buy a set of condos that were on the verge of being condemned thanks to repeated hurricane damage. They rebuilt and repurposed it into a hotel and had a steady stream of guests from the first of the year to the end.

So, not only was he the weird, new Deaf kid, but he was the weird, new Deaf kid who lived in a motel and could never have friends over because his parents forced him to work the sports rental kiosk every waking hour he had free.

When he was ready for college, he took a page out of Levi's book and fled like a cartoon whose ass had caught fire.

He never expected to come back.

But he also never expected Levi to do something like drink a fifth of Jim Beam and get behind the wheel of his motorcycle after his girlfriend dumped him. He didn't expect to be twenty-seven, standing at the edge of Levi's grave and watching as they lowered him down, knowing Levi wouldn't be there for any more important milestones in his life.

The pain wasn't less now, but it was easier to handle. His brain managed to give him a decent shot of endorphins every morning, which got him through the day, and eventually, he just went...numb. Or something like it.

He spent his days cleaning rooms and trying to train his new part-time accountant on all the books. He spent most nights watching TV until he passed out on the couch and occasional ones in wild sex with the only other Deaf guy who was around.

He'd met Theo, the ridiculously hot pilot who spent most of his time flying rich guys to the private airfield, one night at a bar. Theo had spotted his cochlear implants, hesitantly asked if he could sign, and somehow, they ended up making out in a bathroom stall until the bar manager kicked them out. Luckily, Ben's motel wasn't too far. Ben had woken up the next morning to an empty bed and a note from Theo saying he wasn't interested in a relationship, but he'd like to see Ben again soon.

That had worked perfectly for him. At that time, he didn't want to date. He just wanted someone to take his mind off how much the hole in his chest shaped like his brother hurt.

After almost a year, though, sex with Theo was starting to feel a bit more...empty.

He could feel a pressing loneliness that had nothing to do with grief. It was an old, familiar friend who had been with him while he was living and working in Orlando. The little voice inside him that told him he wanted more than just casual hookups and wild flings. Ben had always been the long-term kind of guy, which wasn't conducive to young queer culture in his generation. Whenever he mentioned he thought about marriage and commitment to his dates, they looked at him like he had some sort of plague that might be catching.

A few of his friends took pity on him and told him that eventually he'd reach an age where more guys would be ready to settle down and get serious. But he didn't want to resign himself to two decades of being alone before someone was willing to give up the partying ghost and put a ring on it.

Or...whatever the kids were calling it these days. But it was what it was. He couldn't change other people to suit his needs, so he accepted life for what it was. For now, he had Theo. An amazing friend and a great hookup and the perfect end to a long day.

His doorbell flashed around eight, and he grabbed his phone instead of getting up because he was feeling lazy and full from the sushi delivery he'd consumed.

Ben: Door's open.

Theo walked in a second later, looking harried from a long week of jetting across the US, ferrying the rich and not-so-famous from one end of the country to the other. He was ridiculously hot in spite of his jet lag, and Ben felt his dick take immediate interest as Theo lifted up his shirt and scratched his belly with one hand while lifting the other. 'What's up?'

Ben shrugged. 'Nothing. Hungry? I ordered sushi and got you a bento bowl.'

Theo grinned and hopped over the coffee table with a renewed burst of energy, pinning Ben to the sofa and kissing his neck. "Mm," Theo groaned aloud. Ben didn't have his implants on, so he could only feel the vibrations, but Theo also didn't speak, so he knew he wasn't talking. Theo pulled back. 'Salmon?'

'Yeah,' Ben said, nodding his fist. 'Use the wood chopsticks, though. I don't want to do more dishes.'

'Lazy asshole,' Theo shot over his shoulder as he shuffled into the little kitchenette. Not for the first time, Ben thought maybe he should consider moving out of the motel. Not just from the whole reliving his high school days like some kind of loser, but also, he was a grown-ass man. At twenty-eight, he should probably have, like, a dishwasher and a four-burner stove. He should have a dining room table and a sofa that didn't match the other ones in the sixteen other units.

He should have walls that weren't so thin he could smell every bong hit the guests took next door.

Theo wasn't someone who was going to care where he lived. *He* got a kick out of it. But his situation definitely wasn't marriage material, and that was going to matter if Ben met anyone he was actually interested in.

Ben shifted over when Theo appeared, his little plastic bowl clenched in his hands, the chopsticks clenched between his teeth. He settled down with a happy wiggle, then freed his teeth so he could tear open the little packet of soy sauce.

'So,' Theo signed after shoveling a massive bite into his mouth, 'give me gossip. Did you find any corpses this week?' Theo was obsessed with the idea of a guest dying because all he watched were crime shows, and he seemed to think that was a real and constant issue for Ben.

He'd tried to explain to Theo once that he ran a tiny motel on the side of the road, not some big resort with rich old men in the throes of heart failure. That shit did happen, just not to him. And he'd prefer it to stay that way.

Kicking his feet up on the table, he twisted his body to better face Theo. Being near him brought up old feelings of inadequacy in his own deafness, though he tried to keep that shit to himself most days. He hadn't learned to sign until college, and half the shit about Deaf culture still confused him.

It was something he bore with a sort of quiet smile and lies tripping off his tongue as readily as the truth. *Sure*, he'd tell anyone who asked. *I love being part of both worlds.*

In reality, he felt like an outsider on both sides of the line, and the only thing that made it feel better was the nights Theo was behind him, railing him into oblivion. If only Theo would have been a better boyfriend. Life would have been a lot easier that way.

'You're giving me the look,' Theo pointed out.

Ben sighed. 'Are we fucking tonight?'

At that, Theo's grin went predatory. 'How much do you want this dick, gorgeous?'

Ben shivered. That was the problem right there. Not just how fucking filthy Theo was but also how sweet. How he offered Ben bits and pieces of what he was so desperately craving without the promise it could ever be something more.

He wanted to be precious to someone, damn it. He wanted to be as adored as he was capable of adoring someone. He wanted to be cherished. Instead, he was a twenty-eight-year-old gay man on someone else's timeline for romance, and it made him want to scream.

So he would, but not in the way that would make him feel better in the end.

Ben woke alone the way he always did when Theo fucked him into unconsciousness. He had a vague memory of the bed shifting and of cracking open one eye to see Theo rummaging around the room for his discarded clothes. Ben had long since stopped asking him to stay over because the answer was always a sweet kiss and a polite decline, and he got his feelings hurt every single time, despite knowing Theo's rule.

Starfishing, he stretched his back and reveled in the ache in his ass because Theo always left a mark behind. It was something he particularly enjoyed, so he basked in it before finally rolling off the side of the bed and shuffling to the bathroom. The shower was a little on the warm side, which didn't feel great with how humid it already was, but it was nice to get clean.

He had a long day of mundane tasks, just like every other morning, and he wanted to check on Aya, who was running the front desk that morning. She was the only other person who had stayed on after his parents bailed in their grief, and he was eternally grateful because he really didn't want to do this alone.

He was struggling to retain housekeeping staff as it was, and for the last six months, he and Aya had been picking up the slack. Which, he realized with a small groan, was his morning task. He got dressed in his worst pair of jeans and a motel-branded T-shirt, then slipped his feet into his work boots.

He had a long debate with himself about food, then decided there were probably some mostly-not-stale pastries in the lobby—their sad mockery of a continental breakfast. Swiping his processors off the table, he shoved his box of batteries into his pocket, then headed out the door.

The thick morning air hit him in the face, and he grimaced as he pressed his hand to the wood and waited to feel the lock engaged. He took one step forward, then froze when his boot slid through something...thick. And wet.

Please be iguana shit. Please be iguana shit.

What even was his life that that was his morning mantra?

He held his breath and looked down, his heart sinking when he realized that yeah, it was shit, but it was definitely not from an iguana. It was the phantom dog who targeted his doorstep every goddamn time. This was the fourth time in two weeks it had left him a goddamn gift on his front stoop, and he'd done everything to try and catch the little bastard, but to no avail.

Stomping through the little overhang, he shoved his foot into a pile of leaves and began to scrape his heel. He glanced over to his boat to find three of his morning iguanas lounging.

"No chance you wanna keep watch for that little fucker, is there?" he asked. His voice always felt strange and thick when he couldn't hear it, and he wasn't sure if he was speaking loud enough for the little bastards to hear him. Not that it mattered.

Even if they could understand, they wouldn't help. They were dickheads like that.

With a sigh, he turned, then jumped half a foot when he noticed a guy standing two feet away, his mouth moving with some morning rant. Ben recognized him from the check-in two weeks prior. The guy had booked the room next to Ben for three months, and he remembered being both turned on and a little scared because the stranger looked intimidating as hell.

He was tall, broad, covered in tattoos, his hair kind of shaggy and always falling into his eyes. His name was Paris—not something Ben was going to forget on a whim—and he was unfairly hot. Like, to the point it made Ben uncomfortable.

Right then, he looked like he wanted to wrap his hands around Ben's neck and start choking him. And not in the fun way.

Ben watched his lips for a long moment, but Paris was too far into his tirade for Ben to catch more than a few words, so he held up his finger, then dug his processors out of his pocket and switched them on.

It always took a bit for the world to calibrate and for his brain to start processing noise into sound, and he saw the look of shame on Paris's face when he realized what was happening.

"Sorry," Ben said. "I'm getting a slow start. Just give it a..." Suddenly, there was the wind, and birds in the distance, and Paris's stuttered breathing. "Okay. Sorry. You were yelling at me?"

Paris took a step back and cleared his throat. "Uh. Just." He rubbed the back of his neck, and he looked even more embarrassed, which was...interesting.

"Hey, what's up?" Ben asked, a little softer this time. "Is everything okay?"

Paris tugged on the lapels of his leather jacket, and Ben was tempted to ask why the fuck he was wearing that when it was so goddamn swampy, but he kept that to himself. "The walls here are thin."

Ben tried not to sigh. "I know. Trust me. The amount of contact high I almost get every time some stoner kids from Miami visit..."

Paris's gaze flicked toward the side of Ben's head, and Ben knew what he was looking at, and his chest burned. “The walls are thin,” he repeated.

Ben blinked slowly. “Yes. I *know*. Is there something specific you need me to do about it? I could probably move you to an end unit if you—”

“No,” Paris said, then took a step back. “I...forget I said anything.” He turned and started to walk off, then froze and glanced over his shoulder. “Do you know there’s a dog that keeps shitting on the sidewalk?”

Ben groaned and looked down at his shoe. “Yeah. Yeah, I’m afraid I do.”

“Okay, then,” Paris said, and a second later, he was gone.

Ben stared at him for another long moment before shaking his head. “Fucking weird guy.” And absurdly hot, but he wasn’t going to say that aloud and risk Paris being around the corner. With a sigh, he turned back around to find the hose so he could clean himself off and then get back to his never-ending work.

2

THERE WAS A HANDFUL OF SMELLS THAT MADE PARIS FEEL LIKE HE WAS home. One was the scent of construction. Freshly mixed concrete and wood shavings, and the metal tang of a nail gun. Sometimes it was fresh paint, and tile grout, and a thick layer of floor sealant.

The other was the scent of tattoo ink, Green Soap, witch hazel, and even the sting of rubbing alcohol. That with the buzzing sound of a tattoo machine and the creak of leather on a chair, and he was transported to the only place in the world that felt safe.

Tattooing had saved his life. Literally. It had been the bridge between eating and not eating. Between having a roof over his head and making sure his little brother had somewhere soft and kind to live, and being homeless and watching some asshole from the state take Max away from him.

He was sixteen with a fake ID when he'd gotten the apprenticeship. He was living in a fucking hovel in La Mesa, and he worked overnights stocking at Walmart, the breakfast ship at Guero's Breakfast Burrito's, and then his evenings doing all the bitch work around Bonsai Tattoo.

He learned piercings first, because it was quickest, and the first time he pushed a needle through some waify-thin co-ed's navel, he knew that his life had changed. He saw the startled pain in her eyes and the sudden rush of endorphins. He watched as a tremor of disbelief shot through her as she turned from left to right in the mirror, admiring her new metal.

It was the same feeling the first time he laid needles to his boss's skin and etched out an image that would be there for the rest of his life. Jax didn't believe in tattoo removal, so anything Paris put on there would be inked forever. Even if Jax covered it up—and he had a fuckload of cover-ups—it would still be there.

Paris didn't really know what the fuck to do with that feeling except embrace it and work his ass off to get better.

And he did.

He'd gone from wonky Sailor Jerry style to photorealistic portraits, which had earned him some kind of notoriety around the world. He had appointments booked years in advance from people who flew to the West Coast just to see him. He had money, and he got custody of his little brother. They rented a nice house and bought his dream truck, and he'd forgotten what hunger pangs felt like except on days when he was so busy he forgot to eat.

He knew what it was like to be lonely, but that was easy to shut down. He could tuck that garbage emotion away in a tiny box inside the shadows of his mind because everything else was so much better.

Until it wasn't.

Until he realized that everything around them was starting to feel mundane and tired. He could even see the pressure weighing down on Max as the years crept by. Paris was turning into an Old Green Man but without any kind of real experience. They never left the damn valley. They just...settled, and that was killing him.

It was why the day Zeke and Tony showed up from their little place in Colorado and asked Paris if he might be interested in packing up his life and turning his shit entirely upside down for a dream, he said yes. It was why he looked at Max and saw the hope in his brother's eyes, and he didn't hesitate to burn his life to the ground just to be able to feel something new again.

He hadn't been sure what the fuck to expect out of Key Largo. The most he knew about it was some song on the radio his stepmom used to play when she was on one of her white wine binges. She'd put on some flowy skirt and dance around their house, smiling at Paris like she gave a shit about him.

But she hadn't. No one had. And that was fine.

But he was starting to wonder if all that was about to change as he and Max drove over the long bridge and saw the open water. It was nothing like the West Coast, and he realized that was the only thing that mattered. That, and the look of wonder on Max's face. Neither of them was young anymore. Max had apprenticed under him a year after he graduated from the community college's culinary program and failed miserably trying to work in a kitchen.

They spent two decades in California building their brand at Bonsai, and they were both a little jaded. But Max had retained a sort of hopeful outlook on life, which Paris could never understand, but he wanted to protect it. If the shit their dad and stepmom put them through could bounce off Max and allow him to have healthy, stable relationships, Paris would fight to the death to make sure nothing ever took that away from his brother.

And he wanted to think that maybe this place—this new shop—was the catalyst to Max's happily ever after.

Paris would breathe easy if he got to see that happen.

Shoving his keys into his pocket, Paris stared up at the newly hung sign on the building. It was made from wrought iron, and it didn't really stand out, but he didn't mind that. They weren't really flashy guys. The handful who had been poached from Bonsai had been the quiet sort, which was why Paris got along with them so well over the years.

It felt nice to bring part of his old world with him—the part that didn't make him want to pull his own face off—and it didn't feel as strange. Even if the parent shop had a long, long history that didn't belong to any of them.

Zeke was the only one with any real connection to the original Irons and Works. After leaving Bonsai, he almost settled in Colorado, but Paris didn't need to see him there to know that Zeke wasn't going to feel settled in the mountains. The guy had spent all of his free time on his damn surfboard. There was no way he was giving up the ocean.

Even if he was trading waves for Jet Skis and paddleboards.

Paris shoved his shades up into his hair, then pulled the shop door open. It was almost time for their grand opening, but it was hard to visualize it since it was still half a mess. But his appointment book was already full for the last half of the year, and he knew Max was struggling to find open spots in his.

He imagined the other guys were the same. Even the fresh meat who had just been hired on to apprentice with them were probably struggling to make room for walk-ins.

"Yo! You're in early."

Paris turned to find Tony, Irons and Works' owner, and Jamie, the new part-timer who'd come over from South Carolina. They were both leaning against the newly installed reception counter, which had glass display windows for art any of the guys wanted to sell. The only thing in it right then were two long strips of black velvet liner, but he could imagine some of his pieces sitting there.

Paris tried for a smile, only because it was impossible for anyone not to smile at Tony. The guy was fucking infectious like a goddamn happiness plague, and Paris could never shake it off. "Yeah. My fucking hotel has walls made out of goddamn cardboard, I swear."

Tony grimaced. "Rough."

"You have no idea." The one thing Paris had done his best not to think about on the drive over was his neighbor—who also happened to be the motel manager or whatever. He knew the guy's name was Ben, thanks to the badge he wore at the desk. He was short and muscular, tanned from how much time he spent on the water. His hair was brown with golden highlights—something Paris couldn't believe he'd noticed.

He was deaf, but he wore big-ass hearing aid things, but he was pretty sure that was the problem.

Not that the guy was deaf, but that he had no fucking idea how loud he was.

He and his hookup, boyfriend—whatever—had been going at it all night. They were loud and enthusiastic, and eventually, Paris had to turn on his TV to drown them out. He'd ended up rubbing one out, unable to keep his dick soft with the impromptu porn going on, and then he passed out and woke up to blissful silence at midnight.

Which was great, until the fuckers next door also woke up and started going at it again.

Eventually, he just left, storming up and down the neighborhood streets until he was so exhausted he had no choice but to go unconscious. He woke again to the sound of Ben in the shower, and that was the point he gave up on any idea of getting any rest.

The sleep deprivation left him pissed as fuck, and he was bound and determined to tell the little fucker that while he was thrilled that their relationship was so goddamn healthy, people needed to get some shut-eye. But it only took a second to realize that Ben had no idea Paris could hear him, and Paris couldn't get the words out.

To put the cherry on the fucking cake, he'd thoroughly embarrassed himself by talking about dog shit before he fled into the morning.

"Paris?"

He glanced up and realized he'd zoned out. "Sorry. I got about two hours of actual sleep last night. My neighbor had someone over, and they were, uh..."

Jamie grinned widely. "Smashing 'til dawn?"

"Seriously?" Paris asked flatly.

"That's what the kids are calling it these days," Tony answered sagely. "I should know. I'm surrounded by them."

Paris did his best not to shudder, but a grip of kids sounded like a fucking nightmare—even if they weren't his. He was barely functional as a child, let alone trying to raise one. Max had been enough experience for the rest of his literal eternity, and they were only six years apart.

"Anyway, I haven't had coffee yet, and I feel like I'm going to lose my mind," Paris said.

Jamie immediately looked excited. "Oh shit. Let's head over to Midnight Snack. They have a brunch menu now *and* this dulce de leche coffee that I would literally kill someone for."

"Let's not get that dramatic," Tony said, clapping Jamie on the shoulder, "but I'm in. I need to live it up before I get home and Kat forbids me from eating out."

Once again, Paris hid his grimace and thought about the freedom of not being chained to a partner and their whims. But maybe he was being a little unfair. Granted, most of his attitude had to do with the man his father had become after marrying their stepmom and having kids with her. The moment that happened, Paris and Max had become the shameful extras. The castoffs from their dad's former life.

And Helen had made sure they knew it every single minute of every single day.

He knew he shouldn't let that dictate how he felt about other couples, but it was hard to see them so happy and not assume it came at the expense of other people being neglected and treated like shit.

"How far is this place?" Tony was asking as they headed for the door. He'd only just arrived a few days ago, so he was getting caught up and would be hanging out for the first two weeks that the shop was running.

Paris thought maybe it would feel a little claustrophobic, having the Big Boss hovering over them, but Tony's presence was like a goddamn warm hug, and it was throwing Paris for a loop. He liked the guys he worked with. A lot.

But he had no idea what to do with this sort of unconditional affection Tony seemed to give out as easily as breathing.

"It's right there," Jamie said, shielding his eyes and pointing two little shopping strips down.

Key Largo wasn't the most walkable place in Florida, but there was a cluster of restaurants and little surf shops in the area that Paris was getting to know. He hadn't really been much of a water guy when he was in California. Everyone assumed that if you lived on the coast there, you were a surfer with ready access to the beach.

For him, it was an hour and fifteen minutes to Pacific Beach, and that was on a good day, which didn't exist with the SoCal freeway system. If it wasn't tourists, it was rush hour, and he never had the patience for it.

Things here were different, though. Calmer. More relaxing. He'd woken up more than once to peer out the window and see Ben either on his boat trying to chase off iguanas that should be in a goddamn zoo or hopping on one of the kayaks and cruising out into the open water.

Paris was starting to get the itch to try new things, and it was a sensation he wasn't entirely comfortable with.

He snapped back to the conversation when Tony elbowed him, and he grinned like he hadn't lost the thread again. Neither he nor Jamie seemed to notice—and if they did, they didn't care—so he walked along and nodded and smiled in all the right places.

Jamie got the door at the restaurant and held it open, and Paris stepped in. He'd been there a few times before—the owner a really friendly guy who liked to stop and chat with people after they ate—and Paris didn't actually mind that. Jeremiah wasn't nosy like a lot of people in the area were, and he'd even made an appointment with Linc to get his eyebrow pierced during their grand opening.

Paris found an open table near the window, taking a seat on one of the white benches while Jamie and Tony squeezed into the one opposite him. The menus were stacked against the wall, and Paris grabbed one, scanning the large print next to artistically done photos of the sex-innuendo food.

"Bro, look at the new special. French Maid Toast," Jamie said with a groan. "Nutella and bananas. Sign me the fuck up."

Paris wasn't the kind of person who ever really indulged in sweets. He didn't have a problem with sugar, but he'd grown up not being allowed to touch anything with any sort of flavor, and while Max had binged on every single candy bar he could get his hands on the moment Paris had gotten him out of that house, Paris had just... kept to his routine. Sweets and snacks all felt like forbidden fruit, but he wasn't tempted the way he should have been. That was probably his first sign that he was fucked-up, but he was too busy to care.

And now...well. Now, it was all one big, annoying habit.

He eyed the omelets and settled on Debbie Does Denver before moving to the coffee menu. "I need something that's going to peel the lining from my stomach."

Tony snorted a laugh. "Midnight Mass looks good. It says it's Turkish, and I heard that shit is strong."

"If it's made right," Jamie said, which told Paris that the guy had grown up with a silver spoon tucked neatly between his front teeth. But he couldn't hate the guy for it. Jamie was one of the kindest guys Paris had ever met. Jamie had been open about being tormented as a kid for coming out as trans when he was in grade school. Instead of going the opposite way and becoming a dickhead, Jamie had become the dad friend to everyone, going out of his way to comfort anyone he thought might be in pain. "You should try it. You look like you need some serious caffeine."

"I love your polite way of telling me I look like absolute shit," Paris said as he set his menu back and leaned his head against the soft cushion of the booth, closing his eyes.

"I wouldn't say shit," came another voice that Paris recognized. He opened one eye to see Jeremiah standing there with one hand on his hip. He was wearing a chef's coat, which was open, showing off a stained white T-shirt, and he was grinning down at them, his eyes wide behind his thick glasses. "I'd say you look like you had a rough night. Or maybe a good one."

"His neighbor did. Kept him up," Jamie said with a fake somber tone.

Paris flipped him off and sat up straight. "Tell me this Midnight Mass coffee is gonna keep my ass awake for the day."

"For a few hours, at least," Jeremiah said with a wink. He took the rest of their orders, then made his way back into the kitchen, knocking a chair over with his hip on the way.

"Dude's clumsier than...I don't know, some Southern phrase James would say," Tony said.

Paris only knew of James by proxy—the wild, Southern beau who'd lost both legs in a military accident. All the guys from Denver had plans to visit the shop and tattoo with them all for a few days. It had been Tony's request so the rest of the West Coasters could actually get to know the veterans who'd started their brand.

Paris was keeping it to himself, but he was looking forward to it. He wasn't sure it would change anything for any of them, but at the very least, he could allow himself a little spark of hope that this was exactly what he and Max needed.

The coffee did help. At least, it helped enough for Paris to get through the early afternoon of setting up his stall and making sure he had everything he needed. He could afford to live off a handful of clients a week, but he wanted to do something better in Key Largo. He wanted to build something stable. Even if it wasn't a home, he wanted it to feel that way.

Max had, of course, wasted no time settling in. He started rooming with another one of the former other Bonsai artists, Felix, who needed the help around his house. Max was a bleeding-heart sort of guy who didn't hesitate when Felix announced he was looking for a roommate. The guy had some neurological condition, and about six months after he started renting a stall at Bonsai, he had some sort of massive seizure that almost ruined his brain.

He came back to work the same artist as before, but his visual memory was fucked. It reminded Paris of some movie where the guy couldn't recall events the day after they happened—except for Felix, he couldn't remember anyone's face. He'd been terrified at first, but more than that, he was being smothered by his family, who were making it damn near impossible for him to learn how to cope.

So when Zeke showed up with the offer to move, Felix had pulled Max aside and asked him quietly if he'd be willing to stay with him. Max hadn't hesitated, and Paris couldn't blame him for it. He would forever be in awe of his brother's kindness and how many people turned to him for help.

So they'd moved, and Max and Felix had gotten a place together, and Paris had made the mistake of getting a cheap motel room with paper-thin walls and a neighbor so hot it drove him to distraction. He was now realizing he couldn't keep living like this. He needed to move, and he needed to do it soon.

It would require him to work his fingers down to the bone. It would require stuffing his schedule and eating like shit and praying for sleep so he could make sure he had a down payment big enough to secure a loan. And that required a bit longer in that motel by the water, listening to the owner get railed all night long.

"Yo. Neighbor."

Paris looked up from his stool to find Harley leaning over the short partition. Harley was deceptive. At first glance, he seemed average. Then he stood up, and suddenly, he was broad and was so goddamn tall most people got a pinched neck from staring up at him.

He was one of the few guys who hadn't come from Bonsai. He'd been at the shop Zeke apprenticed at when he was in DC, and while Paris was a little unsure about him, he turned out to be nice. And while he didn't let Paris get away with being a dickhead in his worst moods, he had more patience for it than most people.

"You all set?" Paris asked, standing up and stretching his back.

His coffee was starting to wear off, and he couldn't stop dreaming of a nice, long nap. Maybe if he got some shut-eye in the afternoon, he wouldn't feel so wrecked if Ben had his "friend" over that night.

"Yeah. I was about to grab some tacos or something. I told Tony I'd help him with the flooring in the drawing room. Wanna come along?"

Paris shook his head, and when Harley gave him a look, he put his hands up in surrender. "I'm not being an ass. I need to catch a nap, or I'm gonna collapse."

Harley smirked. "Yeah. Heard about your neighbor."

"Jesus, y'all are worse than a knitting circle," Paris complained, reaching for his keys.

"You ever see that guy's dick in person, be sure to let me know. I have to live vicariously. Ever since Kaylee and I split up, I've been in a dry spell. In every way you can imagine."

Paris grimaced. "Seriously? I'm pretty sure you can get all the sex gossip you want through Linc. He and Ryder can't seem to stop sucking face every time they're within five miles of each other."

Harley laughed. "They're cute."

Paris certainly wouldn't call it cute. He called it a quiet torture that constantly reminded him of how lonely he was. But luckily, most of the guys at the shop were either casually dating or tragically single, and it made him feel less alone.

Paris startled when Harley clapped his hands, but the bigger man didn't seem to notice. "Well, if you change your mind, you know where to find us."

Paris nodded as he grabbed his phone off the desk and checked it for messages. There was one from Max letting him know he'd be by with dinner later, and that was it. But then again, that had been his life for the last twenty years. He didn't make friends easily, and the ones he did tended to abandon ship when they realized he really was a giant, grumpy asshole who had no plans to change.

"I'll probably be by later. Max is gonna swing by for dinner, so I'll try and talk him into stopping by."

Harley grinned. "Love that kid. Check you later."

It settled something in Paris to know that all these guys loved his brother as much as he did, and that feeling stayed with him on the drive back to the motel. The parking lot was fairly empty, so he was able to snag one of the overhang spots next to his unit, and he pawed around for his room key before he found it in the glove box.

He was looking forward to a day when he could use a real key in his real house and not survive with a tiny little kitchenette and a shower with the worst water pressure in the world. He hadn't gotten brave enough to look at real estate yet, but the more time that passed, the more desperate he was starting to feel.

Stepping out of his truck, he headed for the door, then froze when he heard a loud, rhythmic thud and soft swearing from the other side of the wall. He told himself to keep walking. This wasn't his business, but Paris had always been pretty crap about keeping his nose where it belonged.

He moved around the corner where the water rental kiosk sat, and it took him a second to find what was happening. Ben was there, standing over his row of kayaks, smacking one of them repeatedly with a broom.

Paris reacted before he could stop himself. "Uh. What are you doing?"

Ben whipped around with his free hand pressed to his chest. "Jesus, you scared me."

It was obvious by the following silence that Ben hadn't understood him, so he cleared his throat. "Why...uh...why are you beating your kayak with a broom?"

His gaze flicked down to the broom, and even from where he was standing, Paris could see the guy blush as he offered a sheepish grin. "I—yeah. So, there's this asshole iguana who likes to hide in there and bite the tourists. I'm not really looking for that kind of drama right now, you know?"

Paris walked forward and peered into the little hole where the seat was. He could see the fucker crouched in the nook, more orange than it was green, its little eyes telling Paris it wouldn't hesitate to commit murder.

"You want some help?" he offered, hating himself since this was the guy responsible for his lack of sleep.

Ben's face softened. "Better not. I don't want to get sued if this asshole takes a chunk out of you."

Paris felt a little insulted that Ben thought he'd sue him, but Paris also knew he hadn't been the most friendly of guests either. "I wouldn't sue you, trust me."

Ben hesitated, his fingers drumming on the broom handle. "If you're sure...?"

Paris rolled his eyes. "Fuck yeah, man. If anything, it'll be a hilarious story to tell the guys later. Here." He wriggled his fingers until Ben relinquished the broom, then walked over to the other side of the kayak and stuck the handle in. "Get out, you little fucker!" He smacked the handle on the sides until he heard claws scrabbling, and then the iguana shot out of the kayak and began its awkward run down the sidewalk.

Paris tapped the broom bristles on the ground. "Anyone else hiding out?"

Ben laughed, shaking his head. "I don't think so. But I owe you. You'd think I'd be used to these little dickheads for as long as I've lived here, but they still scare the shit out of me. And I know that's totally irrational."

Paris shrugged as he handed the broom back. "Yeah, it's not. I think I'm just reckless." He took a step back, then hesitated because God help him, but he kind of liked talking to Ben. "Is it true they freeze and fall out of trees?"

Ben let out a startled laugh as he walked over to the kiosk and set the broom against it. "Yeah. I mean, it doesn't happen a lot, but whenever we get a nasty cold front, they end up all over the sidewalk."

"Not dead?" Paris asked.

Ben had turned around, and when he looked back, his brows were furrowed. "Sorry, I missed that."

"Not dead?" Paris repeated.

"Oh!" Ben grinned. "No. Just frosty. There are people who think we should take the opportunity to kill them while they're down since they're an invasive species, but..."

"Jesus. What kind of sociopath wants to go on an iguana-killing spree?"

Ben shrugged, pulling a face. "I know, right? I mean, they're not my favorite. They're always fucking with the boat, and hiding in the kayaks, and costing me actual money. But, like, lizard murder? I think I'll pass."

Paris felt something stir in his gut, and he quickly stamped it down. "Well, if you need anything else—"

"I'd like to find a way to thank you," Ben said suddenly, his tone surprisingly low.

Paris froze, not sure what the guy was implying because it couldn't possibly be—

"How about a free rental. Anything you want."

He did his best to ignore the unexpected surge of disappointment, though he knew a decent guy with a boyfriend wouldn't *actually* proposition him. "Uh, yeah. I'm not really a water kind of guy."

Ben frowned. "But you moved to Key Largo."

"Yeah. To tattoo people. Not to scuba dive or do water yoga or whatever," he said, feeling a little defensive.

Ben cocked his head to the side. "Okay, but have you even tried it?"

Paris opened his mouth to tell this little shit that he lived in California, so of course, he tried it. But he didn't think the two times his work buddies convinced him to miserably fail at surfing really counted.

"Maybe just give it some thought," Ben said. He turned again and grabbed something off his little kiosk desk, then moved closer. Paris could see him holding one of the brochures he'd been given when he first checked in. "Read through this. And hey, if you're nervous, I can go with you."

Rejection was on the tip of his tongue. Crushing on the guy he could hear fucking all night was bad enough, and torturing himself with his presence alone in the ocean would be a bad decision. But something about Ben's big, soft brown eyes made it impossible to tell him to fuck off.

So, against his better judgment, he took the damn pamphlet and tucked it into his back pocket.

"Fine. I'll think about it."

Ben laughed very softly, making Paris's heart pound a little bit harder. "See you around?"

Paris said nothing because anything he could say would be either snarky or it would give away feelings he had no business feeling at all.

3

Ben hated going out. He liked his friends okay, but everywhere on Key Largo was loud. Even the low-key restaurants always had blaring music and tourist chatter, and it made it impossible for him to understand anything that was going on.

In Orlando, he had a nice group of Deaf friends who knew all the best places to hang out and all signed, so he never had to pretend like he was following along. But there, he only had Theo, and he was only around every so often when his schedule allowed it. And it wasn't like Ben didn't enjoy hanging out with everyone, but none of them quite understood what it was like for him.

They wrote him off as being distracted, and he heard the phrase "I'll just tell you later" so many times that it started to give him an eye twitch. But he also knew he needed outside stimulus. He was no good to himself or anyone if he existed for work, sleep, and the occasional orgasm.

So, when Andrew texted him and said they were all meeting at Sushi Hana that night after work, he resigned himself to a few hours of smiling and nodding. Even if the conversation sucked, he could get a couple of drinks and fill himself with good food so the good outweighed the bad. And frankly, he was in the mood for a distraction.

He'd been in his head all day after Paris had helped him with the damn iguana, unable to get his adorable frown out of his head. Ben told himself he had absolutely no business lusting after a guest. That was his policy, and he'd been able to stick to it perfectly well. Until the tattooed, leather-jacket-wearing, grumpy asshole had strolled up to his front desk and booked a full month.

Ben had done his best to keep his distance, but the more Paris approached him, the harder it was to keep a level head. Paris was the last person Ben assumed would ever want something stable, but goddamn, he couldn't help the fantasy.

So now he headed over to meet his friends on Islamorada and prayed that a couple of drinks and some heavy carbs would be enough to keep his mind on other things.

It was a Tuesday, and while it was always tourist season, the parking lot was fairly empty, which allowed him to breathe a little easier. Sushi Hana was one of his favorite places because it had a wraparound outdoor dining patio and a tiki bar, which meant he didn't have to deal with noises bouncing off the restaurant walls.

He saw the twins, Andrew and Amelia, waiting for him as he walked up the steps. He bypassed the hostess and sat down, glancing over at the five other place settings, and he raised a brow. "Are we having a party?"

Amelia laughed. "No. I just got hired at that new tattoo shop. Irons and Works. Have you seen it?"

Ben laughed and shook his head. "Babe, if I'm not scrubbing gunk off the bottom of kayaks, I'm scrubbing shit off bathroom walls because guests who stay in motels are disgusting."

She pulled a face. "Okay, no thank you *forever*."

Ben shrugged. "It is what it is. But hey, I'm excited for you. Are you learning to tattoo?"

She shook her head. "Nope. I'm working as the receptionist for now, but I'm going to learn piercings. Their piercer there is, like, super famous or some shit, and he agreed to take me under his wing."

Andrew rolled his eyes. "Yeah, sure, you and needles. She literally screamed the roof off the mall when she got her ears done," he said, shooting Ben a smirk.

"They used a piercing gun, not a needle. And it was traumatic," she answered with a sniff. "One of the tattoo guys is living at your place, though, you know."

And that fucking figured. Of course it would be Paris.

Ben took a breath and tried his best not to blush. "I think I know who you mean. Leather jacket? Octopus tattoo on his hand? Drives a truck?"

Amelia laughed. "I think they all drive trucks, but yeah. Paris. He and his brother, Max, just moved here."

Ben almost choked on his sip of water. Paris had a *brother*? God help anyone who was single. "Well, he seems nice."

Amelia gave him a skeptical look. "Um. Maybe we're talking about a different guy? I mean, he's not like some creepy racist or anything, but—"

"Who are we talking about?" came a voice from directly behind Ben, and he startled, looking over his shoulder at a full-on salt-and-pepper Daddy-type wearing ripped jeans and an ink-stained shirt. He was grinning like his smile was made out of literal sunshine, and he had his gaze locked on Ben.

"Um...no one," Ben said, then looked back at Amelia, who was quickly jumping to her feet.

"Everyone, this is Tony. He's the owner of the shop."

"Co-owner. Or...well. More like sponsor," Tony said. His gaze roamed over Ben for a second, and then he plopped down. "You sign?"

Ben blinked at him. "What?"

Tony raised his hands into fists, then flicked his fingers out and back in twice. 'Sign?'

Ben felt his entire being startle. "Yeah," he said, then glanced over at Andrew and Amelia before raising his own hands and feeling self-conscious the way he always did with his hearing friends. 'I sign.'

'Cool. My daughter's Deaf, so our home language is ASL,' Tony went on, his hands almost as fast and fluid as Theo's, though with what Ben had come to learn was a distinct hearing accent to his movements.

"Um. Are you going to share with the class, or...?" Amelia said loudly.

Ben ducked his head and sighed before signing, 'I don't have Deaf friends here. Talking's fine.'

Tony looked unsure, but he still dropped his hands to the table and offered the other two a grin. "I'm a...PODK." The word blended together weirdly enough that Ben wasn't sure if he'd heard it right. At his frown, Tony laughed. "Parent of a Deaf Kid."

"Oh. Sweet," Amelia said. "I keep meaning to learn, but that shit's hard, you know?"

Ben watched as Tony's expression fell, and he laid his hands on the table. "You know what's harder? A Deaf person trying to follow a conversation they can't hear."

Amelia looked nervously over at Ben like she was waiting for him to say something, but his tongue felt stuck to the roof of his mouth. "Oh. Well. I mean, he has the implants, so..."

"It's fine," Ben said in a rush. "Seriously."

Tony didn't look thrilled. "We can talk about it at work tomorrow."

Amelia looked like she'd just been called to the principal's office, and Ben didn't know whether to laugh or cry. Luckily, the mood shattered when a handful of inked-up guys and one woman with bright blue hair trudged up the deck, and all of them grabbed seats.

For a moment, Ben didn't see Paris, and his heart sank, but then the last chair was drawn out, and the familiar, leather-wearing hottie dropped into his seat and caught Ben's eye, nodding once before turning his gaze to the younger man beside him.

Ben could only assume that was Paris's younger brother. They didn't look much alike, but they had the same wild green eyes that he could get lost in for days. The guy opened his mouth to say something, but his voice was way too quiet for Ben to catch anything, and he settled back into his disappointment.

It was a familiar feeling, though, and easy to tuck away.

The server came over shortly after, and everyone placed drink orders, then a handful of apps. Ben's appetite was effectively dead at the sight of Paris, but he forced himself to order some miso soup just so he had something to do with his hands as he watched the conversation volley across the table.

Once or twice, he caught Tony staring at him, and he started to feel like his skin was crawling.

'You okay?' Tony asked between them.

Ben closed his eyes and took a breath. "Can you just use your voice, please?"

Tony dropped his hands immediately. "Sure. Wanna come to the bar with me so I can check out the drink menu there? You can recommend something to me."

Now Ben knew how Amelia felt, and every single eye was on him as they stood up and walked down the little ramp and into the grassy lawn between the patio and the bar. He felt awkward and shoved his hands into his pockets, and Tony came to a stop beside the support beam and leaned against it.

"I won't sign if you don't want me to," Tony said, "but you're obviously fluent."

Ben licked his lips. "Yeah. I'm fluent in English too, though."

"I'm not going to be the hearing dickhead who tells you how to communicate, but I will be the over*bearing* dickhead who tells you that you're allowed to put the demand to learn your language on your hearing friends."

Ben scoffed. "Is that so?"

Tony shrugged. "Every guy in my Colorado shop took ASL classes for four years. We have several Deaf members of our little tattoo family, and each and every one of them is accommodated. And if your friends aren't willing to learn..."

"Please don't tell me they're not worth having," Ben said from behind a sigh. "If I said shit like that, I'd be alone."

Tony's face fell but only for a second. "I won't pretend like I get it. Seriously. I know I got lucky as hell with my guys. But I picked the people to come work at this shop for a reason. Just because they don't know shit now doesn't mean they're not willing. All of them understand what it's like to be...you know. Other."

Ben winced, but he didn't know what the fuck to say to that. It was starting to sound like the anti-bullying PSA ads that his third grade teacher would play during friend week at school. And it didn't feel good because they always used him as the example of someone "different."

He glanced back at the table, and he could feel all the eyes on him. "They know what you're talking to me about, don't they?"

Tony looked up, then laughed. "Oh, shit. No. It's because of you and Paris."

Ben's face went white-hot, and he cleared his throat. "What about me and Paris?"

"He's still pretty annoyed that you and your boyfriend kept him up all night, and I think they're worried he's going to be a dick and call you out."

Ben frowned, completely confused since he didn't actually have a boyfriend, but that only lasted a second before realization slammed into him. "Oh my God. Oh my *God*. He...he heard us?"

"I thought he talked to you about it. He said he ran into you, and you chatted," Tony blurted, then slapped his face. "Oh fuck. He didn't, did he?"

Ben shook his head, wanting to dissolve into the ground. "They all know?" he whispered.

Tony's mouth opened, and then it shut again before he cleared his throat. "Kind of?"

Ben didn't look back this time. He just patted his pockets and felt a punch of relief that he had his keys on him. "Yeah. So. I'm gonna go. I can't—yeah. Sorry." He fumbled through the world's worst goodbye, and then he fled. The only relief he had was the fact that no one tried to stop him.

But then again, after all that, who the fuck would?

As he waited for the video call to connect, Ben paced in front of the kitchen table, his hands shaking with the adrenaline that hadn't stopped firing since he left the restaurant. He'd never been so humiliated in his entire life, and he had no idea how to handle it.

The light on his screen flashed, and he turned to see Theo's face there, looking obviously concerned for Ben's state of being.

'What's up? Are you okay?'

Ben dropped into a chair. 'No, I'm not okay! My neighbor heard us!'

Theo frowned, and then his lips twitched into a tiny smirk. 'You mean when we were fucking?'

'Yes!' Ben said, jumping up again because he couldn't sit still with all this raging in his chest.

Theo scoffed and waved him off. 'Who cares? He's just a guest. It's not like he knows anyone you know. And everyone knows we're fucking.'

'He's a long-term guest. And I ended up having dinner with him and his friends last night, and they all knew about it!'

Theo threw his head back and laughed, his hands still shaking a bit as he leaned forward toward the screen. 'Who cares? If they gave you shit about it, you know that means they're just jealous.'

Ben plopped down, the wind gone from his sails. Yeah, it was slightly embarrassing, but he was a grown adult and allowed to have sex. This wasn't like when he was a kid and he didn't realize people could hear more subtle sounds. Like his stomach growling or farts he thought were silent but deadly.

Then he thought about Paris being next door and listening to him and Theo. He'd heard every groan and every grunt the pair of them made while Theo was fucking him into oblivion. He realized it wasn't mortification he was feeling. At least, not entirely.

It was something a little closer to regret because there was something about Paris that made him want in a way no one had in a long, long time.

Theo's face softened immediately. 'You like him.'

Ben raised his hands to argue, but he couldn't. It was like being hit with a freight train of sexual awakening. 'I like him.'

There was a flash of something on Theo's face—almost sad, though Ben knew it was just from the potential loss of a decent hookup. Theo wasn't in love with him, and Ben was fine with that because he could never fall in love with a guy like Theo. But he hadn't expected the conversation to take this turn.

'What do I do?'

'Talk to him,' Theo offered simply. 'Does he know how you feel?'

'He probably does now. When I found out everyone knew, I ran. Literally. I took off like a bat out of hell.'

Theo looked at him like he was a pathetic fluffy kitten. 'Poor baby.'

'Fuck off,' Ben signed irritably. 'It was mortifying to look at him and know that you and I *literally* kept him up all night with how loud we were.'

Theo sighed loudly and waved his hand to regain Ben's attention. 'Talk to him,' he said. 'It's already awkward, right? It can't get much worse.'

Ben doubted that, but Theo was right. He needed to be able to learn to live with it and confront awkward problems head-on. 'I wish he'd come to me instead of telling all of his friends.'

Theo shrugged. 'What would you do if someone was fucking in their front window where you could see.'

Ben's hands dropped to the table in resignation. Theo probably would have been his first call. 'Shit. I should apologize.'

'For what? Orgasming?'

Ben rolled his eyes. 'For keeping him awake. We should have been more careful.'

Theo gave him a flat look as he made a fist, stuck his thumb against his ear, then flung his fingers out wide. 'Profoundly Deaf. We have an excuse, Ben. If he doesn't understand that, he doesn't deserve to know you.'

The words felt a little better coming from Theo—someone who understood his reality—than they did from Tony. He knew the guy meant well, but he was still reeling a bit over the lecture from a total stranger.

'I'm going to talk to him tomorrow,' Ben decided.

Theo nodded, and then his expression went serious. 'Is this a goodbye call?'

Ben almost choked on his own tongue. 'What?'

Leaning forward again, Theo tilted his head to the side. 'I always knew you'd find someone. You're precious, and someone good deserves you. I'm okay if that's what this is.'

Ben felt a rush of panic. 'I don't want to lose you.'

Theo laughed and waved him off. 'You're not going to lose me. But maybe it's better if I don't make any more late-night calls.'

Ben wanted to tell him that was jumping the gun a bit, but he realized Theo was right. If he felt this bad about knowing that Paris had heard them, God only knew how he'd feel if Paris saw Theo come back to his room.

'Maybe for now,' he agreed. 'But please promise me...'

'Hey. I'm not going anywhere,' Theo interrupted, his signs sharp and pointed. 'Do you understand? You are one of my best friends, and I love you.'

Ben hoarded those words close to his heart, and that allowed him to breathe a little easier. 'Wish me luck?'

'I wish you something dramatic enough to keep me interested next time we talk, but not so dramatic it hurts your feelings,' Theo said.

Ben laughed, knowing that was the best he was going to get. 'I'll text you after.'

'You'd better.' He shot him a quick ILY, kissing the back of his hand before the screen went black, and Ben sat back with a sigh.

He wasn't sure he felt better—not entirely. But at least he felt like he had a goal, and that was something he could focus on until morning and he had to confront the hottest guy he'd ever met with the most embarrassing thing he'd ever done.

Morning came, and Ben rolled out of bed after a night of broken sleep. He'd stayed up with his processors on in hopes he'd hear Paris come home, but by midnight, he gave up and attempted to sleep. He wasn't sure if it would be mortifying to know that Paris had fled the damn city instead of coming back to the place of his apparent torment or if that would just solve his problem for him.

But when he stepped out that morning, careful to avoid yet another dog shit deposit, he saw Paris's truck parked at the far end of the lot.

While he cleaned up the mess, he debated about knocking on the guy's door, but it seemed needlessly cruel after he'd already disturbed the poor guy's peace and quiet. That thought carried with him as he opened the kiosk, then went to the front desk to check in with Aya on how many reservations they had and how many checkouts.

He had a stack of resumes for housekeepers to look at, so he took those with him back to the kiosk and settled on his stool. As the sun got higher in the sky, the humidity started to thicken the air around him, so he turned on his fan and got to work.

It was almost eleven when he heard a room door open and close, and he looked up just in time to see Paris tucking his key card into his back pocket. Ben's heart was racing, but he steeled his reserve and pushed out of the swinging door, waving his hand to catch Paris's eye.

It was clear by the expression on the man's face Tony had been very clear about why Ben had taken off. Paris shoved one hand into his pocket and lifted the other in a sheepish wave.

"Hey," Ben said, a little breathless.

Paris licked his lips and seemed to be having trouble making eye contact. "Uh. Hey."

Ben closed his eyes and tried to use the panic racing through his gut like fuel. "I'm so sorry," he started babbling. "I have this thing with this guy, and when I take off my implants, we're both totally deaf, so sometimes we don't think about making noise. And I *know* the walls here are thin, but I didn't even think, and I kept you up... and...and I'm sure that was *so* uncomfortable, and *Jesus*, I don't know what to say except that I'm more than happy to move you to a new room if you—"

"Whoa," Paris said, and Ben's jaw snapped shut. "Dude. Can you take a breath for just a second? You look like you're going to pass out."

Ben realized he actually was light-headed, and he forced himself to take a couple of shallow breaths before clearing his throat. "Sorry. Again."

Paris shook his head. "*I'm* sorry that Tony has a big fucking mouth and apparently went all dad mode on you last night."

Ben laughed, which felt on the verge of hysterical, but he was starting to calm down.

A little.

"Yeah, well. When this hot old guy tells me that the entire table of equally hot tattoo artists are aware that my sex noises can be heard through their friend's wall, there's no recovering from that."

"If it helps," Paris said with a very small, very crooked smile, "they all thought you were adorable and wished they could swap places with me."

"Uh, no, that doesn't help," Ben said, his voice rising. "Oh my God. Excuse me, but I have to go throw myself into the ocean now."

Paris chuckled, and the sound was deep and almost consuming. Ben normally didn't get what all the fuss was about with laughter since he was pretty sure he could never hear it right, but Paris's was like a rumble of thunder.

"Please don't," Paris said through a grin. "If you do, there won't be anyone who can teach me how to stand-up paddleboard."

Ben started to laugh, but the sound died on the edges of his tongue. "I...wait. Are you saying that because you feel bad for me?"

"Yep," Paris said. "But also because my brother says it's the most fun thing he's done since we moved, and he basically threatened me until I agreed to try it."

Ben bit his lip and glanced over his shoulder before meeting Paris's gaze. The moment didn't feel so heavy anymore. "I have plenty of boards. And I do owe you one free rental."

"And what about the offer to go with me?" Paris said, sounding only slightly unsure. "I, uh...I'm kind of scared I'll make a fool of myself and drown."

Ben grinned, his heart racing for a whole new reason now. "I could make some time. As you can see, I'm not being overwhelmed by customers this week."

Paris's smile faltered a little. "Rough times?"

"More like I don't know what the fuck I'm doing in the motel business, but I'm trying. It's a long story full of grief and sighs, and I don't want to bore you."

"I doubt you could," Paris said, "but we can table it for later. I have to run to the shop for a team meeting with Tony. He's gone some bee in his bonnet about something, and it's mandatory."

Fuck. Ben knew what it was. "Um. Good luck. And I'm sorry?"

"Doubt it was your fault," Paris said as he stepped back. "But catch you later this afternoon? I should be done around two."

"I'll be here all day," Ben called after him as Paris started toward his truck. "If I'm not out here, find me in the office."

Paris gave a half salute before climbing into his truck cab, and Ben watched with a thirsty pulse in his chest as Paris rolled down his window, shot him one last smile, then pulled out onto the main street.

He had no idea what the fuck to do with himself now, but something had sparked a little flame of hope in his gut as bright as Paris's grin.

4

Paris stirred his straw around his iced tea, watching as the condensation on the glass continued to thicken. The drops drew patterns that almost immediately filled in from the humid air coming off the water, and he stared out of the open window, hoping to absorb some of the sun since he'd been avoiding spending time outside.

He didn't look over until he felt a sharp kick against his thigh, and his gaze immediately turned to Max, who was grinning at him.

"God, you're such a child."

Max shrugged, unrepentant. "And you're zoning out. Still having a panic attack about the neighbor?"

Paris dragged his hand down his face with a soft groan. All morning, he'd been getting shit from the team. At least, until Tony showed up and told them that under no circumstances would they get away with saying the same shit that their new receptionist had said the night before.

"I understand y'all aren't family the way my shop is," Tony had said, pacing in front of them. "I get that you've been islands up until now. But this isn't the business I'm here to run. That ain't the Irons and Works brand. You make a new friend who needs a different way to communicate, I sure as shit better hear that all of your asses are signing up for a class."

Paris had a feeling it was about Ben, though he wasn't entirely sure how Ben was connected to the shop. Paris had seen a lot of Ben's bare skin, and apart from glimpsing a tongue ring the first morning they met, he was a blank canvas.

But Amelia had left the meeting looking upset, so Paris figured Tony had hit a sensitive nerve.

Tony was also right, and Paris knew it. Ben had no problems communicating with speech, but he'd also seen the guy using sign a handful of times, and he couldn't always understand Paris when they were talking. If Ben was going to be around, it would only be fair for them to learn it.

That wasn't really Paris's problem. It was the fact that all roads seemed to lead to Ben, and it was starting to make him feel...things. Uncomfortable things. Deeper than a crush. Feelings he'd been avoiding most of his life.

He didn't know what the hell had come over him when he had spent the morning flirting with him either. He told himself he was just trying to deflect the utter mortification he felt when Ben actually brought up the sex thing, but he was never great at lying to himself.

He'd been flirting because it felt good.

Never mind Ben had a boyfriend. One who was really good at taking care of his needs, if those noises were anything to go by. Paris knew damn well he could never compete with that, even if he was the sort of guy who'd be willing to break people up. Which he wasn't. He didn't think.

Paris took a long drink before he finally spoke again. "I agreed to do that paddleboard thing with him."

Max lit up like it was Christmas. He looked like a kid again, and Paris felt a pang in his chest. "Seriously? Trust me, you're going to love it. Felix and I brought snorkel masks with us, and I'm pretty sure I saw a lobster."

His brother's enthusiasm might have been infectious if he was actually capable of getting excited about crap like snorkeling. But he wasn't about to rain on Max's parade. "Well, I figure I could use some vitamin D." He paused, then growled, "Shut up," when Max's smile turned into a smirk.

"Not saying a word." He made a zipper motion at his lips, then sat back with a satisfied grin. "I'm glad you like him, though."

Paris scoffed and nodded at the server who came to sweep up their plates. "I don't like him. I don't like anyone. I barely tolerate you."

"Fucking liar. And yeah, you do like him. You're completely obsessed. Which I get it. He's goddamn cute."

Paris bit the inside of his cheek because it was true. Ben was a lot of things, and cute was one of them. He had a damn dimple, for fuck's sake. "He's got a boyfriend, and I'm not here to start dating, so don't get your hopes up."

Max sighed, but he didn't push it. Instead, he leaned on his elbow and lifted his hand, twisting into shapes. "I learned the ASL alphabet back in school. You think Tony's right about that whole thing?"

Paris bit his lip, then finally nodded. "Seems fair, right? I don't know what the deal is with Amelia and Ben—"

"They're old friends, I guess. They grew up here together. Harley told me he overheard Amelia and Tony talking at dinner. She said that Ben has those implants, so she didn't need to learn sign, and Tony just lost his damn mind."

Paris winced. He'd seen the tense conversation, but the patio had been too loud for him to make any of it out. Then Ben and Tony had moved to the bar right before Ben ran like his ass was on fire.

"Then he's right. Tony's got a Deaf kid. He's not going to fuck around with assholes who act like learning sign is an inconvenience."

Max nodded. "Let's sign up, then. I'll see what I can find."

Paris frowned. "You planning to be friends with this guy?"

Max grinned widely, making Paris roll his eyes. "Depends. But it can't hurt, right? And even if you two aren't going to date, you might become friends. Plus, Tony said some Deaf guys work at the Colorado shop, right?"

Paris nodded, drumming his fingers on the table in thought. He didn't have a lot of hope they'd find classes on any of the Keys, but he also didn't mind a drive up to Miami every so often. He knew getting away from the shop would be a good thing every once in a while, and if he was actually going to be friends with Ben, it seemed the decent thing to do.

"In the meantime, maybe Benny-boy can teach you a few things while y'all are out on the water." Max waggled his brows.

Paris balled up his napkin and hit him in the face with it. "Don't call him that."

Max shrugged and sat back, resting his hands on his stomach. "Anyway..."

"How's things living with Felix?" Paris asked, desperate to change the subject.

Max sobered almost instantly. "Good. I mean...I feel like an asshole if I say things are hard, but it's not really about me. He's not making any real progress with his memory issues, and he just...he's struggling."

Paris closed his eyes in a deep sigh. He barely remembered Felix from before the seizure that changed everything, but he knew it had to be hell on the guy. "Is he still freaking out when he sees you?" Paris asked. He knew it wasn't just memory issues anymore. The face blindness was what almost had Felix ready to give up all hope of working ever again.

"Not anymore. We came up with a phrase that I use in the morning so he knows it's me. I also think he's getting used to the smell of my soap and cologne, so it's been easier on him."

Paris looked at his brother for a long moment. "You into him?"

Max laughed, and then he realized Paris was serious because his face sobered. "Honestly, no. I mean, he's hot and he's nice, but neither one of us is feeling that, you know? He's more like a brother to me."

Paris tried not to feel a hot rush of jealousy, but it was hard to ignore it. He was possessive over his brother. He'd sacrificed every single waking hour of his life to make sure that Max didn't suffer as deeply as he'd suffered at the hands of his shit-for-brains dad and wicked stepmother.

Hearing someone had come along and settled into his spot made him want to put his fist through the wall.

But he kept that shit in check because Max deserved the best.

"You should come over this weekend. We can throw something on the grill," Max said.

Paris nodded in spite of wanting to turtle in his apartment and do jack shit until the shop opened. "Sounds good." He checked his phone, then sighed. "I should head."

"Ocean date?" Max said.

Paris flipped him off as he stood up and grabbed his wallet out of his back pocket. He tossed a wad of cash on the table that would more than cover the meal, then held his fist out for Max to knock knuckles. "Let me know if you need anything later."

"And you let me know if you get your dick sucked."

"Not a fuckin' chance," Paris said, then turned on his heel and headed for his truck. He always felt better when he spent time with his brother, and even with the ugly green monster sitting on his shoulder, some of the weight had sloughed off during the meal.

He didn't think this place was paradise. Not really. It wasn't full of some sort of magical sea air that was going to heal his childhood trauma. But he could see them all settled for a good, long while.

There was the smallest part of Paris that hoped Ben would have forgotten about the afternoon by the time he got back to the motel, but as he pulled into the parking lot, he caught a glimpse of Ben by the dock, kneeling beside one of the paddleboards. His heart ticked up a few beats as he took his favorite parking spot, and by the time he was climbing out of his truck, Ben was there.

He looked as delicious as ever—soft and sweet with his smile showing off his dimple. He was leaning against the side of the wall with his arms crossed, the expression on his face almost like a challenge.

"You didn't chicken out," he said when Paris shut the truck door and took a few steps closer.

"I didn't chicken out," Paris echoed and left off the bit where he almost did. Deep down, he knew he wouldn't have missed it for the world, but there had been that part of him tempting him to just... run. He ruffled his hair, feeling a little uncertain, then glanced over toward his room. "Should I, uh...change, or...?"

"I've got a few things you can borrow," Ben started, but Paris was overwhelmed by a sudden wave of panic.

"Actually, let me throw something on," Paris interrupted in a rush, not meaning to cut him off, but he needed a second. He turned after Ben gave him a confused nod, and he fumbled with the key card before getting his door open.

The moment it shut, he covered his face with his hands and fought the urge to scream. Ben might be Deaf, but with his implants and the thin-as-fuck walls, he'd probably hear it.

"This isn't a bad thing," he murmured to himself. "You're not proposing to the guy. You're not asking him out. You're just going for a fucking cruise on the water. *So don't be a dipshit.*"

With his half-cocked pep talk, Paris walked into his room and dug around in the cheap little dresser for the single pair of board shorts he owned. They were a little bit too big, and one side was white and went completely see-through if they got even slightly damp, but they covered his dick and balls, so they would have to be good enough.

He swapped to one of his cleaner T-shirts—a blue one with a faint hibiscus pattern that Max had gotten him one day as a joke—

and stared at himself in the mirror. He looked ridiculous without his jacket and jeans. He was pasty and on the thin side from constantly forgetting to eat and lack of working out. It was hard to imagine a guy like Ben would ever look twice at him, even if Paris wanted him to.

But this wasn't a date, he reminded himself. This was a sort of apology for being an epic dick. And maybe to make things less awkward when he eventually had to see Ben with his boyfriend.

He took a breath, then rummaged around for his flip-flops and finally made his way out the door and back toward the dock, where Ben was still waiting.

Paris's mouth went dry.

Ben had changed into a pair of wet suit pants and an impossibly tight T-shirt that showed off every line and curve of his body. His hair was a little mussed from the slight breeze, and he was smiling again like he was a fucking Greek God who ruled the ocean.

His dick twitched.

"You okay?" Ben eventually asked, and to his horror, Paris realized he'd been staring.

He cleared his throat. "Uh...yeah. Sorry. I'm nervous, I think. About falling into the water," he lied so Ben didn't get any ideas, even if they might be true.

Ben laughed and shuffled closer in his bare feet, holding out a long paddle. "Relax. It's just the ocean." He gave Paris an up-and-down look, then said, "I have a spare set of pants if you want to borrow—"

"No, thanks," Paris interrupted sharply. He hadn't meant to be rude, but he was having a hard enough time controlling his half chub behind his loose shorts. God knows what it would look like in spandex. "I'm good."

"If you're sure. I'm only suggesting it because—"

"Dude. I'm sure," Paris said.

Ben deflated, his face falling, which made Paris's stomach ache. But he perked up only a second later and clapped his hands. "Okay.

Then let's go over some basics and then test your balance. Then we can take a little tour around the mangroves and see if we can find some stingrays."

Paris didn't hate that idea. In fact, it sounded close to the paradise he'd been promised when Zeke proposed the idea of working at the shop on the island.

This place was nothing like the Caribbean islands he'd seen online. The water was darker and greener and murkier. There was no sand, no waves, too fucking many mosquitos, and the humidity made him sweat so much he wanted to peel his skin off just to get some relief.

But it was also calming in a way he wasn't expecting, especially right then. Though, he did have a feeling that had everything to do with Ben and nothing to do with where he was.

Doing his best to pay attention to Ben's lessons, Paris took three spills directly into the water before he finally managed to stand up on his board without feeling like he was going to go flying. It took him another ten minutes to get the hang of paddling, but it wasn't long before Ben was sliding onto his own board and gliding up to his side like it was nothing.

Jesus, he even moved like a fucking sea god.

"You ready?" Ben asked.

Paris hesitated, glancing at the little devices Ben had in his hair. "Do you need to take those off in case you fall in?"

Ben laughed. "I'm not going to fall in. But no. My parents were kind enough to pay for the upgrades a couple years ago as a birthday gift."

"That was...nice of them?" Paris offered.

Ben snorted. "They were like thirty-five grand, so yeah."

Paris almost choked on his own tongue. "Jesus, dude."

Ben shrugged and glanced away. "They could afford it that year. Anyway, um...ready?"

With Ben's strange tone, Paris had a feeling there was a story there that carried pain, though he couldn't begin to think what it was. But it was obvious Ben didn't want to talk about it, and Paris was more than happy not to pry.

"Let's go. Just promise you'll come back for me if I tumble into the ocean and a shark starts heading my way," Paris said.

Ben grinned. "Sorry, man. I make no promises when it comes to sharks." And with that, he shoved his paddle into the water and took off in a smooth glide.

Paris was nowhere near as suave or graceful as he followed. He wobbled more than once, panic rising in him that he was going to tumble into the open water, but eventually, he was steadier. He wasn't keeping up with Ben, but he was close. His arms burned with the effort, but the late-afternoon sun on his shoulders felt amazing.

"Let's go this way," Ben said, turning his head back toward Paris. "We'll probably get to see some dolphins around that bend."

The mangroves were like a maze, but as he followed Ben's path, they soon came to open water, and Paris's heart stuttered in his chest. The vast, still ocean stood in front of them—the sun glinting off the water, a few clouds in the distance, the sky a shade of blue he wasn't sure he'd ever seen before. It was nothing like the Pacific with the winds, fog, and wild water, but it still gave him the same feeling of being alive.

It wasn't perfect because nothing was ever perfect, but it was the first time in a long time he felt at peace.

Glancing over, he saw Ben had dropped down to sit on his board, one leg hanging over the side, the other pulled toward his chest. Paris paddled himself closer, then chuckled when Ben leaned over to grab the tether on his board.

"Try to sit," he suggested, and Paris did so—wobbling a bit but eventually managing to get down. "Just give them a few minutes. This is their feeding time."

Paris sat cross-legged at the front of his board, and when he felt the brush of something warm against his side, he realized it was Ben's hand still holding his tether. His breath hitched in his chest, and he felt a wild urge to do something outrageous—like lean over and kiss the guy and promise he could make him scream louder than his boyfriend ever could.

God, what the fuck was wrong with him? He didn't do this. Ever.

"You okay?" Ben asked.

Paris cleared his throat. "Yeah. Uh...I don't do this a lot."

Ben chuckled softly. "Falling off the board when it wasn't moving was kind of an indication."

Rolling his eyes, Paris elbowed Ben's arm gently. The contact sent sparks shooting up to the back of his neck. "I mean this," he said, waving his hand toward the water. "All of this. I lived in LA for most of my life, but I never spent time by the ocean."

Ben tilted his head to the side. "Really? Why?"

"Work," Paris said. "When I was seventeen, I had three jobs so I could pay rent. Then, when I finished my tattoo apprenticeship and my work started getting popular, I didn't have the time." He didn't mention that he'd spent most of his life knowing—no, believing—it was better for him to never, ever get close to people. Because people always let him down.

Ben nodded, his expression a little somber but not full of the pity Paris hated so much. "I recently met this guy, Callisto, whose story sounds a little like that. He works part-time for me doing accounting and the rest of his time at the aquatic rescue center. His mom died when he was like two, and his dad dove into the bottle and never came back out of it. Now he's got this kid to take care of, so his entire life is just surviving moment to moment."

Paris's cheeks heated. "Yeah, my story isn't really like—"

"Dolphins!" Ben's excited shout cut Paris off, and he was grateful for it. This was no place for his childhood trauma. "Sorry, but..."

"No, no. That's what we came out here for," Paris said. He turned toward the front of his board and balanced on his hands and knees as Ben hopped to his feet. "I don't see them."

"Just there," Ben said. "Give them a second. Stand up, you'll get a better view."

Paris was nervous about moving, but just as he lifted up to his knees, he saw them. They weren't close, but he could see their dorsal fins glinting in the sun as they breached the water, then dove back down. Their arcing dives were beautiful, and they made him feel something soft, and warm, and new.

He slipped one foot flat onto the board, then carefully pushed to his feet...

And promptly fell over.

The water rushed around him, racing up his nose and making him want to choke on the briny liquid. His eyes burned as he scrambled for the surface, definitely not the strongest swimmer, and feeling a momentary wave of panic that he wasn't going to make it back to his board.

Then his face reached air, and he gulped a breath, squinting to see as a wet, slippery hand had grabbed his.

"Relax," Ben's commanding voice told him. "It's not deep. Put your feet straight down."

Paris did, almost on instinct, and his toes scraped the slimy bottom as he steadied himself. He managed to get both eyes open and used his free hand to swipe at his face as he pulled his feet up to tread water. "It's gross in here."

Ben laughed and tugged him close. "Yeah, it doesn't feel amazing. Let's get you back up on your board. Give me a second, okay?"

Paris nodded and grabbed the edge of the board as Ben hopped back onto his, and he looked to his left, but from this low to the water, he couldn't see the dolphins. Beneath his tucked knees, he could see ocean floor. There was kelp growing and small fish darting around in massive schools. It was both terrifying and beautiful all at the same time.

He kicked his feet a bit more, then felt something strange. Like sharp, electric sparks on his thigh, moving upward. He sucked in a breath, and then it happened again...on his dick. "The fuck?" he muttered.

Before he could ask again, Ben was back, offering him a hand.

He'd secured the boards together, and with careful movements, he got Paris back up on his and flat on his back.

"How much water did you swallow?" Ben asked, kneeling beside him.

Paris shrugged, closing his eyes against the sun. "Less than a mouthful. Felt something on my...um...on my thigh, though," he said. "Like a tiny little sting." Now that he was thinking about it, his dick was itching and burning. "It's kind of uncomfortable."

"Fuck. That's what I was afraid of," Ben groaned.

Paris felt a wave of panic and pushed up on his elbows, his gaze locking on Paris. "Afraid of what?"

"Stinging water," Ben said.

"Stinging *water*?"

Ben licked his lips. "Yeah. Uh...it's not actually the water. It's jellyfish venom floating around."

Horror rushed through Paris's body as he stared down at his crotch. "Please tell me I don't need a hospital."

"Probably not," Ben said. "If they just got you on the thigh, you're fine. It could be a lot worse."

Paris slapped his hand over his face and fell back, his head hitting the board. "Can we go back now?"

"Yeah," Ben said with a quiet laugh. "Need a hand?"

The itching and burning was getting worse, but Paris wasn't ready to show it yet. He wasn't sure how the hell he was supposed to confess to this man that he had jellyfish venom in his dick. Rolling up, he carefully wobbled to his feet, then picked up his paddle. His knees wanted to buckle, but he managed to keep it together as they made their way back into the maze of mangroves and eventually to the dock.

5

Paris wanted to cry when it came into view, and it was taking everything in him not to start pawing at his poor cock, which was now throbbing with a steady burn.

"So, uh, is there any relief?" he asked as the board thunked quietly against the wood.

Ben hopped up, then offered his hand. "Yeah. Apple cider vinegar usually takes care of it. If it gets infected, you might have to get it looked at, but it's happened to me more than once."

Paris tried not to do the piss dance. "Yeah?"

Ben's smile got bigger. "Got me in the balls, though."

Letting out a rush of air, Paris couldn't hold the truth back anymore. "It's my dick. It's...it hurts."

Ben pulled a face, and he laid his hand on Paris's arm. "Come to my place. I'll get something mixed up for you, okay?"

Paris nodded, but he didn't move, even as Ben tugged on him. "It's not, like...*in* me, is it? It didn't float up my piss hole, right?"

Ben stared, then burst into laughter, stepping forward and wrapping an arm around Paris's neck. "No. It's not inside you. It just stung you, and I know it hurts, but I promise I can help."

The pain was persistent enough that Paris couldn't feel embarrassment, though he knew it was coming. For now, it was easy to let Ben take the lead, opening the door next to his and gesturing for him to step inside.

"Let me grab some boxers for you," Ben said, giving him a quick glance up and down. "I have a pair that'll fit."

Paris nodded, trying not to think about how badly he wanted to scratch himself, and instead paced around the room a bit. It was definitely more lived-in than his own hotel room but not as homey as he would have expected for a guy who actually lived there. The furniture was the same as the shit in his room, and even the kitchen had the tiny two-burner nook with no cupboard space and a half-sized fridge.

He was more curious about Ben's story now. Why he'd bought this place. Why he stayed. If it was what he'd envisioned for his future.

Not that Paris could have answered those questions if Ben turned them around on him, but Ben seemed far more settled than he was. He clearly had parents who loved him, and he was willing to bet a sibling or two that he was close to.

So why be so isolated?

He startled when Ben appeared next to him, holding a pair of black boxers. "Hopefully, these will fit. And I've got a blanket you can use while you soak."

Paris didn't know what the hell Ben was talking about, but he was too afraid to ask, so he just ducked into the bathroom and peeled off his wet clothes, leaving them in the tub. The boxers were snug, but not impossibly so, and he felt a little exposed as he stepped out of the bathroom and found Ben draping a large, fluffy blanket over the arm of the sofa. He fought the urge to tug on his dick just to relieve some of the burning, but he didn't think it would work, and he didn't want to look like a creep.

"Um."

Ben's head whipped toward him, and his cheeks darkened with a blush. He was very obviously trying not to stare, and Paris didn't quite know how he felt about that. "Okay, so, sit there. You can cover up with the blanket, and I'll be right back. You'll have to take your—uh—um—whatever got stung out."

Paris wanted to sink into the floor and die. Instead, he brushed past Ben and flopped down, pulling the blanket over his lap. He hadn't examined himself in the bathroom like he probably should have, but just by poking at himself, most of the pain was along the tip of his dick.

He slid it through the slit in the boxers and wondered, thanks to this utter humiliation, if he would ever be able to get hard again.

"Okay," Ben said a second later. He was holding a small Styrofoam cup that housekeeping left every time they came by. "So, you're gonna...um..."

Paris stared for a second before he realized what Ben was trying to say. "I gotta teabag my dick into that cup?"

Ben burst into laughter, covering his face with his free hand. "Oh my *God*. I mean, *yes*, but Jesus, man."

Paris couldn't help his own chuckle. The situation was so absurd. He'd wanted a way for the universe to put a barrier between him and Ben, and if the boyfriend hadn't done it, this sure as shit had. "Just hand me the cup, and let me get this over with."

Ben was still trying to smother his giggles as he passed the cup over, and then he took a seat in the armchair, deliberately looking away as Paris scooted to the edge of the cushion. By feel alone, he carefully submerged his poor, abused, jellyfish-ravaged cock into the vinegar.

"How's it feel?" Ben asked after a beat.

Paris grimaced. "Stings, but not as bad as I thought it was going to be. How long do I have to do this?"

"I don't know. Like, ten minutes or so. I had to do it for a few days before it really started feeling better."

Paris groaned, but he was resigned to his fate. "Well, better than letting my dick fall off, right?"

Ben rolled his eyes, though he was grinning widely. "Your dick wouldn't fall off. It's just a little sting. Think of it as your welcome to the Keys initiation."

"I'd like a damn refund," Paris grumbled, though his mouth was twitching. He settled as comfortably as he could, feeling some type of way knowing that Ben knew what was happening under the blankets. "So, um. This place. You like it?"

Ben snorted. "You're terrible at small talk."

Paris shrugged. "Dude, I tattoo for a living. People sit in my chair, and suddenly, they start confessing like I'm their fucking priest. I don't know how to start normal conversations."

"What's the weirdest thing someone's said to you?"

"There's a lot of jerking-off confessions," Paris admitted. "Like weird, weird shit. One chick really got her rocks off watching videos of people cutting up dick-shaped vegetables. I have no idea why the fuck she felt comfortable telling me that."

Ben choked on a laugh. "Seriously?"

Paris shrugged. "I've heard worse, but that was definitely one of the weirdest."

Ben's smile softened. "It must be nice. I mean, not cutting up dick-shaped vegetables to get off."

Paris laughed hard enough his ears heated up. "Yeah, I could have done without that one."

Ben grinned, his dimple so fucking adorable Paris couldn't stop staring at it. "I just mean having a job like that where people trust you with themselves. And from what I noticed, everyone there seems like family, which must be nice. You know...having a bunch of people who care about you like that?"

Tilting his head to the side, Paris tried to shift to face Ben better without spilling his little cup. "Your family seems pretty good to you. Not that you wouldn't deserve those implants or whatever, but..."

Ben immediately sobered. "No, yeah. They do love me. The upgrades were sort of a onetime deal. My brother died, and they got money from his life insurance."

Paris felt like the world's biggest jackass. "Shit. I'm *so* sorry. I didn't mean—"

"No," Ben said from behind a sigh, waving his hand. His fingers twisted in what Paris knew were ASL signs, and he wished he'd done at least some YouTube on them. "They are good parents. Really. I tried to fight them when they wanted to buy these"—he tapped the little round disc on the side of his head—"but they pointed out Levi would have wanted that. And they were right."

Paris licked his lips. "Is that how you got this motel?"

Ben chuckled, the sound kind of sad but also maybe a little nostalgic. "No. My parents bought this place when Levi and I were kids, and we kind of grew up here. After he died, they couldn't handle it. They were going to sell it, and for some reason, I couldn't stand the thought of some asshole buying it and changing everything. It was a stupid move on my part."

"How do you figure?" Paris asked.

Ben let out a humorless laugh. "Because I very clearly have no idea what the hell I'm doing. This place is a shithole."

Paris frowned. "Not even close. I mean, it's not the fuckin' Ritz or anything, but it's decent."

"Apart from the walls so thin you can hear your neighbor going at it all night?" Ben asked with a quirked brow.

"Oh, fuck *off*," Paris said, but he laughed so hard he almost spilled the vinegar and pulled himself out of the cup. "Can I stop now? I don't want pickle dick."

Ben blinked at him, then laughed again as he stood up. "I like you."

Paris's entire body flushed hotly, and he quickly turned his attention to tucking himself away and slipping the blankets down so he didn't spill the cup. "Thanks?"

Ben chuckled. "Let me get rid of that for you."

"Dude. No. It's dick juice," Paris protested, but Ben was quicker than he was and managed to snatch it away, taking it into the kitchen and appearing with a shirt draped over his shoulder. He tossed it to Paris, who caught it and looked down. "You got clothes stashed all over or what?"

"Oh," Ben said, and then his cheeks went pink, "Theo tends to kind of throw stuff around while he's here, and he always forgets it when he leaves. But don't worry, he won't care that you're wearing his stuff."

Fan-fucking-tastic. Not only was Paris suffering his first real crush since he was a dipshit teenager, but now he was wearing the guy's boyfriend's clothes? He wouldn't complain if God struck him dead right then.

"So, your boyfriend—"

"He's not my boyfriend," Ben said in a rush. He sat the moment Paris pulled the shirt over his head. "We just..." He stopped and sighed, shrugging. "He's the only Deaf person I know around here. We kind of connected, and we hook up sometimes. It's a nice distraction from when I feel like I'm going to drown in my grief."

Paris deflated immediately. He knew what that was like. He was anti-relationship, but he was no stranger to hooking up in order to make all the loud voices just a little bit softer. "Sorry."

Ben leaned back and kicked one foot up onto the table. "It's fine. It's not as bad as it used to be. Levi and I were really close, and I don't think anything can ever prepare you for losing someone like that. The brain does really weird things when it happens."

"Not as weird as getting off to chopping vegetables, right?" Paris said.

Ben laughed. "Okay, no. Not that weird."

Letting out a quiet breath, Paris settled back and realized they were just inches apart. He wanted to reach over and touch him more than anything, but he knew that would only end in disaster.

"My brother's the only person that's ever really mattered to me," he said after a beat. His chest felt warm with the confession. "My mom died in a car crash just after I turned six—two weeks after Max was born. He obviously doesn't remember her. He just remembers our wicked stepmother, who popped out a couple of kids and made sure Max and I never felt like we had a home with them."

Ben frowned. "Seriously?"

Paris sighed. "Yeah. I mean, I know people can be shitty to decent stepparents, but she was a damn monster. The last birthday party I had was when I was five, right before my mom died. The next year, my dad told me we couldn't have one because he and Helen were wedding planning. The year after that, she planned a date night and made me stay home to watch Max. I realized pretty quick she was doing it on purpose and that things were never going to be like they were."

"Jesus," Ben breathed.

Paris never talked about this with anyone. Ever. He had no idea why it was all coming out now. He shifted and rubbed a hand down his face. "We never got Christmas presents, never had a birthday. We weren't allowed to have friends or sleepovers. They'd take her kids to the movies or out to dinner, and she'd leave us freezer-burned left-overs. And my dad was such a fucking spineless worm he never said anything to her. He just let her do whatever the fuck she wanted."

"Paris," Ben said quietly. "I'm so sorry."

He shook his head. "Don't be. I moved out when I was sixteen. I knew this guy at school who could print really good fake IDs, so he doctored me one that said I was nineteen, and I was able to get a couple of jobs and an apartment. I went back for Max on his eleventh birthday and brought him to my place. He got his first cake that night."

Ben said nothing for a really long time. Then he took a deep breath. "He's so fucking lucky to have you."

Paris had never heard that before. He'd never, ever consider someone was lucky to know a cold, emotionless bastard like him. He wasn't quite sure what to do with the feeling those words caused. "I did my best to make up for what happened for all those years."

"What about you?" Ben asked.

Paris blinked. "What about me?"

"I mean, obviously, Max threw you birthdays and bought you Christmas presents..." He trailed off, likely at the expression on Paris's face. "Didn't he?"

"He was a kid," Paris said, hugging his middle. "He literally didn't know any different. We were both super fucked-up, you know? I don't blame him."

"So, you've never—"

"No."

Ben gave him a flat look. "You don't know what I was going to ask."

At that, Paris managed a small grin. "Whatever it was, the answer's probably no. No, I didn't ever have a birthday party, or sleepovers, or any kind of holiday. I don't get gifts on Christmas, and I've never had a Thanksgiving dinner. But I swear to you, it's fine. I got Max out of that house, and things have been good for us. Maybe not normal, but who needs that." He laughed, even if it didn't feel very funny at the moment.

Ben pulled both of his lips between his teeth and bit down, letting them go slowly. They were all red and slick, and fuck, Paris wanted to kiss him. "I'm sorry. I'm being really intense right now." Ben's hand lifted, and he signed something else.

"Where do you go to learn that?" Paris asked.

Ben frowned. "Learn what?"

"Sign. ASL, right? That's the right term for it?"

Ben let out a tense laugh. "Oh God. Trust me, you don't have to—"

"Yeah, dude. I do. Where do I go?"

"I learned it in college," Ben answered with a slightly awkward shrug. "But there's community centers that teach it and sometimes online classes run by Deaf people." He took a breath, then met Paris's gaze. "I really am okay with speaking, though."

Paris's lips stretched into a small smile. "Yeah, I know. And I like the sound of your voice. But I like *you*. So I want to learn."

Ben glanced away, and then suddenly, he was taking Paris's face between his hands, and those warm, bitten, slightly damp lips were on his. It took a second for Paris to get with the program, but just as he felt Ben start to stiffen and pull away, he was on him. It was everything he both wanted and didn't want, and now that the line had been crossed, he was willing to obliterate it.

He dug his fingers into Ben's sides, pulling him onto his lap. Ben ground his hips down as his lips parted, and his tongue came out to taste Paris's, and though it stung, Paris held him tighter.

"Fuck," he groaned.

Ben ripped himself back, his eyes wide and shocked. "Fuck. I am so sorry. I can't believe I just *jumped* you like that. Jesus, I—"

"Hey, hey. It's okay," Paris said quietly, prepared to release him as he stroked tender fingers over Ben's sides. Ben didn't seem to want to move back any further, and Paris wasn't in a hurry to let him. "I liked it."

Ben let out a tight, sheepish laugh. "So did I, but that was...I never do that. God. I'm sorry. I've been, like, lusting after you for weeks now, and after what you said, I think I just snapped."

Paris felt his dick twitch, though there was no chance in hell it was getting hard right then. "Weeks?"

"God," he groaned, "please don't make me admit that out loud again." Ben dropped his forehead to Paris's. "But yeah. You're ridiculously hot, and I'm still mortified that you heard me and Theo, and—"

"He's not going to care that you did this with me, right? He's not your boyfriend."

"Not my boyfriend," Ben confirmed, then pulled back. "Actually, we talked last night and pretty much ended things."

Pretty much wasn't a hundred percent, but Paris also wasn't about to ask Ben to give him more than that. He couldn't ask for what he wasn't sure he was capable of giving himself. "Okay. But... you should know I probably can't do much tonight."

"Right," Ben said with his absurdly sweet, dimpled smile. "Jellyfish dick."

Paris lunged forward and bit him on the neck, making Ben laugh. "Shut the fuck up," he mumbled against the warm, salty skin.

Ben's laughter died off, and when he pulled back, his face was a bit more somber. "I'd like to see you again. Like, more than just in passing. I want to take you out."

Paris felt a wave of panic race up his spine, but he also knew there was no chance in hell he could tell Ben no. "Okay, but I'm not getting in that water ever again."

Ben snorted. "If you wore the wet suit pants like I tried to suggest, you'd have been fine. But don't worry, I won't make you relive your trauma just yet." He sat back and toyed with his bottom lip with one thin finger that Paris wanted to take into his own mouth.

"What kind of date?" Paris asked once he was able to tear his gaze from Ben's lips.

Ben smiled wider. "Can I surprise you?"

"I don't know." Paris bit the inside of his cheek to stave off his nerves. "I'm not really a surprise kind of guy. I kind of have trust issues."

"I understand," Ben said, then leaned in and kissed him once more—this time slower, longer, deeper. Paris's head was spinning by the time he pulled back. "But maybe we can start small. How about you tell me everything you're not willing to do and I work around that."

It took him a second to regain his composure, but after a beat, Paris nodded. "Okay. The shop is opening this weekend, though, so my schedule is gonna be tight. I think Tuesday's my shortest day. I should be done around seven."

"That's fine. We can keep the first date simple. Dinner with me. Just come over here as soon as you get in."

Paris lifted his brows again, but Ben just grinned and shrugged, so Paris kissed him one last time before extracting himself from Ben's grip. "If I don't leave now, things are gonna get physical, and I think I might regret it."

Ben laughed as he stood up, then darted into the kitchen and came back with a bottle of amber-colored liquid. “Here. The vinegar. Just do a soak whenever it starts to bother you.”

Paris took the bottle and twisted it in his hands. “Promise me that when you get to know the guys, you’ll never tell them this story.”

“I’ll take your secret to the grave,” Ben vowed, signing along with his words.

Paris looked at him and told himself to just leave, but instead, he crowded Ben against the wall and kissed him until neither one of them could breathe.

6

Ben opened his mouth, then shut it again for the fifth time in the last ten minutes. Callisto, who'd been in the office working for the last two hours, raised a brow above the rim of his red-tinted glasses.

"You can just ask," Callisto said, leaning his elbow on the desk. He was currently doing Ben's accounting since Ben's brain didn't get along with numbers and math. "Whatever it is, I'm not going to get offended."

Ben flushed lightly and rolled his eyes, glancing away. "It's not that. It just sounds, uh...I don't know." He rubbed both hands down his face and leaned back in the little rolling chair. He couldn't see over the lobby desk, and he couldn't hear the little bell on the door when it opened, but he trusted Callisto to let him know if a guest came in.

Callisto dropped the pen he was using to make notes in his accounting notebook and leaned his hip on the counter, turning to face Ben. 'What's up?' His signs were rudimentary at best and, at worst, clearly taught by some level one student on the internet, but he was one of the few people who tried, and Ben appreciated that.

He leaned forward over his knees. "You had a pretty typical childhood, right?"

Callisto blinked in surprise. "I guess? Whatever a typical childhood is."

"I mean, like, you had friends. Birthday parties. Holidays."

Callisto looked even more confused. "Ye-es? And if I remember right, so did you. Or did I miss some huge traumatic thing that was going on with you in fifth grade?"

Ben laughed. "No. This isn't about me. I met this guy..." He trailed off, trying not to think of Paris and their afternoon together and that kiss. *Damn*, that kiss. Ben had gone to bed and jerked off, trying to muffle his cries into his pillow, though a small part of him had wanted Paris to hear it through the walls.

They were still practically strangers, and while Ben wanted him with a ferocity in his chest he didn't know what to do with, he had no idea what Paris expected to happen between them.

"You met this guy?" Callisto prompted.

"Right. I met this guy." Ben rubbed a hand down his face. "There's that new tattoo shop that just opened up near Midnight Snack," Ben said. "All those guys from the West Coast."

Callisto shrugged, his eyes moving slightly from side to side behind his Coke-bottle-thick lenses. "I hadn't noticed, but okay. So you're getting ink from this guy?"

Ben shook his head. "No. The guy I'm talking about rented the room here for three months."

Raising his brows, Callisto glanced at the computer as though Paris's story might be there on the screen. "Okay."

"We had a—" He stopped. It hadn't been a date, but it hadn't been really platonic either, even if he took out the way he'd pretty much mauled the poor guy with his mouth. God, everything with Paris felt like it had twenty layers he had to peel back just to make it all make sense. "We spent the afternoon together," he clarified. "And I...I think I like him."

Callisto's face softened into something sweeter, almost happy. It was rare to see him smile, considering his situation. The motel was his second job, which did very little to help his situation. He'd gotten saddled with single parenthood after his ex unceremoniously dumped their three-month-old daughter on his couch and took off four years ago. She was a good kid, but Ben had watched his friend slowly crack under the weight of his responsibilities.

They'd only just reconnected after Ben had come back to Key Largo, and he was a shadow of the man he'd been. In high school, Callisto had been hot, strange, and unattainable. His glasses and shit eyesight were from the fact that he was totally colorblind, but where Ben's deaf accent and giant processors made him a weirdo to most people, Callisto's red glasses and dancing eyes made him sort of mysterious.

Callisto had been one of the few people who genuinely liked Ben, though. And he was slightly clueless about the mechanics of the high school social circus. He would get high and make out with anyone willing, but he'd never date. He spent most of his free time painting as a way of trying to relate to color, and he always had a rainbow of acrylics smeared on his arms and under his nails.

Ben had crushed on him just a little, but they'd been better friends back then

and far better friends now. Ben wasn't really into the whole kid thing, but he liked Lila. And he was glad that Callisto was back in his life.

"You know you're cute, right?" Callisto said after a beat. "And funny. And really sweet."

Ben felt his cheeks heat. "Um? No, but thank you?"

Callisto laughed and stepped closer so he could knock Ben's knee with his own. "I'm saying you're a catch. I had a huge crush on you in high school, and you're still the same guy from back then."

Ben cleared his throat. "Oh. Uh..."

Callisto rolled his eyes. "I'm not hitting on you, Ben. I'm saying you don't have anything to worry about. But considering my life is an absolute shit-show right now, I don't know that I'm the right guy to give you dating advice."

That startled a laugh out of Ben. "First of all, I'd totally come to you for advice. Your situation isn't exactly your fault. But this whole thing is kind of...unconventional. I don't know him that well, and I don't even know if he wants to do more than just sleep with me. He's had..." Ben bit his lip, cutting himself off because it wasn't his story to tell. "Let's just say he didn't have a typical childhood, and I got this idea in my head that might be ridiculous, but I don't know. Maybe he'd appreciate it?"

Callisto stared at him for a long moment, then turned and grabbed the second chair, pulling it close to Ben. "Don't worry. I'll hear the door," he assured him when Ben shot him a worried look.

Ben let out a breath. "Thanks."

With a nod, Callisto made a "go on" gesture. "Tell me your ideas, and I'll tell you honestly if I think they're bad."

It took Ben a moment to gather his courage, but after a few breaths, he did. The words poured from him like he'd been holding them in for weeks instead of hours, and he felt a thousand times better when he was done. As he trailed off, he searched Callisto's face, feeling a mixture of hopeful and a little silly.

His friends had always accused him of being too extra—going too far with the idea of romance. And shit, maybe they were right because Callisto's face was unreadable.

"You can tell me if that idea's—"

"No," Callisto said, then stopped and cleared his throat. "I mean. Yes? I don't know what you were going to say, but I think it's amazing. I don't know how he'll react because trauma like that runs pretty deep, but he's lucky to have met you, Ben."

His chest felt warm, and he couldn't stop staring at Callisto's lips like maybe he'd misheard something. But the look in his friend's eyes said otherwise. "Yeah?"

Callisto laughed and shook his head. "God, Ben, you are wasted on the people who never make you feel good enough."

Ben blinked at him, not sure what to say to that, but it didn't matter. Callisto just took a breath and went on.

"I think what you're suggesting is a huge risk. It could backfire. But it might also be the best thing that ever happened to him."

Ben watched his lips carefully, pairing it with sound, trying to make sure it all made sense in his head. "That's what I'm afraid of."

Callisto gave him a long, considering look. "So start small. Don't go balls to the wall with it."

Picking at his cuticle, Ben ran through one of the thousand different scenarios he'd come up with in his head after Paris left his place the night before. "Like a sleepover. Pizza, popcorn, movies?"

"Yeah," Callisto said with a small laugh. "That'll at least get you laid."

Ben's cheeks heated, and he glanced down at his hands. "I'm definitely not doing this to get laid. I really just...like him."

He looked up when Callisto gently tapped his arm. 'I'm sorry,' Callisto signed. 'I don't...' He froze, clearly at the end of his sign lexicon. "I didn't mean it like that. What you want to do for him is kind of the dream, Ben. I don't know what I'd give for someone to come in and look at my shit-show of a life and soothe all the painful parts."

Ben didn't quite know what to say to that. "Cal—"

"I'm not asking you to woo me," Callisto said with a laugh, nudging him softly against his knee. "I'm saying maybe don't overthink this too much. I don't think there's a right or wrong answer here. Start small, read the room, see if he's in a place he can handle what you want to give him."

It was fair advice. It was sound, at the very least, and he needed to be better at taking it from his friends who actually cared about him. "I should—" His words were cut off when the desk phone started ringing, and he sighed. He was great one-on-one with people, but speakers just sounded like garbled noise.

"Let me," Callisto said. He snagged it from the receiver, and after a beat, his face fell. "Got it." He cradled it and looked at Ben. "Crisis in room fourteen."

"It never fucking ends," Ben said. "Mind watching the desk for me?"

"You know I never do."

And that was true. As Ben left the lobby, he reminded himself to do a bit more caring about the people who cared for him right back.

As he pulled up to the new tattoo shop, Ben's heart beat against the inside of his throat. He didn't see Paris's truck anywhere, but there was every chance the employees were saving the front space for their customers. Amelia had told him that they were running the soft opening that week to prepare for the grand one on Saturday. Not all the tattoo artists had booked clients, and they were still dealing with a few building problems, which was why Andrew was there and Ben needed to pick him up.

Ben hadn't actually been inside of a tattoo shop before his tongue piercing, and that had been such a quick in-and-out that he didn't retain much apart from the sterile smell, the loud music which made it hard to understand the speech around him, and the cacophony of art covering the walls.

He stared up at the sign hanging at the top of the building. *Irons and Works*. He wondered if there was some significance to that. Most of the shops he'd seen around were things like Epic Dragon, or NeedlePoint, or Black Rose.

This place felt very different as he stepped up to the door and pulled it open.

There was music, though it wasn't blaring—just sort of a soft background hum that he could almost feel in his bones. He wriggled his right processor, which was the one that worked best, but nothing changed, so the place really must have been that quiet.

"Hey!"

Ben's gaze whipped to the right, then to the left, and it settled on Amelia, who was leaning against a tall counter.

She bit her lip, then raised her hand and made a fist, circling it over her chest. 'Sorry,' her hands said in signed English. 'Thanks for driving.'

Ben's brows dipped, and he walked up to her so he didn't have to raise his voice. "You're signing?"

She shrugged and looked vaguely embarrassed. "I know I should have been doing it before. Tony made me feel like shit about it." When Ben's mouth dropped open to argue, she quickly shook her head. "No. Seriously. I should have."

He didn't have it in him to argue with her, mostly because it would make him sound like an asshole. But the truth was, he didn't consider her or Andrew a close enough friend to warrant language acquisition. It would be good for her job, but hell, he hadn't even become slightly conversational until college, and even now, he felt leaps and bounds behind people like Theo.

But it was what it was, and he certainly wasn't going to tell her to stop.

'Thanks,' he signed back, then switched to his voice since he was pretty damn sure that she'd only mastered basic greetings. "Is your brother still here?" Amelia looked torn, and Ben let out a ragged sigh. "You can speak. It's fine."

"Just...there's a Deaf guy here right now, and I think we all kind of feel like assholes since most of us barely know the alphabet. And Tony pointed out that we never, uh...we never asked you what you preferred."

"Well, I'm telling you right now that I need to know if your brother's here because I have a hotel emergency, and he said he needed a ride. And since you can't sign it, you can say it," he said, letting his irritation show.

Amelia sagged back into a rolling chair and swallowed heavily. "Uh. Yeah. Everyone's out back behind the shop. There's a barbeque going. You should meet the guys. They're fun."

Ben wasn't sure he was in the mood, but there was every chance Paris was back there, so he let Amelia gesture him past the counter, and she pointed to the door with the big signed marked EXIT. Feeling his nerves firing because he wasn't used to this, he passed the stalls, trying not to look at the few people in there giving tattoos. His social circle was tragically small, and for as much as he'd teased Paris about it, he also had no real idea how to make small talk with strangers like that.

Ben's heart gave a couple of hard thuds in his chest as he pushed out the back door and stepped into the overflow parking lot. Everyone there was so...hot. Maybe not entirely his type, but he was coming to realize he definitely had a thing for ripped jeans, pierced faces, and skin covered in ink.

Several people stared at him as he searched the crowd for a familiar face, and the first person he landed on was Tony. He was at a cheap standing charcoal grill, the grey in his hair glinting like silver in the bright afternoon. He had a pair of tongs, and he waved them at Ben, jerking his head for emphasis.

Ben sighed to himself. He liked Tony. Or, well, he wanted to like Tony, but the guy was a little overbearing for a total stranger. Still, Ben felt compelled to walk over, and he let out a short laugh when Tony wrapped him in a one-armed hug.

"I was hoping you were coming by," Tony said aloud. "Andrew said he asked you for a ride back to the motel."

Ben nodded. "Um. Yeah."

Tony set the tongs down. 'I wanted to say sorry. I hope signing is okay.'

'It's fine,' Ben said. And it was. It was just—he didn't like to make a damn issue of shit with a bunch of people who probably wouldn't remember his name the next day. To them, he'd just be that Deaf motel guy like he was to most people.

Tony gave him a look. 'I know what I'm like. My boys tell me all the time. I'm in everyone's business, and I take on problems that don't belong to me. I won't dump my childhood trauma on you, but that's part of it, and I'm trying to be better. So I *am* sorry.'

Ben debated about arguing with him, considering he'd

continued to make Amelia feel bad about not knowing even the basics, but he decided it wasn't worth it. 'Apology accepted,' he offered.

Tony grinned and hooked his arm around Ben's neck, yanking him in for another hug, and despite everything, Ben leaned into it because it felt good. It felt like one of his dad's hugs, back when he and Levi were kids and having a bad day.

His throat got a little hot as he pulled back, and he did his best not to think about his brother right then.

"Miguel!"

Ben jumped at the sound of Tony's shout, and a second later, a hulking guy who looked like he could be a Hell's Angel walked up. He was in tight jeans, riding boots, and a black T-shirt that read Irons and Works on the front with two crossing tattoo machines. He was also taller than Ben by several inches and had massive scars down one side of his face.

'This is Ben,' Tony signed. 'Ben, this is Miguel. He's here with his husband for two weeks while the shop opens. He's going to be doing some guest ink here.'

'Are you looking to book a tattoo?' Miguel signed.

It took Ben a second to follow the signs once he realized that Miguel only had fingers on one hand, but it wasn't the first time he'd used adaptive ASL. He grinned, shaking his head as he licked his lips. 'No. I'm here for Andrew.'

Miguel frowned, so Tony jumped in and explained that Andrew was the guy who'd been hired to do maintenance on the shop all day.

'I run a motel. He's also my handyman, and we're in the middle of a busted pipe crisis,' Ben explained.

'That sucks,' Miguel signed. He was clearly a man of few words in any language, and just as Ben was starting to feel slightly uncomfortable, another person walked up.

He was tall and thin, wearing leggings and an off-the-shoulder top in purple, showing off a light brown shoulder that displayed some abstract watercolor ink. He was wearing a light dusting of highlighter on his cheeks, which matched the shimmer on his purple hearing aids.

"Hey."

Tony grinned and lifted one hand as the other adjusted the burgers. 'This is Amit,' he spelled, then offered the guy's name sign. 'He's Miguel's husband.'

Amit stuck out his fist, and Ben knocked knuckles with him. 'Nice to meet you,' Amit signed with all the fluency of a native speaker. 'You going to be around a lot?'

'I don't—' Ben started, but Tony stepped in.

'This is Paris's new friend.'

Ben's entire face went tingling hot, and he wondered just how much these guys knew about him and Paris and the drama of the afternoon before. 'Is he here?'

Tony shook his head. 'He and a couple of the guys had to run an errand in Miami. They'll be back later if you want to hang around and wait.'

Amit actually looked excited at the prospect, and Ben could understand why. It was the exact reason why he'd clung to Theo when they first met. In fact, he was sorely tempted to ignore a burst pipe in room fourteen to do it. But he couldn't run his little motel into the ground for the sake of conversation.

'I'm having a maintenance crisis,' he admitted. 'Sorry. I have to grab Andrew.'

Tony's gaze scanned the crowd, and then he picked up the tongs and pointed to the few people clustered around a massive cooler before leaning over to flip the hot dogs. 'Tell him to give me a call later.'

Ben nodded, then waved a quick goodbye to Miguel and Amit before making his way over. He could still feel the heavy weight of everyone's eyes on him as he approached Andrew, who was talking to the guy he recognized as Paris's brother.

Max, if he remembered right.

Max gave him a slow up-and-down look before smirking. "Ben?"

He sighed. "Yeah. I'm sorry to steal your friend, but one of my motel rooms is about to turn into Noah's flood."

Max grimaced and gave Andrew a pat on the arm. "Catch you later?"

"Yeah. Shoot me a text, and I'll reserve a couple of the wave runners." He offered a sheepish grin to Ben. "If you don't mind."

Ben rolled his eyes. "Better you than me." He could ride them. He just hated them with a fiery passion. He started around the building with Andrew close at his heels, and when the conversation died down, he looked over his shoulder. "Sorry to ruin your afternoon."

Andrew scoffed and waved a hand at him. "Dude, no. I need the money. I can't afford days off right now."

Ben climbed into his car and waited for Andrew to slide in before asking, "Are you two okay?"

Andrew stared at him before bursting into laughter. "Dude, yes. It's nothing like that. I'm sort of...dating someone. I think. She's apprenticing at the shop, and Amelia introduced me to her a couple weeks ago."

Ben deflated, feeling somewhat relieved that his friend didn't need a raise because he didn't have it in the budget. Not with having to pay Callisto for the accounting help. "I'm happy for you."

Andrew gave him a soft smile. "Yeah. Her name is Eve, and I think I love her."

"Dramatic since you just met her, but okay," Ben said as he darted across the road and took the side streets back to the motel.

Silence carried them to the parking lot, but before Ben could get out of the car, Andrew stopped him. "So, I guess I owe you an apology for not learning to—"

"No," Ben interrupted in a rush. He was in no mood to have this conversation twice. "I mean, yeah, people using ASL with me is nice because listening is such a fucking chore most days, but I don't expect it from you."

Andrew stared at him for a long moment. "Why not?"

Ben froze. He didn't have an answer for that. Or, well, he did, but it was a shitty one.

His parents had taught him that his communication was the exception, not the rule, and if he wanted his life to be easy, assimilation was best. And his brother—who loved him arguably more than anyone else in his life ever had—only learned the basics because he liked the idea of talking shit about people in public. No one ever had given him more, no matter how close he got to them. His only friends who used it were already immersed in the language and culture.

Ben had never been important enough to anyone for them to make the effort, so there was no reason to expect that would change.

Except...he thought about what Paris had said just before Ben kissed him. How he wanted to learn for him as though making the effort was not an inconvenience at all.

Shit.

"Sorry," Andrew said, so soft Ben almost didn't catch it. "I never really thought about it before today. I mean, you seem to be able to understand everyone just fine."

Ben laughed, only because it was obvious Andrew didn't understand at all. But then again, no one did. Ben understood what hearing was like with his implants on. He understood what totally deaf was like when they were off. It was his entire world since he was a baby, and when he lost the thread of conversations, he was really good at playing along until he caught up again.

It worked for him. Even if he didn't always like it.

"We fucked up, didn't we?" Andrew asked.

Ben wanted to know why the hell Andrew cared so much, but it seemed cruel, so he just kept his mouth shut and shook his head. "Seriously, don't worry about it."

Andrew sighed. "We can talk about it later. I better go fix that pipe before animals start showing up to board the ship."

At that, Ben laughed. "Thanks. Come by the office when you're done. Callisto is there right now. Maybe we can order some takeout or something and hang for a bit."

Andrew brightened. "Yeah. That sounds good. I can tell you both about Eva and how amazing she is."

Ben wanted to groan, but he realized that if he felt any sort of confidence about his upcoming date with Paris, he might be doing the exact same thing.

7

Paris sat in the back next to Harley, with Jamie in the front and Eva behind the wheel. He and Harley had worked together for years at Bonsai, starting around the same time. Paris was still a kid then, though, while Harley was getting out of his job as a therapist after an incident he refused to talk about. He'd opened up a bit after a few years, but even now, he was looking a little haggard and exhausted. Paris didn't want to know what shit was like outside of the shop doors, and he felt a little bad about not asking.

And hell, maybe he should start checking in more. Maybe he should do better about taking care of these guys who were going to become his family. Tony had given them a soul-crushing lecture about taking care of each other, and while Paris's first instinct was to crawl into his metaphorical turtle shell and ignore anything even close to resembling responsibility, that wasn't the life he wanted to live.

Not anymore.

It wasn't just the feelings Ben had awakened in him, but they were a big part of it.

"You sure you're good, man?" It had been the longest day, but they were finally done on their supply run, and Harley was currently trying to find a place to stop and eat before they headed back to the key.

Harley lifted his head up, then laughed. "Yeah. Sorry, I just haven't been getting much sleep lately. My sister's going through some shit right now. Her boyfriend tried to hit her, so she's staying with me, and the fucker keeps showing up at my place at all hours of the night."

"Fuck," Paris breathed out.

Harley grunted. "And it doesn't help that she keeps trying to drink her problems away at the bar they both used to hang out at. I don't know what to do with that shit, you know?"

"Dude, I don't do drama," Paris said, "so I have no advice."

"Yeah, I know," Harley said. Not all the guys at Bonsai were understanding, but Harley knew him better than a lot of the guys at the new shop.

Paris wanted to believe that he had a new opportunity to be different this time around. He knew Tony had helped Zeke choose everyone who would fit under the Irons and Works brand, so maybe this really was his shot.

"What about you?" Harley asked as he went back to scrolling.

Paris blinked. "What about me?"

"He wants to know why you've been a morose asshole all afternoon," Jamie said, turning around in his seat and grinning.

"He's freaking out because he has a date," Eva said, glancing at him in the rearview mirror.

"Fuck off. Paris doesn't date," Harley said, then froze when he caught Paris's eye and saw the truth there. "Fuck off," he repeated. "You have a date?"

Jamie was grinning, still holding on to the headrest as his gaze darted between Paris and Eva. "Who is he? Have we met him?"

"We met him at dinner the other night," Harley said. "That adorable little fucker that Tony scared off."

"Oh," Eva said, looking slightly more awake now. "I remember him. Why'd he take off? Tony's not that much of a dick."

Paris was pretty sure Tony didn't have a cruel bone in his body, but it was also obvious that Ben didn't enjoy the kind of attention Tony gave people. "He probably just had shit to do. He owns the motel I'm staying at, and I think he pretty much runs it by himself."

Jamie let out a low whistle. "Damn. Maybe we should offer to give him a hand."

Paris was startled at the utter sincerity in Jamie's voice. It didn't sound like a bullshit offer just to sound like he was kind. "He might like that."

There was something else he knew Ben would like. Something Paris needed to do, but he wasn't sure he was ready to talk about it yet. Hell, he was barely able to admit he had a date with Ben, and the thought of considering it something serious still had him breaking into a cold sweat.

"Hey. How about bao buns?" Harley said.

That distracted the car immediately, and Paris grabbed his phone, doing a quick Google search while they debated the merits of a restaurant dedicated solely to the art of different-flavored bao.

To: Paris Marin

From: ASLBIZ

Thank you for your inquiry. I have Zoom classes for ASL level one available every Wednesday and Friday at eight a.m. Each session lasts one and a half hours, and does require additional work outside of the classes to further your education on both the language and the Deaf Community.

If you wish to move forward, please fill out the attached form and send your payment to the following Zelle link.

Best regards,

Alice Davis
Ph.D Deaf Studies

Well, that was fast, Paris thought as he tapped his fingers on the side of his phone. He'd sent the email over lunch, and by the time they got back to the shop, the email was waiting for him. He didn't read it until he'd gotten back to the motel, and even then, he took a shower first, then changed into lounge pants and called his brother.

It had been the longest day in the world, and he was reeling from the fact that Ben had apparently shown up at the shop after they'd taken off to run errands.

He felt both relieved, because he wasn't quite sure he was ready to see Ben, and also slightly disappointed because although it had only been a day, he hadn't seen Ben since the kiss. The email was the next bridge into something important he wasn't quite sure he was ready to admit.

His stomach was in knots, and every couple of minutes, he could hear laughter from the other side of the wall. The only reason Paris didn't want to pull his own face off was because there were at least two other guys over there with Ben, which likely meant it wasn't Ben's ex...or whatever he was supposed to be.

Not that he had any right to be possessive or jealous, but he wasn't a fool. At least, not one who could lie to himself.

He stared down at the email again, and his gaze snapped up when there was a knock on his door. He almost tripped over his own socked feet getting there, and then he came face-to-face with his brother, then Felix, who was hanging back a few feet behind him.

Paris tried to imagine what it would be like to live with the inability to remember anyone's face, and the thought was almost impossible.

"Hey," Paris said, standing aside.

Max just nodded at him, his arms heavy with bags of takeout, and Felix slipped in right behind. His voice was quiet as he offered his fist to bump. "Hey, Paris." When Paris's brows shot up, Felix rolled his eyes. "I'm not that chick from the terrible movie about forgetting my entire life every time I go to sleep. I knew we were heading to your place."

Paris offered him a sheepish smile. "Sorry. I just don't want to freak you out, man."

Felix waved him off as he dropped his coat on the armchair and followed Max to the kitchenette. "It's getting easier. Y'all have tells, and Max is helping me come up with a system."

Paris kind of wanted to know how the whole thing worked, but he had a feeling Felix needed a safe space from being watched like a damn zoo animal, and Irons and Works should be that place for him. He brushed past Max, who was unloading boxes of Greek food, and grabbed a stack of paper plates from the cabinet.

"Here."

Max gasped as he took them. "Bro. These kill sea turtles and shit."

"I thought that was plastic straws," Felix said with a frown. He brushed a lock of dark curls from his forehead back into the collection that was thick with product. He had a bit of a fifties greaser look to him, which Paris felt suited his whole aesthetic. He was always in skinny jeans and white T-shirts, and he had a lot of Sailor Jerry ink to match.

Max shrugged and shoved a plate at his roommate. "I think Paris hates all living things."

"Not all of them," Paris said.

Max grinned. "Just baby jellyfish."

Face heating up, Paris took a step back. "*Dude*."

"Relax. Felix and I haven't told anyone."

Felix offered him a pained smile. "Yeah. That's not something I'd want anyone to talk about. How's, uh...*it* feeling?"

Paris fought the urge to rub at his crotch. The itch was better, though he was still teabagging the tip of his dick in vinegar every couple of hours. "Getting better, I guess. I'm not sure there's any amount of money that would get me back in that fuckin' water, though."

Max snorted, then burst into laughter, grabbing the chair as he howled. "Bro," he said when he caught his breath. "Only you."

Paris flipped him off and stole the paper bag full of pita and the container with the tzatziki and threw himself on the couch. "Eat shit."

Max eventually calmed himself and loaded up his plate before sitting on the floor with his back pressed against the wall. Felix took the chair where he'd dropped his coat, and silence settled down. It only lasted a moment, though, before the next room over erupted into more laughter.

Max winced. "Is he on a date?"

"Nah. Friends over," Paris said, his mouth full. He swallowed thickly, then grabbed his glass of water and took a long swallow. "We haven't talked since the other night, though."

The look on Max's face was a mixture of hope and pity, and Paris hated them both. "You know, Felix has one more room, and—"

"I told you I want to figure my own shit out," Paris snapped, then softened and took a breath. "I don't want this to be like LA, okay?" He knew Max wouldn't take it personally because Max wasn't the one who had slipped into a heavy codependency with borderline agoraphobia. Paris was a few days away from suggesting his brother find a new place to stay so he could deal with it when Zeke appeared with his offer.

And even then, he hadn't allowed himself to feel hope that it was going to work out until he woke up one morning to have his coffee out on his terrace and realized he didn't need to struggle for breath.

"I might start looking soon, though. Once the shop's on regular hours," he added.

Felix smiled at him. "It's nice here."

"Yeah," Max said, stretching his legs out. He took a massive bite of chicken and chewed noisily before speaking again. "I could get used to this. I mean, I miss the surfing, but it feels so different. Like, in a good way."

Paris knew what he meant. There was peace to be found on the West Coast like this, but even with the amount of money they'd both started making, only celebrities could afford it. This was something new and different. And maybe it wasn't meant to last forever, but he'd take even a little while.

"We haven't had our first hurricane yet," Felix reminded them both, and Paris groaned while Max threw a corner of spanakopita at his friend.

"Fuck you, bro. Let us live in ignorance until we have to face it."

Paris snorted. "He's scared of storms. When he was twelve, he used to sleep under my bed with his Super Mario blanket whenever there was thunder."

Max looked pissed as Felix laughed. "Fuck off."

"I think it's cute," Felix said. "Little Mario."

"It's-a-me, the guy who's gonna rip-a-your dick off if you keep talking shit," Max said, making Felix laugh harder.

"He was a pain in my ass, but luckily, we didn't have to deal with it as much as we probably do here," Paris said. He stared at his phone again, which lit up with some junk mail. His heart thudded, and he bit his lip. He became profoundly aware that he had the full attention of both men in the room. "I think I signed up for an ASL class."

Max perked up. "Dude. Where? I looked, like, fucking everywhere, and there was nothing closer than Miami."

Paris set his plate down and ran his thumb over the octopus tattoo that twisted around his finger. "It's actually this Zoom thing. This Deaf woman on Instagram runs classes. She's got, like, a PhD and shit. It's pretty pricey, so I think it's legit."

"Yo, send me the link," Max said. "Are there good times?"

"They're not great," Paris said, but his disappointment was

starting to ease a bit because if he didn't have to do this alone, maybe it wouldn't feel so heavy. "It's at eight in the morning."

Max groaned, but he didn't look deterred. "It'll suck getting up that early, but at least it won't cut into shop time."

Paris's shoulders sagged. "That's what I was thinking. You really wanna do it with me?"

"Yes," Max said like it was a ridiculous question. "Felix, you in?"

"I might try," he said, sounding hesitant. He picked at the sides of his jeans. "I've been struggling to retain new information, so...I don't know."

"Let me try it first," Max said. "Maybe you can sit in and check it out."

Felix's face softened, and Paris realized that this was it. This was how it started. The whole new family thing when his blood relatives were absolute shit and he had to create something for himself. Max was way ahead of him, but maybe he wasn't too far gone yet.

"I bet it'll be like my French class," Max said after a beat. "Where you get to learn all the bad words at the end of the semester if you do a good enough job. Then you can talk dirty to your boyfriend."

Paris's cheeks went tingly hot. "Shut up. I don't need a teacher to show me dirty talk."

"Yeah. Let's hope he learns all that well before the semester is up," Felix said with a small grin. "I feel like Ben would be a damn good hands-on teacher."

Paris threw half a pita at him, then laughed along when Felix burst into giggles.

Felix and Max left a couple of hours later, and while Paris knew he should probably crawl into his bed and sleep, instead, he found himself on the terrace with his sketch pad. He was covered in bug spray because the mosquitos were fucking real there, but he didn't even mind it that much. The air was thick and humid, with a slight breeze off the water cooling it down. There was no porch light, but the bright one from the kitchen was enough to brighten his workspace, and he began to get lost in the lines of his designs.

His current stall at Irons and Works was pretty bare. He'd left a lot of his work back at Bonsai, wanting to leave a piece of himself behind while also starting fresh. This wasn't exactly a clean slate because he didn't believe those existed, but it was as close as he was ever going to get.

He was halfway to finishing up the phoenix on the first page when he heard a soft tapping noise. He ignored it the first time, and then the second, but by the third, he stood up and walked to the edge, startling when he found Ben leaning over his own metal railing, grinning at him.

"I wasn't sure if I was hearing you or hallucinating."

Paris lifted a brow. "Do you hallucinate a lot?"

"Side effect of these," he said, tapping one of his processors. "The doctors told my parents it wouldn't last, but apparently, doctors who don't have cochlear implants don't know as much as they think they do."

"Imagine that," Paris said flatly, sparks flying through his belly when Ben dropped his head and laughed.

"Yeah. Anyway, I hope I'm not interrupting anything important. Callisto said he heard voices over here, so I figured you had friends over. Or, like...a date...or something?"

"Subtle," Paris said, though he couldn't hide his smile. "It wasn't a date. It was my brother and his roommate."

Paris couldn't pretend like he didn't feel almost fucking giddy at the relief on Ben's face. "Cool. Yeah. Uh..."

"Do you want to come over?" Paris blurted.

Ben bit his lip like he was trying to hide his smile, and then after a long beat, he nodded. "You don't mind?"

"Fuck no. I've been thinking about you non-stop since the kiss."

Ben blinked, then took a step back and vanished from Paris's line of sight. "Go open the door for me."

Paris had never made it across his living room faster, and he was wrenching the door open the second Ben appeared, and he only had time enough to slam it shut before Ben's mouth was on his. He had no idea what he was actually doing, but Jesus Christ, it felt so fucking good to be kissing him again. His entire body felt like he had roman candles going off under his skin, and he couldn't do anything except shove Ben up against the wall and get a hand in his hair.

"God," Ben murmured against his lips. "You're so fucking hot I don't know what to do with myself."

Paris forced himself to pull back and take a breath. "Do you mind if we slow down?"

Ben blinked almost sleepily. "Repeat that?"

"Can we slow down?"

He deflated in Paris's arms, but he didn't try to get away. "Yeah. Sorry. I'm such a fucking lunatic sometimes, I swear to God. I'm so, so—"

Paris pressed a finger to Ben's lips, feeling the plush wetness of them that he put there. Fuck. "Don't apologize. Don't you fucking dare. You have no idea how much I wanted that. I'm just, uh...I don't do this a lot, and I'm trying not to fuck it up."

Ben looked up at him, sweet and kind of soft. "Oh. Yeah. I mean, me either. The best I've gotten is fairly decent sex with a friend who does an okay job of not making it awkward once we finished hooking up."

Paris tried not to feel the stab of jealousy in his stomach, but it was there. He clung to the fact that Ben said it was over, and he grabbed his hand, pulling him to the sofa before glancing over to make sure he'd remembered to close the back door.

Ben sat with a heavy breath, looking at the remnants of the meal left on Paris's table. "Y'all can put it away."

Paris rolled his eyes. "You were at the shop today. You saw those fucking beasts."

Ben snorted a laugh, and when Paris sat, he inched forward until their knees were touching. In a bold move, Ben reached over and took Paris's hand in his. Ben's fingers—calloused but thin apart from his big knuckles—traced a touch over the lines on Paris's palm. "Is this okay?"

"More than," Paris said, slightly breathy.

Ben leaned his head back against the top of the cushions and looked at him with heavy eyes. "I liked your friends. Tony's a bit much, but everyone else was pretty nice."

Paris smiled. "Yeah. He's not staying, though."

"Really?"

With a nod, Paris got a bit more comfortable, kicking his leg up on the coffee table and hoping Ben didn't mind since technically it was all his furniture. He supposed other guests—the short-term ones—probably did a lot worse. "He owns the franchise, but Zeke is running the shop. Have you met him? Big, nerdy dude with glasses who looks like a cross between a linebacker and a librarian?"

Ben covered his mouth as he laughed. "No. Was he there yesterday?"

"Nah, he's back in Colorado doing more management training, but he'll be here in a couple of weeks." Paris fought back the urge to lean in and take another kiss. "You'll like him. He's a really good guy. He's only been tattooing a couple of years, but he noticed that some of the guys weren't happy at our old spot, so he got together with Tony and suggested we open a shop here. His other place is in Denver. Or, like, near it in some small town in the Rockies."

Ben got a wistful look on his face. "I've never been, but the pictures look amazing."

Paris twisted their hands so he could run his thumb over the tendon in Ben's wrist. It was tight with tension, but he didn't think it was the bad kind. "I haven't either. I was working a bunch of jobs because I had to, and then after that, it just became easier not to. I think Max resents me a little bit for it. He always had the travel bug. But he forgave me when I said yes to Key Largo."

Ben met his gaze and held it. "I'm glad you did."

Paris's resolve broke. He leaned in, carefully cupping Ben's cheek as he brought their lips together. His instinct was to devour. It was to pin Ben to the sofa and consume him until there was nothing left of either of them. Instead, he kept it a careful dance—a push-pull of lips and tongue, tasting everything Ben allowed him to have.

And it was intoxicating.

He was falling hard and fast, and that was maybe the most terrifying sensation he'd ever felt.

"I hope your brother gets to do some exploring while he's here," Ben said once the kiss broke. He shuffled even closer, shifting so he could drape his legs over Paris's lap, and he just let himself be held. Paris felt awkward and clumsy, like one wrong move would break the precious man in his arms, but he decided it was time to trust himself. After all, he was owed that little bit of faith after this long.

Curling his hand around Ben's ankle, Paris ran his thumb over the exposed skin on the top of his foot. It was rough and a little hairy, and he could feel the echo of Ben's pulse in the thick vein that ran beside the bone.

"Am I being weird?" Ben asked.

Paris blinked in surprise, then realized he'd been quiet for too long. "No. *God* no. I'm, uh...I'm kind of a hot mess. That's something you should probably know about me before you decide you want to do this."

Ben looked vaguely amused, his brows lifted high on his forehead. "No offense, but I definitely already knew that."

Paris choked a little. "Am I that obvious?"

"You're living in this shithole motel, which is clearly way under your budget. That alone says enough about you," Ben told him with a tiny grin.

Paris squeezed his calf, making Ben jump and laugh. "This is *your* motel."

"Like I said. A shithole." Ben's face sobered after a beat, and Paris realized they were touching on something serious. Something tender. "It could be better. I know that. I mean, I'm not broke or anything. We're almost always at capacity, even if the walls are cardboard and annoying neighbors fuck late at night."

Paris's cheeks heated a bit, and he had to glance away. "It might not have been as awful as I made it sound."

Ben cleared his throat. "Yeah, well. I'm just saying I know it's not the best, and I know I could afford to make it better."

"Is it because of your brother?" Paris asked carefully.

Ben closed his eyes, and his shoulders tensed. "I'm not actually a sentimental guy. I can be romantic, but I don't feel like I need to cling to material stuff, you know? I'm happy enough to collect pretty stones and put them on Levi's headstone whenever I visit." He finally looked at Paris, and his eyes were dry and pained. "My grief therapist said it would manifest in weird ways. She told me a bunch of times it wouldn't be like the movies with some montage and old letters that crack me open and help me get over it."

"It's paralyzing," Paris said, hating that he understood. His own grief of losing not only his mother but his entire way of life was different, but he could still relate. The hollow ache that lived in his chest made up of the knowledge that nothing could ever change his past.

Just like nothing Ben did would ever bring his brother back.

Inevitability and mortality was a fucking bitch.

And so was reality.

"Someday, I'll either sell this place, or I'll save a bunch of money to dump into it and turn it into a place people want to stay when they come back."

Paris didn't know what to say. He wasn't great with feelings. He didn't know how to make people feel better. So he just reached out and cupped Ben's cheek again. "I happen to know one person who has a massive amount of incentive to come back again. Or...to stay."

"Even with a jellyfish dick?" Ben shot back.

Paris's mouth dropped open in surprise. "Are you fucking—"

Before he could get the rest of the words out, Ben was on him. He was grinding down on Paris's still-sore dick, which was the strangest mix of pain and pleasure. His hands moved into Paris's hair, holding tight, lips parted, tongue tasting.

It was as good as the other night, that kiss.

No, it was better. Now, Paris knew what Ben liked. He knew how to push his tongue in, and to bite Ben's lips, and to hold him by the waist and squeeze. He pulled small, thoughtless moans from Ben's lungs and hoarded them in his own as he breathed in deep.

"Fuck," Ben said, pulling back.

Paris tried to regain his composure as their foreheads knocked together. His dick was throbbing but only half-hard, and he knew he needed more time. Not just physically, though. This was something new—it was important, and just like Ben, the possibilities with him were precious and endless. He was fucking terrified that he would barrel forward like a goddamn rabid bull in a china shop and ruin everything.

Paris didn't want to think about what life would be like there if he could no longer even look at Ben.

"We should slow down," Paris said, bracing himself for Ben to get offended.

But Ben only nodded, sagging against Paris's chest. "Yeah. That's...yeah."

Paris made no move to let him go, though. Instead, he wrapped his arms tight around Ben's back and held him.

"I can hear your heart," Ben said after a moment. He lifted his face with a huge grin. "I don't think I've ever heard someone's heartbeat before."

Paris didn't know what to say. He just stared at Ben as his would-be lover turned his gaze down to Paris's chest, then traced a finger over his left pec. He had a raven there—the ink done by Max, who had a talent for colors. He'd managed to get it to look iridescent, like black feathers in a stream of sunlight, and it was one of Paris's favorite pieces.

"How many tattoos do you have?" Ben asked.

Paris laughed. "I've lost count. I have a lot more bare skin than most of the guys in the shop, but that's because I was too busy giving ink to get much." He ran the tips of his fingers up and down Ben's back, smiling lightly when Ben sagged against him again. "You have anything?"

Ben laughed. "Nah. The bravest I ever got was after I took a bite of a weed gummy and went into a piercing shop." Paris heard a soft clicking sound of Ben tapping his barbell against his teeth. "My mom about lost her mind."

Paris snorted. "Yeah. Sometimes I wonder what my mom would think if she saw me like this."

Ben stiffened just a bit and turned his head. "You think she'd be disappointed?"

"I think she'd be more pissed at what my dad let happen to me and Max than how I decorated my skin. But I was really young when she died, so I don't remember her as much as I wish I could. And Max doesn't remember her at all."

Ben sighed quietly and went back to tracing patterns on Paris's chest. "Sometimes it hurts more to think of all the people Levi will never meet. And all the people who won't meet him. He would have liked you."

That was a weight Paris was afraid to bear, but he also knew the words were important, so he held them close to his chest. "I'm sorry life dealt you a shit hand."

Ben pulled back. "Seriously?"

Paris sucked in a breath. "Sorry, I told you I'm no good at—"

He was cut off by another kiss, this one almost desperate. Ben's lips were trembling, and his breath was coming a bit too fast. Paris carefully slowed him down, petting fingers through the back of his hair, easing their lips into gentle pecks.

"No one has ever," Ben started, but his voice wavered, so he stopped and waited a beat. "People never just say sorry. They always feed me some bullshit line about how Levi would be happy for me, or proud of me, or whatever. And that's probably true. Like, he was a pretty pragmatic guy, and if he's some ghost aware of his own death,

I'm sure he'd be glad I'm able to function after losing him. But he's not here. He made a mistake that cost him everything, and I hate when people say shit like that because there's no way to know."

Paris cupped Ben's cheeks with both hands. "I get that."

Ben leaned into Paris's touch. "Yeah, you do. Better than most people. Life dealt a lot of us a shit hand, and I'd prefer to just, you know, accept it."

"Well, I'm good at that. Like I said, I'm really fucking bad at being normal."

Ben surged up and kissed him one more time. "That's fine by me. Normal sounds boring as hell."

8

"You're panicking."

Ben looked over at Callisto, who was watching him with a careful expression. He was leaning on the cart with Lila in the front, the toddler distracted by her little can of kid-friendly cheese puffs made out of sweet potato or some other abomination.

Running a hand over his face, he sighed. "I can't help it. I don't really remember what sleepovers were like. It's probably no surprise I didn't get invited to them a lot. If I wasn't hanging out with you, my mom had to bully Levi's friends into including me."

Callisto's face fell. "I'm sorry, man. Kids are shitty."

Ben just laughed and shrugged. He was well over the middle school tormentors who never got more clever than making fun of his deaf accent and calling him the r-word while smacking their chest with their hands. Back then, it had been the height of insult, but now, Ben looked back and realized those were the kids who peaked at twelve.

Maybe his life wasn't anything to write books about, but it was a shitload better than the lives they were all living now. Except the panicking part, but that was only because he needed to make this good for Paris. He'd been consumed with the idea of helping his new lover relive all the things he'd been denied as a kid.

He couldn't get over the fact that Paris and Max had lived some real-life Cinderella story, minus the handsome prince sweeping in to save them from their evil stepfamily. Instead, Paris had become his own white knight, but it left behind gaping holes and obvious scars.

Ben wasn't a fool. He knew he couldn't rewrite Paris's past or take away his pain, but he could at least give him this. Tenderness, kindness, and maybe some sex that Ben wasn't sure he'd survive because those kisses were enough to ruin him already.

He could only imagine what Paris was like in bed.

Ben turned when he felt a tap on his shoulder, and Callisto was smiling at him. 'Lost?' Callisto signed.

Ben fought the urge to flip him off, but only because the tiny toddler with her innocent eyes and wispy curls was watching. "Okay. So we've got pizza rolls, Popsicles, ice cream...you really think chocolate chip cookie dough is the right one?"

Callisto scoffed. "If he doesn't like cookie dough ice cream, he's a fucking monster and needs to be driven from the island."

Ben grinned. "Not before I have my wicked way with him."

"Wicked," Lila repeated.

Ben slapped his face, and she copied him.

"She's a sponge," Callisto said with a small sigh. "Eat your Cheetos, peanut."

She threw one on the floor in protest, and Ben was reminded once again why he would never, ever choose the parent life.

"Next is chips and popcorn," Callisto said. "Do you have movies ready to go?"

Ben bit his lip. "I mean, I have streaming, so yeah, pretty much. Andrew said he was going to come up with a list of date movies from back when we were in high school so I can give Paris the proper experience."

Callisto's smile softened into something almost wistful. "He's going to love this."

Ben wanted to tell him that something like this would happen for him one day, but he didn't want to make some empty, bullshit promise because he didn't know that. Most queer men their age cringed at the idea of kids, let alone dating a single dad. It would probably happen for him someday because Callisto was devastatingly good-looking and one of the kindest people Ben had ever met.

But he also had very little time to himself, no support system, and he wasn't willing to compromise on the things he couldn't change.

He followed Callisto a few aisles over and loaded up the cart with various chips. "I hope you and Andrew are going to come over after all this and help me finish this shit off. I can't have this junk sitting around my house."

Callisto laughed. "Give me two hours with my trash compactor toddler."

Ben was willing to bet if he did that, most of it would end up ground into the carpet by tiny feet, but he didn't mind that idea that much. Callisto deserved friends who let his kid be a kid. "I'll take it."

They finished their shopping, Callisto picking up a few things for his house and trying to protest when Ben gathered it all and paid for it together, but Ben wasn't having it. He just pulled his processors off his head and gave him a grin before swiping his card.

He put them back on as they were heading into the parking lot, and the noise returned with an annoying pulse against the back of his skull. He ignored it as he loaded up the food, then climbed into the driver's seat while he waited for Callisto to finish strapping Lila in.

The passenger door slammed with a bit too much vigor, and Ben carefully turned to look at his friend. "Don't be pissed."

Callisto just stared, looking put out.

Ben groaned gently. "Can you let me help once in a while without resenting me for it? You're working two full-time jobs, and my bills are so tight right now I can't afford to give you a raise." Ben swallowed heavily and hated himself for having to say that, but it was true. Even at capacity, his employee budget was stretched to the max. "The least I can do is buy the peanut a bag of chicken nuggets every once in a while."

After a long, tense moment, Callisto sagged against his seat. "I'm sorry. I'm just really tired and really frustrated."

"I know. I wish I could do more."

Callisto shook his head and pulled his glasses off before tapping his thumb on his chest. 'I'm fine.'

Ben didn't push the issue. Instead, he stayed quiet and let Callisto feel whatever it was he was feeling as he made his way to his little one-room cottage to drop him off. He didn't help him inside. Callisto hated having people over, and Ben didn't need to ask why.

He gave a quick wave right before Callisto shut his front door, and then he backed out and headed to his place, trying not to panic about the upcoming date. If that's what he was willing to call it—and if what Paris was willing to accept.

They'd seen each other sporadically since the tattoo shop opened, usually just in passing but a couple of times for a quick make-out session before bed. Ben was desperate for more, but Paris kept pulling back, and Ben knew that whatever trauma Paris was keeping close to his chest was the reason for it. And he sure as hell wasn't going to push.

Hell, if that's all Paris wanted to do for the rest of their lives together, Ben would take it. He loved sex, and he was pretty damn good at it, but it wasn't the end-all, be-all of what he wanted. Not for his future, and as little as he knew Paris still, something told him he should cling to hope.

Ben looked around at the bedroom and had a quiet, internal crisis that Paris was going to take one look at it and bolt. He'd head right over to the tattoo shop and tell everyone what an absolute fucking weirdo Ben was, and slowly but surely, the entire island would cut him off.

He was well aware that he didn't actually believe Paris would be capable of doing something like that, but the self-doubt was crushing. He and Levi had spent a good chunk of their summers in elementary school living inside blanket forts. He was pretty sure his parents still had several old quilts with round burn marks from where they accidentally let the fabric rest against a naked lightbulb.

The memory made his chest ache in the best way.

This fort was a bit more luxurious than the ones they had as kids. They'd been stuck with old, beat-up eighties cushions from their grandparents' old couch, and they were only allowed to use the emergency sheets and the old blankets that no one was brave enough to sleep with. They'd build it with the rickety old kitchen chairs and piles of their dad's coffee table travel books to hold the blankets in place.

This setup had come from an actual blanket fort kit that Callisto had been given when Lila was born. It was a thin PVC pipe frame with hooks to hold the nice set of silky sheets that Ben dug out from his closet. It had space for a hanging lantern, which he took out of the hurricane kit, and he grabbed every spare pillow the motel had to offer, along with a couple of his downy blankets to line the floors.

He had put all the snacks into bowls, hoping the humidity wouldn't make the chips all chewy before Paris finally got home, the pizza was timed for delivery, and the ice cream was in the freezer, waiting for him to take it out. The only thing left was to cue up a movie on his laptop and hope that Paris was willing to accept this as cute and quirky instead of creepy and strange.

His forehead broke out into a cold sweat, and he rushed into the bathroom to look at himself for the sixteenth time in half an hour.

Ben had taken time on his hair, trying to order his slightly frizzy curls into something attractive. He'd washed his face and put on a lightly scented lotion, slipped into his most comfortable pair of sweats and a T-shirt, and hoped that Paris got his text about dressing in pajamas.

He was kind of hoping that would give it away, but considering Paris had no experience with shit like this, he didn't hold out hope.

Pulling down the skin beneath his eyes, he stared at the whites and then let go just as something flashed in his periphery.

The doorbell.

It definitely wasn't the pizza, which meant he'd missed Paris's text, and he swore he could feel his heartbeat pounding in his throat as he tried to appear calm and collected. He leaned on the door handle as he pulled it open and let out a rush of relieved breath when he saw Paris was dressed in flannel pants and a black T-shirt.

Paris's eyes moved up and down Ben's body, a tiny smile playing at his lips. "Okay. So you weren't kidding about pajamas and staying in."

Ben shook his head and motioned for him to come in. "Nope. I mean, we can get dressed and go out if you'd prefer to do that, but—"

"No offense, but I just spent every single hour of my day talking to strangers," Paris said, sounding exhausted. "The last thing I want to do is sit at a table surrounded by more."

Ben offered him a sympathetic smile. "Well, I've got pizza on the way. And um. Some other stuff."

Paris lifted a brow. "Some other stuff?"

"It's—" But Ben didn't get to finish his sentence. His doorbell flashed again, and he scrambled for the cash in his wallet. He recognized the kid at the door and felt bad for yanking the boxes out of his hand and shoving the cash at him, but he had no space in his brain to be polite. "Sorry. Thanks. Keep all the change," he said in a rush, then slammed the door.

Paris was watching him carefully, his brow still high on his forehead. "Um. What was that?"

"Me being a fucking nightmare," Ben said with a hollow laugh. "I think I'm nervous."

Paris's smile widened. "I meant the..." He gestured to the little light above the door.

"Oh. My doorbell. I don't wear my processors at home after work very often."

At that, Paris's face fell. "Do you want to take them off? We could...I don't know. I mean, I've only picked up a little bit so far, but we could write? Or text? I could—"

"You're sweet," Ben interrupted, his voice coming out soft against the back of his throat. "But honestly, this is fine."

Paris looked like he didn't quite believe him, but he still moved to take the pizza from his hands. "Where do you want this?"

"Um." Ben swallowed thickly. *Stop saying um, you moron,* he shouted internally at himself. "The bedroom?"

Paris's eyes widened. "Okay?"

"It's not a sex thing," Ben blurted, then slapped a hand over his face. "It's a non-sex surprise. And you can tell me that I'm being a jackass and totally leave if you hate it. I just...I had this idea. Now I'm thinking it was wrong, and I don't—"

His words cut off when he felt a gentle touch against his jaw and looked up to see that Paris had closed the distance between them. He was balancing both boxes on the palm of one hand, his body turned to the side.

Ben had just enough time to think, *That has to be burning his hand,* before he was kissed long, and slow, and careful. When Paris pulled away, Ben was slightly breathless and smiling helplessly. "Oh."

Paris laughed softly. "Ben. I really want to see your surprise."

Ben fought back the urge to once again remind Paris that he would totally understand if he turned around and walked right back out. He wouldn't be offended either. Maybe a little devastated, sure, and halfway to heartbreak, but he could deal with that.

He'd been through worse.

Squaring his shoulders, he grabbed the door handle to his room and pushed in, then held his breath and closed his eyes as Paris came up behind him. He could feel the heat from Paris's body and the weight of his stare as the man took in the room.

"It's a blanket fort," Ben finally said into the silence.

"I can...see that," Paris said slowly.

"Because you," Ben went on, stammering gently. "Because you said your whole life, you were never allowed to have stuff like this. And I know it's kind of—whatever. Immature. But my brother and I spent every summer living in one of these, and I just couldn't stand the thought that you never got to have one. And if you hate it, we can just tear it down and eat on the couch and pretend like this never happened."

Paris remained silent, but he pushed Ben to the side and walked to the bed, dropping the pizzas down on the comforter with a hard thud. Ben's heart sank to his feet, but only until Paris had him by the waist, backing him against the wall and kissing the literal breath from his lungs.

"I don't know what to say," Paris finally murmured, right against his lips.

Ben was too afraid to move, too afraid it wasn't real. "You don't hate it?"

"No. I don't know what the fuck this emotion is, but no. I don't hate it. Is there room for two grown men in there?"

Ben laughed, the sound probably on the edge of hysterical, but he was struggling to process noise right then with how badly his nerves were firing. "Um, yeah. There's already snacks inside, and pillows. I thought we could watch a movie and...whatever."

"And whatever," Paris echoed before kissing him again.

Ben was fully hard in his sweats and starting to feel a little desperate, but he didn't do anything about it. He just let Paris kiss him until they had to break apart to breathe, and then Paris laughed and swiped his thumb over Ben's lips.

"Sorry."

"Please don't ever apologize for kissing me," Ben said. "Like. Ever."

Paris's smile turned a little darker, but he didn't step close again. Instead, he turned and dropped to his knees at the entrance of the little tent. His ass was round and pert, and Ben had a quick fantasy of sinking his teeth into his skin there before Paris disappeared from view.

"Holy shit," Paris said, his voice slightly muffled. "Are you serious?"

Ben laughed, then grabbed the pizzas and handed them through the flap before he crawled inside himself. The light at the top gave a sort of hazy yellow glow, and Paris sat under it with a shit-eating grin on his face. It was everything Ben's queer, teenage heart had ever wanted, and he was struggling to believe he'd gotten it now.

Even if it ended after tonight, this was something he'd take with him until the day he died.

Paris looked so fucking happy. His smile rarely reached his eyes, but in that moment, his entire face lit up like an eighth-night menorah.

"So this is a lot nicer than the ones my brother and I used to build," Ben said, getting settled against a pile of pillows. "We weren't allowed to use any of the good shit, so the cushions always smelled like my grandpa's stale cigars, and we definitely didn't have a laptop."

Paris laughed softly and shifted closer so their hips were touching. He turned on his side and ran the tips of his fingers over Ben's collarbone. "Ever take a date in one?"

Ben snorted. "I definitely didn't have dates back then. No one even looked at me twice until college."

Paris pulled back with a look of disbelief. "That can't possibly be true."

Ben shrugged. "They thought I was weird. I had a couple of actual friends, but in high school, most of the people who talked to me just wanted to write 'friends with a disabled kid' on their college applications."

Paris's face went stormy. "People are the worst."

Ben laughed and shrugged again. "It got better. I tried to apply to Gallaudet, but I didn't qualify for financial aid, and I didn't want to take out loans for that much. So I went to school in Orlando and met a bunch of queer Deafs who introduced me to the joys of hookup culture."

"Why did you make that sound like it was your worst nightmare?" Paris asked.

Ben hadn't realized how raw he sounded, and he flushed, glancing away. He grabbed a chip bowl and picked one out just for something to do with his hands. "I never quite fit in with anyone, you know? Like, I went fully deaf when I was a baby, and my parents panicked and got me the implants so I could fit in. But it took me forever to learn how to hear, and by then, I had a weird accent, and I was struggling in school." Ben stopped abruptly. "Sorry. This isn't great first-date conversation."

"Getting to know you is perfect first-date conversation," Paris argued. He seized Ben's wrist and tugged his hand close, carefully biting the chip from his fingers and smirking. "Keep going."

"Jesus," Ben breathed, trying to control his raging hard-on. "Um. So, they had this really great marriage, right? And I went to college knowing I probably wasn't going to marry my first boyfriend, but I figured I'd at least *have* one."

"And that didn't happen," Paris said.

Ben shrugged. "There were plenty of guys in our friend group who were in relationships, but no one else there was interested in anything more than sex. And it was fine for a while. Like scratching an itch. But I started to wonder if maybe it was me."

"Maybe it was a bunch of morons who had no idea how to appreciate you for the gift you are," Paris growled. He leaned forward. "Chip, please."

Ben had to work hard to keep his fingers from trembling as he fed Paris another bite. "Um. So. Um."

Paris smiled at him, indulgent and way too goddamn sexy.

Ben cleared his throat. "So, yeah. I got a job working in PR, then my brother died, and my parents kind of fell apart, and I ended up here." He met Paris's gaze. "Long story really long, I never had the chance to build a blanket fort for any boyfriends because I've never had one."

"Neither have I," Paris said after a small beat of silence. "But you probably figured that out already."

Ben laughed a little breathlessly and set the chip bowl aside, swiping his fingers on his sweats. "I'm sure plenty of people tried. You're hotter than the fucking sun and maybe one of the nicest guys I've ever met."

Paris looked almost unsure, and he rubbed the back of his neck, ducking his head. "Yeah, you might be the only person on the planet who has ever called me nice. I'm not a dick, but I'm not the easiest person to be around most of the time."

Ben didn't want to outright call him a liar, but he struggled to believe that he was a totally different person with everyone else. Yeah, Paris had been abrasive and almost skittish when Ben first met him, but he'd softened, almost like he was desperate to.

"Well, then they're not paying close enough attention," Ben told him, and Paris bit his lip hard enough Ben was afraid he might break the skin. "Anyway, we should eat and watch a movie. I promised you the whole experience, and that's part of it."

Paris let out the smallest laugh, then nodded. "You start the movie. I'll get the pizza ready."

Ben tried not to stare out of the corner of his eye as Paris did, but he couldn't help himself. He was falling so hard and so fast, if Paris wasn't there to catch him when he hit the ground, he'd definitely shatter.

9

Paris did his absolute fucking best to pay attention to the movie. It was some eighties flick with a bunch of actors who looked thirty, all playing high school students in detention. He got the distinct impression he was supposed to know the movie, but he hadn't been lying about how much he'd missed out on.

His childhood had been garbage, and from sixteen on, his every waking hour had been consumed with earning enough money to take Max and then making sure Max was taken care of. He'd seen a couple of *Star Wars* movies and the occasional car-racing film whenever one of the guys put something on in the studio, but that was where his pop culture education ended.

And if he had been with anyone else but Ben, he might have been embarrassed. With him, Paris was helplessly charmed. Ben laughed at all the wrong parts, ranted whenever the movie got a little bit sexist—which was a lot—and then told the story of the first time he'd smoked weed and then had to go to gym class.

"I was pretty sure I was going to vomit," Ben said quietly, his cheek pressed against Paris's pec. "I was doing those dip things—I forget what they're called. You hold yourself up between two bars and use your arms to lower yourself?"

Paris shrugged. "I dropped out of high school, and when I was there, I sure as fuck didn't go to *gym*."

Ben snort-laughed and tilted his head up to look at Paris. "God, you would have been the worst influence on me. It's too bad we didn't know each other then. Though you probably would have thrown me in a trash can or something."

"Or I would have tried to kiss you behind the bleachers," Paris murmured, leaning in to demonstrate.

Ben groaned, but he pushed Paris away after a lingering moment and laid his head back down. "Anyway, the dips were done in front of the mirror, and I know I wasn't hallucinating, but my brain was all fucked-up. Everything sounded really wrong, and my face looked all...I don't know. Distorted. I started to have a panic attack and ran to the locker room and stayed there until my next period."

Paris gently carded fingers through Ben's hair, careful not to knock his processors off, which was easier said than done. He'd already done it twice while they were trying to exchange pizza slices, and while Ben just laughed it off, Paris felt like a clumsy ogre.

"Your teacher didn't get pissed?"

"I don't think he noticed. He was the football coach, so he was busy going over plays or whatever with the kids on the freshman team." Ben let out a slow breath. "By the time high school rolled around, people outgrew the name-calling and moved on to ignoring me. It was a lot easier to deal with."

Paris clenched one hand into a fist and only just managed not to ask Ben the names of those little fuck-faces so he could pay them a visit. "If we ever see one of those assholes from your middle school, feel free to point them out."

Ben laughed again, turning to push up on his elbow. "You want to defend my honor?"

"I want to do a lot of things," Paris told him, his voice a low growl. "But yeah. I'd happily hold them down while you knocked them in the mouth."

Paris hadn't considered the way to Ben's heart was through threats of violence against his former tormentors, but the way he went all soft and pliant, Paris tucked that away for later. He knocked a finger under Ben's chin and lifted his face so he could kiss him, and this time, it went on for longer.

Paris had been desperately hard since he saw Ben in his adorable little pajamas. His sweats were grey, with a little barely there cat pattern along the outside of the legs, and he was perfectly soft and sweet. Then Paris had gotten a look at Ben's surprise, and he wasn't quite sure how to name the feeling in his chest.

All he knew was that he never wanted it to go away.

He wanted to pin Ben down there in that ridiculous little blanket fort and just eat and fuck and breathe the same air and never come out again.

Paris had been trying to move slowly since he agreed to date Ben, not just for his own sake but also because he didn't know exactly what he wanted—or what he was capable of giving. It was clear from Ben's past that he wanted a relationship. He wanted to be swept away and tumbled head over heels, and Paris wanted to vow he could give him all of that.

He could offer him a future and a life and stability.

Hell, he'd done it for Max, so he knew he was capable of being steady and stable. But he wasn't sure he trusted himself with Ben's heart. What if Ben wanted things Paris couldn't stand? Like kids. Or what if he wanted Paris to move away from Max? Not to mention Paris only had two ASL lessons under his belt, and he was still too insecure to use even basic phrases just yet.

Paris felt like a different man when he was with him, but it wouldn't last. Eventually, the sharp edges would come out, and he would hurt Ben, and then...

Fuck.

He'd ruin it.

He pulled back, his chest heaving for breath, and he met Ben's gaze, which was a little concerned. "You okay?" Ben asked.

Nodding, Paris dragged a hand down his face and decided that the very least thing Ben deserved was honesty. "I want you. I want to fuck you so badly."

Ben's cheeks pinked, and his lips parted as he sucked in a breath. "You're not going to hear me argue."

Paris let out a tense laugh and shook his head, dropping his face to Ben's hair and breathing him in. He smelled like soap and lotion—just a subtle hint, and he fucking loved it. "I know you want more than a hookup."

Ben carefully dislodged himself from Paris's arms and sat up, pulling his knees to his chest. It was a defensive position Paris knew a little too well. "You're right. I do. I really like you, Paris. And I don't think I can do casual with you."

"I'm not saying that's what I want," Paris said in a rush. It felt like some invisible force was crushing his heart at the thought that Ben believed Paris was just in it for sex. "I'm saying that I've never done this before. It's not just blanket forts and movies and birthday parties. After my mom died, no one in my entire life told me they loved me."

Ben drew his lip between his teeth and bit down hard.

Paris knew that people who had been loved couldn't fathom the way he'd grown up. The few people in his life he had told his story to looked at him like he was full of cracks, on the edge of shattering like hot glass in a bucket of ice.

But he was stronger than that.

"Max and I love each other, but we never really learned to say it. And it became easier to just accept that about myself than try to fight it," Paris went on. "I really like you. I like you so much it scares the shit out of me, but I don't ever want to hurt you, and I'm afraid I will because I don't know how to be good for anyone."

Ben sat there, his eyes fixed on Paris's lips, his brow furrowed, nose slightly scrunched. He was clearly processing, so Paris went silent and let him.

"I understand what you're saying," Ben eventually told him. "I can't imagine what you've gone through, but I get it. Things can't just change overnight because you met someone you like."

Paris nodded, though he felt a sudden and powerful urge to beg Ben to fight for him.

"So can I ask something from you?"

"Anything," Paris said. "I just can't promise I'll say yes."

Ben's lip twitched. "Yeah, I know. I'm not asking for a yes anyway. I'm asking that maybe...that maybe you trust me a little. Maybe you and I take it really slow, and let me woo you."

Paris felt like there was a hurricane under his skin. "Woo me."

"Shut up. I know I sound like some duke in a romance novel, but I'm serious. I want to show you that love can be easy. I mean, I'm learning too. I wasn't joking when I said no one's ever wanted me for more than just a quick fuck, but I know what it's like to be cared about. I just need some patience to prove that you can do this with me."

Paris squeezed his eyes shut and reached out, finding Ben's fingers with his own. "And if I need you to be patient with me?"

"Can you look at me?" Ben asked.

Paris did. It wasn't a struggle. Paris understood the aesthetics of beauty, but not when it came to people. In the past, when he fucked, it was with someone who was willing and had a condom. He had no idea if the rest of the world wanted to drop to their knees at the sight of Ben, but *he* sure as hell did.

When their gazes locked, Ben carefully climbed to his knees, then swung one leg over Paris's thighs and straddled him. He was hard—Paris could feel his throbbing erection when he laid his weight down, and he groaned softly at the same time Ben did.

"I will be as patient as you need me to be," Ben said softly. He wrapped both hands around the back of Paris's neck and squeezed. "But I need you to answer me. Will you try?"

"Yes," Paris said. He licked his lips, then confessed, "I signed up for ASL. It's this...Zoom class thing. Twice a week. I want to be good for you, Ben. I'm so fucking tired of being lonely and ignored. And I know most of it is my fault. I just...I want it to be different here."

Ben sucked in a breath, then surged forward and kissed Paris. It was on the edge of painful—too biting and sharp—but Paris took the sting without a single second of complaint because he'd give every bit of himself to Ben that he asked for.

Would it still end in disaster? Considering his track record, Paris would be a fool to bet on himself, but Ben gave him hope.

"Does taking it slow mean no sex?" he choked out when Ben pulled back.

With a laugh, Ben rolled his eyes and rubbed their noses together. "I fucking hope not. I want you so bad it feels like my balls are going to burst."

Emboldened, Paris dropped one hand between them and palmed over Ben's crotch. He felt along his hard dick, then lower to his warm sac, which he kneaded gently. Ben let out a loud moan, thrusting against Paris, his arms starting to tremble.

"Condom?"

"No," Paris said. "Fuck. I'm so sorry."

Ben groaned. "I'm out too. Theo usually...sorry. Shit. I don't mean to bring him up right now."

Paris didn't take his hand away. He used the heel of his palm to rub against Ben's dick as he met his gaze. "I'm going to do my best not to be a jealous asshole. And Theo made you feel good. I heard it, and I can't hate him for that."

"God, how are you real?" Ben asked as he continued to rock his hips over Paris's. He stared down at where they were pressed together. "Get off with me like this? And I'll be more prepared next time."

Paris laughed, the sound strained, and he tilted Ben's head up as he urged him to lift higher on his knees. With a swift motion, he had Ben's sweats down to his thighs, and he gave his palm several licks before curling his fingers around Ben's throbbing shaft. His thumb pressed to the slit, and then he slid his hand down to the root, then back up to the tip.

Ben let out a hard groan, his thighs shaking as he held himself up. "I'm going to literally nut all over you in ten seconds." His voice was thready and breathless. "This is going to be embarrassing."

"The fuck it is," Paris said. "That is so goddamn hot." He urged Ben to sit back down, putting his ass right over Paris's dick. The pressure was overwhelming, but he did his best to ignore it as his hand picked up speed, trying to match the way Ben was rocking his hips. The friction was definitely enough to get Paris off, and he felt his balls pulling up as he tried to get Ben over the edge of his orgasm before he shot his load in his sweats.

Ben's neck was pink just above his collar, and he was making the most beautiful punched-out noises as he thrust his dick into Paris's palm. It only took a few moments, and then he was crying out and dropping his head and coming all over Paris's stomach.

Paris let out a sharp breath as Ben pulled away, and suddenly, there were fierce, furious hands tugging at his waistband. "It's fine. It's..." he started to argue.

"Let me," Ben ordered, not looking up.

He seemed singularly focused, and Paris was too fucking needy to argue with him. He lifted his hips when Ben urged him to, and suddenly, his dick was exposed to the humid air of the little blanket fort. Ben's firm hand shoved him back, and his gaze fixed on the lantern, which made the sheets glow.

A moment later, he heard Ben spit, and then warm, wet fingers curled around him. The fingers on Ben's other hand dug into his thigh, forcing him to spread his legs wider, then crept past his balls and pressed hard against his taint.

Paris's mouth opened on a silent cry when he felt Ben's lips press a kiss to his shaft, and though Ben didn't take him in his mouth, he could picture it. He could almost feel the slick slide of his tongue over the head of his dick, and it was enough.

It knocked him right off the edge of the cliff, and he was only barely aware of Ben's hand stroking him until his thighs were shaking and his hands were clawing at the blankets beneath him.

His shirt was filthy from both of them, and he managed to get one eye open, looking down at the mess they'd made. He had the urge to drag his finger through it and taste it, so he did. It was sticky and cooling, and the taste was subtle and salty.

He forced himself to meet Ben's gaze, whose eyes were wide, pupils all but consuming his irises. "Fuck. I'm..."

"Yeah," Paris breathed out. He sat up carefully, pulling his shirt off while trying to contain the mess, and then he flopped back down. Ben only took a second before he was curled up next to him, and he pressed a kiss to Paris's bare pec before laying a hand on his stomach.

"I haven't fucked anyone with my processors on before."

Paris blinked at him. "Never?"

Ben shook his head. "Never fucked a hearing guy."

"Did you...was it...?"

"I like everything about you," Ben said with a tiny smile. "Even your weird noises."

Paris's face erupted with heat, making Ben laugh and curl closer to him. "Thanks for making me feel even more awkward."

Ben pushed up on his elbow and rolled his eyes. "I'm sure my noises were just as strange."

Paris reached out, feeling tender and soft and willing to lean into it, even if everything changed tomorrow. He traced a touch over Ben's slightly swollen lips. "Everything about you was perfect. Is perfect."

"God, don't say that. I can't live up to that," Ben begged.

Paris just shrugged, then hooked his finger under Ben's chin and pulled him in for a kiss. He was in no rush to leave, and from the way Ben held him, Ben was in no rush for him to go.

10

"HEY. YOU DIDN'T FILL OUT THE CALENDAR."

Paris looked up from his client's arm when he realized Jamie was talking to him, and he frowned. "The what?"

"Birthday calendar," Jamie clarified. He was sitting on his rolling stool, darting from stall to stall like he was a little kid on a go-kart. "You didn't fill yours out."

Paris rolled his eyes and looked back down at the young woman who'd flown in from Montreal to get a quarter sleeve done. "Sorry," he told her, setting his machine down and folding his hands between his knees. "Look, bud. I'm kind of in the middle of something right now."

"Right. I just..."

"His birthday is in two weeks," Max piped up from his stall, "but Paris doesn't celebrate it."

"Ever?" Jamie asked, wide-eyed and horrified.

Paris braced himself for the inevitable conversation. No, he didn't want to talk about it. No, he wasn't going to change his mind. *Yes*, he really didn't celebrate.

"Never," Max said, and Paris breathed a small sigh of relief, grateful for his brother, who probably knew Paris didn't want to go over this again. "It's not personal, Jamie."

Paris could feel the other tattoo artist staring at him, and he felt a wave of irritation because he just wanted to get the fucking work done so he could go. Because going meant his second date with Ben. And his second date with Ben meant getting to touch him again, and kiss him, and—if he was very lucky—make him fall apart.

But he also didn't want to be the shop monster either. He took a breath and offered an apologetic look to Kelly or Kaleigh or whatever her name was, and then he looked up at the man still hovering in the stall entrance.

"It's on the sixteenth," he said. "I never celebrated birthdays growing up, so it's not a big thing for me."

Jamie tilted his head. "Jehovah's Witness?"

Max snorted loudly, and Paris's lips twitched. "Shitty family. It would be easier to blame religion. But yeah, it's just not a thing I've ever done."

"Can I write it down anyway?" Jamie asked.

Paris bristled, but it wasn't like Jamie was asking to throw him a surprise party or get a bunch of fucking clowns or some shit. And hell, maybe this could be one of the first steps he took to letting people closer.

"Yeah. You can write it down. But if you fuckers get me a cake, it had better not be carrot. That shit is an abomination."

Jamie brightened up and shoved his feet against the tiled floor, whipping back out of the stall. Paris grinned to himself as he turned back to his client, but he caught a motion out of his periphery, and he glanced over to see Max hovering.

"Paris?"

He waved his brother off. "I'm good."

Max's face did something complicated Paris couldn't quite read, but he swore he saw a little glassy moisture in his brother's eyes before he disappeared back into his own space. Paris decided that was something he could deal with later. For now, he had a floral watercolor piece to finish and then a man across town to sweep off his adorable feet.

"Paris!"

He tried not to groan at the sound of his brother's voice. He knew he wasn't going to be able to sneak out without some kind of interrogation, so he resigned himself to it, turning to lean against his truck as Max came to a skidding halt.

"Nice try, asshole," Max wheezed.

Paris raised a brow at him. "You should probably work out more."

"And you should fucking explain yourself."

Paris twirled his key ring around his finger and tried not to physically feel the passage of time. He needed to get the fuck out of there. Ben had told him they were leaving the motel for this date, and he didn't want to look like a total slob.

"Look, if this is about the birthday thing..."

"The birthday thing," Max repeated. He took a step closer and pressed his wrist to Paris's forehead. "You feeling okay?"

Paris batted him away. "Fuck off. It's not a big deal."

Max choked on a laugh. "When Charlie tried to give you a fucking Applebee's gift card, you threatened to throw his equipment in the ocean. And you meant it."

Letting out a soft sigh, Paris met his brother's gaze. "I don't know what you want me to say, Max. It's about time I stop being such a massive asshole, right? Isn't that what you keep telling me?"

Max bit his lip and glanced away. "I don't want you to feel pressure to be someone else just because I—" He stopped abruptly and took a big breath. "Look, I've been feeling like total shit, okay?"

Paris's brows furrowed. "What the fuck for?"

"Because I gave you an ultimatum," Max said in a rush. "I made you pack up your life and move here even though you were perfectly fine where you were."

Paris gave a hollow laugh and reached for Max, dropping a hand to his shoulder to put the poor fucker out of his misery. "I was not perfectly fine in LA. Jesus, I was such a miserable shithead there I don't know how the fuck you put up with me for so long."

Max rolled his eyes. "Because you saved my life."

There was a warmth in his gut Paris didn't have time to think about right then. "I did a shit-ass job raising you, and somehow, you turned into a good person. You were fucking owed this move, Max. I'm not mad about it. I...shit." He let Max go and rubbed his hand down his face. "If I jinx this and it bites me in the ass, I'm gonna be so pissed, but...I think this might have been good for me too. I think this move might have saved me."

Max said nothing for a long time, and then he cleared his throat. "Still no surprises, right?"

"I know how to torture you. And I know how to make it last," Paris warned, turning to open his door. "No fucking surprise parties. But, uh...a barbeque might be fine. With some cake."

Max's entire face went soft. "Okay."

"No gift cards to garbage restaurants, though," he added, then checked his phone. "Anyway, I gotta take off."

"Have fun on your date tonight," Max called as Paris slid behind the wheel, and it was a testament to Paris's desire to change that he didn't try to deny what it was. He just shot his brother a two-fingered salute from the edge of his forehead, then put his car in gear and pulled out onto the main road.

It didn't take him long to get home, and he immediately hopped in the shower, smiling when he heard music blaring through the walls. He didn't recognize it—it was all heavy bass and vibration, which probably meant Ben was listening to it without his processors on.

Paris had spent one long bout of insomnia reading up on all the Deaf lit that his new teacher had assigned him, and when he finished with that, he fell down the rabbit hole of cochlear implants and the experience of Deaf people who didn't get a chance to grow up within their community.

Some of the things Ben had said while they were together in the little blanket fort echoed what he'd read, and now he was wondering if Ben was carrying around a little ball made of misery to accompany the grief of losing his brother.

Ben had gone out of his way to give something to Paris that he'd been denied all of his life, and he felt like such a shit because he had no idea—other than throwing himself into ASL as best he could—to give something back to Ben. But maybe it was enough?

He wished he was better at being a person so he'd have some idea. And part of him was screaming to just ask the guys because all of them knew better than he did, but the thought was still too humiliating to admit he'd spent all of his life as some sort of emotional hermit.

Paris became profoundly aware that the music had stopped somewhere during his thought spiral, and his nerves started to fizz like popping candy. He took one last look at himself in the mirror, then shoved his phone into his pocket and stepped out just as Ben was closing his own door.

They locked eyes, and Ben laughed before bodily shoving Paris back against the wall and kissing him.

"I hope you checked for dog shit," Paris muttered against his lips.

Ben laughed again as he pulled back. "Yes. And I'm about to bribe one of my damn boat iguanas to sit in wait if that fucker doesn't stop."

Paris had almost stepped in the dog shit more than once, so he was definitely on board with the iguana idea. "Why is that happening? I mean, did you piss someone off? Break someone's heart?"

"Trust me. I did nothing," Ben said, rolling his eyes as he stuck out his hand. It took Paris a second to realize what he was asking for. His neck and ears went a little hot as he let Ben thread their fingers together, and he went pliant as Ben tugged him across the parking lot and toward his small car.

Paris pulled his hand away, a slow drag of fingers, and caught Ben's gaze to find it heated and wanting. He was just about ready to beg that they cancel the date and stay in, but he didn't want to see a look of disappointment on Ben's face. There was time enough for that later.

'Ready?' Paris signed.

Ben's face lit up, and he nodded his fist. 'Yes.'

Paris felt a surge of triumph in his gut as he slid in and buckled his seat belt. He still felt clumsy and ridiculous with his signs. His teacher was kind but constantly correcting him, and he was beginning to wonder if maybe he wasn't capable. He was street-smart, but he'd never been able to hack it in school. Even if he had a set of parents who gave a shit about him, he doubted he would have been a scholar. Reading had always been hard, and numbers were so far beyond him.

He held a small, flickering hope that Ben would never notice just how beneath him Paris was.

He glanced over just in time to see Ben tapping the Y shape on his chin. *Wrong. Mistake.* His stomach dropped.

'I know,' he signed, then faltered because that's where his lexicon ended. "Um. I know I'm not very good right now."

Ben blinked, then let out a tiny laugh. "Honey, no, I'm not correcting you. I'm asking what's wrong."

Paris's entire body flushed at the term of endearment. He'd heard them a few times, but usually in sarcasm or mockery. Coming from Ben's lips, it was wrapped around kindness and sincerity. God, he was not prepared for this.

He cleared his throat. "I'm nervous to sign," he said. "I don't want to fuck it all up."

"Everyone fucks it up," Ben said with a half grin. "You ever heard babies talk?"

"Yeah, but I don't have the privilege of being small and adorable," Paris grumbled.

Ben grinned and leaned over, grabbing the front of Paris's shirt and kissing him soundly. He sighed as he pulled back and rested his head against the seat. "Well, you have the privilege of being hot as fuck, and that does it for me. The fact that you want to learn is enough."

'I'm trying,' Paris signed. 'I promise.' He'd worked hard on those two short sentences. It was something he'd planned to say later, but the moment felt right.

Ben swallowed heavily, then nodded and cleared his throat. "Well, until you master more than what, four classes? We'll work with what we've got."

Paris laughed. "It's been three, actually."

Ben grinned and shook his head. "Then you're doing amazing." And with that, he pulled out onto the street and began the drive south.

11

Paris hadn't been further than Islamorada, so when they passed the key and hopped on the little bridge, he couldn't stop himself from staring out the window. It was sunset, so the water had lost the clear blue-green hue and was now dark, with orange playing along the top like waves of fire. He had a sudden and intense urge to paint it, and he wondered if Ben would think he was a freak for asking to come back one evening as one of their dates.

The one thing that always brought Paris peace was art. Whether he was inking it into someone's skin, or putting it onto a canvas, or sketching random little pencil-led figures into the top of a desk or counter, it settled him in ways nothing else did.

He didn't actually think Ben would judge him for it, but he wasn't sure Ben would understand. The last thing in the world he wanted was to be humored.

"You're quiet," Ben said after an eternal silence.

Paris turned his head and let out a soft laugh. "Can I tell you something?"

"Anything."

For some reason, the events of the afternoon were gnawing at his guts. "This afternoon, I told Jamie when my birthday is."

"Jamie?" Ben repeated.

"Yeah. Another tattoo artist. He was going around the shop with this little fuckin' date book, getting everyone's birthdays." Paris rubbed a hand down his face and glanced around. They'd driven onto another key, and it was less lush and more like an island than where they'd come from. "Where are we?"

"It's still a surprise," Ben said with a tiny smile. "Is the birthday a big deal for you?"

Paris shrugged. "I mean, I told you before I never celebrated, right? And I never really told people when it was because if I did, they wanted to do shit for me."

"Which is...bad?" Ben said slowly.

Paris grinned a bit. "When you tell people you've never gotten a birthday present before, they look at you like you're some sad orphan with an empty bowl in a black-and-white movie."

Ben barked a laugh. "I can see that."

"That's the first thing you thought, isn't it?" Paris challenged.

Ben opened his mouth, then shut it and sighed. "Not...exactly. But yeah, I did feel sorry for you."

"See," Paris groused. He let his head fall back against the seat and looked at Ben out of the corner of his eye. Fuck, he was gorgeous. "Anyway, I hate talking about it. I hate explaining why I didn't start, I don't know, baking myself fuckin' birthday cakes or whatever."

Ben was quiet a long moment, and as they rolled to a stop at a red light, he reached over and grabbed Paris's hand, twisting their fingers together. "I'm sorry. I feel like maybe I'm being too much."

Paris tugged on Ben's hand, twisting it so he could press a kiss to the inside of his wrist. "You're not. This is nice. And I think...hell.," he breathed out, "part of the reason why I could tell Jamie when my birthday is and not have a damn panic attack is because of this. I don't feel like such a freak show when I think about the fact that you actually want to be here with me."

Ben looked tense, but he said nothing. He didn't pull his hand away, though, so Paris kept a tight hold on him, gently mouthing at the tips of his fingers as Ben finally turned down a street and came to a stop in a short queue of cars.

Paris sat up and squinted out the window, though the sun had finally set, and all he could see were taillights. "Now, can you tell me what this is?"

Ben huffed, but he was grinning, and he pulled his hand back. "Tell me how much of this you understand."

His hands began to move, a gentle motion like flowing water, and Paris's gaze moved between them and Ben's face.

'Surprise," Paris said. "Here? Eat...watch?" He tried to put the words together in his head. "It's a surprise?" Paris asked slowly, copying Ben's sign.

Ben grinned and nodded his fist. 'Yes.'

"We're here," Paris said and signed. "To...eat? And watch...something. I missed all the rest."

Ben's hand darted out, seizing Paris by the front of his shirt, and yanked him as far as the seat belt would allow. He met Paris halfway and kissed him soundly and thoroughly. 'You did great,' he signed when he pulled back. "This is a pop-up drive-in."

Paris's brows flew up. "Like...a drive-in movie? Like where we sit in the car and eat dinner and watch a giant fuck-off screen? How the *hell* did you arrange that?"

Ben laughed and grabbed the wheel again when the line began to move forward. "Some guy Andrew knows does this two days a month. He bought some old equipment and a screen from an auction like ten years ago, and he set it up. Andrew gave him a call to let him know we were coming, and the guy agreed to play the movie tonight with captions."

Paris felt a warm sensation in his chest, and after a second, he realized what it was: joy. It was actual *joy*. "This is amazing."

Ben's eyes were slightly shiny as he looked over. "Yeah. I know it's kind of cheating because this is more like a date in the sixties, but

I don't really care. I packed us a picnic, and I figure we can sit in the back seat under a blanket and make out if the movie's boring."

Paris couldn't help a quiet laugh, and he felt almost giddy. He'd known that feeling once, as a very small child when his mom was still alive and he was still loved. It was old and atrophied, but being with Ben made him feel like he was coming back to himself—to the man he should have been.

It didn't take long for them to pull in, and they were directed to a reserved spot that would have the best view of the screen. The guy taking cash at the entrance gave them a little sticker with the radio channel for the sound, and Ben stuck it on the dash while Paris pulled the cooler and blankets out of the trunk.

There were a bunch of people there in pickups, and Paris wondered if maybe he should have brought his.

"Look at all those fuckers on air mattresses," he said when Ben climbed in the back and shut the door behind him.

Ben's brows lifted, and then he looked out the window and scoffed. "Yeah. And they get to be eaten alive by all the tiny vampires out there while we avoid anemia in here."

Paris laughed, pulling Ben close as he got the blanket situated around them. "Good point. The mosquitos here are fucking real."

Ben rolled his eyes as he settled against Paris's side. "Yeah. People will tell you that you get used to them, but you won't. You just hold it inside of you and have dreams of eradicating them from the planet."

Paris tipped Ben's chin up and kissed him. "God. I like you so much."

Ben's cheeks were ruddy enough that Paris could see the color shift even in the dim light. "Did you turn the radio on?"

Paris shook his head and bit his lip for a second. "I, uh...thought it might be nice not to. Unless you wanted the sound?"

Ben's eyes widened a fraction. "I have a really hard time understanding dialogue over speakers, so it doesn't matter to me."

"Then it doesn't matter to me," Paris said. He lifted a hand and brushed his fingers over Ben's left processor. "You can take them off if you want. My teacher said full immersion, and...yeah. I mean, I have like ten phrases, but I want you to be comfortable."

Ben looked torn, and Paris wasn't sure if he'd crossed a line or not until Ben's hand reached up and he plucked the right one from his hair and set it on the top of the console.

'Maybe...that.'

'Why?' Paris asked.

'Worst,' Ben spelled, using painfully slow letters. Then he showed Paris the sign for it.

Paris copied him, and Ben rewarded his efforts with a slow kiss before pulling away. 'Thank you.'

Ben laughed. 'Eat? Hungry?'

Paris felt a sort of thrill because they were communicating. And shit, Ben was right. He had the skills of a goddamn infant, but it was something. No, it was better than something. It was progress.

He shifted away from Ben so he could dig into the cooler and then arranged a space between them for all the little containers. Ben had put something together like a fruit, meat, and cheese board, and Paris couldn't help but laugh when Ben lifted a piece of cut pineapple to his lips.

"Come on," Ben said aloud, "it's tropical."

Paris let Ben set the ripe fruit on his tongue, and he groaned softly at the taste. "Show me pineapple."

Ben lifted his hand, made a circle with his thumb and forefinger, then held it over his eye and rocked his wrist. "But be careful," Ben warned after dropping his hand. He closed his finger and thumb tightly but kept the same hand shape. "This means asshole."

Paris laughed, then reached into the second open container for a cube of cheese and held it up. "Your turn? Sorry I don't know the signs for it."

Ben opened his mouth and took the cheese between his teeth, and Paris got a little hard in his jeans watching him. After chewing, he leaned in and cupped Paris's jaw, letting his thumb brush against his earlobe. "I like speaking with you. I like hearing your voice. I just also like being Deaf. If you can live with having both sides of me in your life..."

"I can live with anything you need me to live with," Paris breathed out. It was as close to a promise as he was willing to make, but from the look on Ben's face, it was enough. He swallowed as Ben shifted closer. "I don't think we've looked up at the movie once."

Ben grinned, the look a little feral and a lot heated. "I don't really give a shit about the movie. We just have to be careful and not rock the boat too much. So to speak."

Paris knew exactly what he was saying. He set the containers back in the cooler and shoved it into the front seat, and Ben urged him to lie back. The car was not made for two grown men to lie down together, but somehow, Ben managed to fit himself right up against Paris with his hand in the perfect position to rub at his aching dick.

"Fuck," Paris moaned.

Ben dropped his forehead to Paris's chest. "I love touching you. Can I—"

"Yes. Fuck yes," Paris said, then lifted one hand and nodded his fist. "Anything you want."

Ben huffed a quiet laugh as he worked at Paris's button, then got the zipper down and his cock out through the slit in his boxers. Paris shut his eyes as warm fingers encircled him, then stroked him from root to tip.

"You seriously did this shit at the movies on dates?" Paris asked, his voice trembling a bit with the struggle it took to keep himself from thrusting his hips.

Ben turned his head, nipping at Paris's cotton-covered nipple. "Once. It was my junior year of college, and we got busted and thrown out because neither one of us realized we were making noise." Ben punctuated his sentence by pressing his thumb just under the head of Paris's cock, sending a rush of pleasure through him. "Seems to be a persistent problem for me."

Paris groaned, his breath coming in a soft pant. "I want to touch you."

"I don't think we can get that creative in the car," Ben said. "But you can blow me after. If you want."

"I fucking want," Paris said. He wanted a lot more than that too. He wanted everything. He wanted to spread Ben out and eat his ass until he was crying into his pillow, and then he wanted to get him loose and sloppy before fucking him into oblivion.

And after that, he wanted Ben to do the same to him. He wanted to spend the rest of his functional life exploring all the ways they could be good for each other and to each other.

"God. God," Ben said. "I do too."

Paris realized he'd said all that aloud, and while a tiny wave of panic crashed over him, it was eclipsed by Ben speeding up his hand and dragging him over the edge. With a soft grunt and a minute flex of his hips, Paris came, the hot spurts of come spreading over Ben's fingers and down his dick.

His head fell against the window, and he wondered if anyone had noticed. His vision was a little blurry, but it didn't look like anyone around them was running for security, so they were probably safe.

"Think I can manage a blowjob without giving us away?" he asked, his voice still a little shaky as Ben tucked him away.

Ben looked up at him. "Repeat that?" So Paris did. With a grin, Ben licked his fingers clean, making Paris's soft, sensitive cock twitch. "I think you can easily suck my dick in here. I like it slow, so you can take your time."

Paris squeezed his eyes shut to collect himself as Ben turned around and pressed his back to the back passenger door. His legs were spread, and he was working his own zipper down when Paris finally looked at him.

His dick was hard and flushed, sitting in a thatch of black curls, and Paris's mouth began to water. He'd never understood the phrase "hungry for dick" until that moment, but he swore he could taste the fantasy of it on the back of his tongue.

"I fucking want you so bad."

Ben lifted his hands and repeated the sentence in sign, which Paris tucked away for later.

Grabbing the blanket, he carefully draped it around his back, then wedged one leg on the floor beneath the driver's seat, and he bent over the other. He was barely flexible enough to hold the position, but it ceased to matter the second the blanket was over his head, and he was close enough to smell the rich musk coming from Ben.

He took a deep breath, then curled his hand around the base of Ben's cock and parted his lips. The first taste was strange. It had been a goddamn long time since he'd done this and never with someone he cared about. He let his lips close around the head, and then he sucked lightly, remembering that Ben liked it slow.

He heard Ben's sharp inhale, then a shaking exhale as he sank an inch deeper. And then another. And another. It took an eternity before he had all of Ben in him, the head grazing the back of his tongue, and he gave a hard suck as he slowly drew up.

Ben let out a soft, sobbing whimper as his hand darted under the blanket and curled into Paris's hair. He didn't tug. He just held Paris tightly like he never wanted him to move, and the possessiveness of it sent Paris into another plane of existence.

People tolerated him. His brother loved him.

But they never really wanted him around. No one wanted to keep him. He was a rain cloud on good days and a thunderstorm on bad ones, but Ben seemed to enjoy that about him. Like he was a storm chaser and Paris was a hurricane.

"Please," Ben murmured the third time Paris brought his lips up.

But he didn't go faster. He squeezed harder, followed his lips with his fist in a tight squeeze, sucking as hard as he could manage and basking in every shudder from Ben's tightly wound body. He could do this all night, though he knew they didn't have that kind of time, but he could tell Ben was getting close.

His breathing was faster, his sighs and gasps and groans all blending together in a symphony of wordless begging, and Paris lifted his hands to feel Ben's balls as they tightened with his impending orgasm. It was only then that he sped up—just a fraction, just to get him there.

Ben let out the softest cry, the noise sudden, and then Paris's mouth filled with his salty come. It was hot and sticky and somewhat unpleasant, but he swallowed down every drop. He swiped his hand over his mouth as he came up for fresh air and was immediately pulled into a kiss, Ben sucking on his tongue like he was taking in the taste of himself.

"Fuck," Paris said when he pulled back. "I'm glad you went first. I would have totally come in my pants if you hadn't."

Ben's pupils dilated even further, and his lips parted just before he pulled Paris into another hot kiss. "Zip me up before I get hard again."

Paris laughed, but he did as Ben asked, and they snuggled back up together to finish the last of the move, sated in ways that Paris didn't think he was capable of feeling.

12

Ben couldn't remember what natural hearing was like. He'd had the misfortune of going deaf in an era where cochlear implants destroyed what little he had left after the infection and medication had affected him the way it did. He had a vague memory of being confused by whatever sounds the implants had him hearing in those early years, and he recalled being petrified of his own screaming.

But most of it was a blur. He was eight months when he lost it all, and three when the first implant was activated.

He did know, though, that music had to sound better than it did in his devices. He had several friends who enjoyed the Bluetooth features that allowed them to stream their nostalgic nineties grunge rock straight into their hearing devices, but he couldn't stand it. The most enjoyment he'd ever gotten from music was going to a rave that Levi had surprised him with.

He took off his implants and moved to the heavy vibrations. He hadn't gotten high—he'd agreed to play babysitter to his brother, who had swallowed a handful of questionable-looking mushrooms—but he felt outside of his body as they moved to the beat.

It was why he preferred to take his implants off when he was cleaning rooms, letting the speaker rest on the floor near his bare feet. The vibrations coursed through him in rapid patterns, and it felt good to move his body to the rhythm as he lost himself in the only motel busywork he actually enjoyed. Most of his friends thought he was a fucking weirdo for liking the housekeeping part, but it was mindless.

It allowed him a sort of meditative state, though right now, he felt anything but peace. His mind kept drifting to the feeling of Paris's mouth around him as he sucked Ben off so slowly he was pretty sure he was going to slip into insanity. He came harder than he could ever remember coming, and watching Paris swallow it down was enough that if he hadn't already fallen before then, that would have done it.

They watched the rest of the movie curled against each other, snaking on his carefully prepared picnic, trading lazy kisses that tasted like salt and sugar. At the end of the night, Ben almost asked Paris to stay over, but Paris had that petrified-deer look in his eyes, so Ben just kissed him at his door and promised to see him later.

That was five days ago.

He had another date planned, but he was starting to worry it was all a bit too one-sided. Paris hadn't given any indication that he wanted to plan dates or that he wanted Ben to stop spoiling him, but Ben also knew he was fucking extra. It was a universal criticism he'd been given by the few people who'd ever gotten past date three.

And never to date four because of it.

The flickering fear became a wildfire by the end of the afternoon, and he wondered if he was driving Paris away. Nothing had changed. Paris saw him whenever he was around. They made out like horny teenagers and spent long nights on each other's couches watching TV and Ben listening to Paris talk about some of his more ridiculously rich clients that flew in from all over just to get a piece done by him.

They practiced Paris's ASL, which got Ben's heart all fluttery because that was also a first, and he had been so fucking sure a guy like Paris—with a chip on his shoulder and trust issues the size of Australia—would have given it up after the dozenth time Ben had to correct his hand placement.

But so far, he hadn't.

He just got a stiff jaw and determined look in his eyes and kept going.

So maybe it wasn't entirely one-sided, but Ben was nervous about their next date because it was...silly. He wasn't sure when he'd have access to the big events—like winter holidays or birthdays. Hell, he managed to refrain from asking when Paris's birthday was after Paris admitted to sharing it with the shop.

But he thought about tiny little Paris and how that child had wanted and deserved to be loved. And how he'd given nothing more than disdain and neglect from two people who were supposed to do everything in their power to take care of him. Ben's heart ached with the knowledge that he could make it better. He thought about all the times he and Levi spent tearing around toy stores and bringing home the most ridiculous crap they played with once and never touched again and wished he could swap places. Maybe not for all of it but for some of it.

Ben couldn't change the past, but he could do this. He could give Paris the future he deserved.

There was one single toy store—a relic of his childhood—which was in a mall near a little petting zoo just outside of Miami. It was an annoying drive, but Paris had texted him that afternoon to let him know that he only had one early afternoon client the next day. Ben took it for the hint it was and told Paris to make sure he blocked off the rest of the day because it was time for his next surprise.

He got a heart emoji in return.

With a sigh, Ben packed up the last of his cleaning supplies and dragged the cart back to the corridor closet, locking it away before heading into the office. Callisto was still behind the desk with Aya, his face buried in his laptop, her nose buried in her phone. She looked up with a quick, guilty smile, but he waved her off and pointed at his ears.

He hadn't bothered putting his processors on, and she gave him a nod and a thumbs-up before he moved past her and slipped into his office. He liked it in there, though it wasn't much bigger than the supply closet. It only fit a tiny laptop desk and a rolling chair, but the wall was covered in photos of Levi and him as kids, and it felt almost like a shrine to what life had been before the grief and loss.

His gaze fell on an old, frayed sticky note that was pinned to the corkboard after the glue stopped working. It had his dad's lazy handwriting across it. It was a reminder to himself to call Levi for his twentieth birthday. Ben took a breath and felt the old, familiar ache in his chest. It wasn't as powerful as before, but there were moments he remembered that Levi was gone.

Forever.

That nothing could bring him back.

That there would always be a hole in the shape of him that no one could ever fill. He hated himself a little for moving on, even if he knew Levi would have smacked him upside the head for feeling that way.

There was movement in his periphery, and he turned to see Callisto in the doorway. 'Someone's here for you.'

Ben hopped up and followed him into the lobby, and it took him a second to recognize the dark-haired man standing with his hands in his pockets. It was Max. Once again, Ben searched out the similarities in the siblings, though they weren't very profound. Max's face was rounder, his hair darker, his skin paler. He was shorter and more slender, and his smile—even his nervous one—was full of mischief.

Max's mouth opened, and he started talking, and Ben quickly held up a finger to stop him.

"Two seconds," he felt himself say. He fumbled in his pocket for his processor case and quickly popped them on. His right one gave him an immediate warning that the battery was dead before shutting off, but his left one flared to life, making his head swim for a second as sound flooded in. "Sorry."

Max looked mortified, and he raised his fist to his chest, rubbing it in a circle. 'Sorry. I'm learning. I'm slow.'

Ben's lip twitched, and he wondered if he and Paris were doing the class together. "You're fine. I was cleaning rooms earlier, so I always take them off. It's Max, right?"

Max's face lit up like he was pleased at being remembered, and Ben reminded himself that Max had spent most of his formative years in that same terrible house. "Yeah. Paris asked me to come by to grab his sketch pad for his client this afternoon, but I can't find the key to his room. I was wondering if you can let me in, though I know that's probably, like, against the law..."

"You're fine," Ben interrupted, smiling at how the brothers both babbled when they were nervous. "I have the master. I can let you in."

Max's shoulders deflated. "Thank you. I told him I had it, and I probably do, but it's God knows where, and he's going to kill me if I don't get this to him."

Ben chuckled as he led the way out. Ben pulled the master key out of his pocket and swiped it against Paris's door. It clicked, and he pushed it open, waving Max inside. "I'm sure he wouldn't *kill* you."

Max grinned as he stopped in the doorway. "Well. Maybe not now that he met you."

Ben didn't know what to say. He stood in the doorway with his mouth slightly open as Max darted in and disappeared into Paris's room. Ben heard him shout something, but he couldn't understand the words, and he just wasn't in the mood to ask Max to repeat himself, only to miss it again.

"...mind, you know." Max appeared in the door as Ben caught the last three words, and then his eyes widened. "Oh my God, I just talked to you out of the room, and you missed it. I'm so sorry."

Ben offered him a smile, a little surprised because even the people who'd known him forever often forgot he couldn't understand them when they walked away. "It's fine. It takes some getting used to."

"No, I know," Max said, tucking the drawing pad under his arm. He raised his fist to his chest. 'I'm sorry. I'm trying.'

'I know,' Ben signed back at him. 'I'm patient.'

Max's brow furrowed. "I don't know the last one."

"Patient," Ben repeated aloud. "I don't expect you to have a robust vocabulary after two and a half weeks. And I don't expect you to remember everything after having met me twice."

Max's cheeks pinked, and he looked a lot like Paris right then. "Um. Anyway, I said I don't think Paris would mind if you came in. I think he likes you in his space."

Ben determinedly looked anywhere but at the sofa because the last time he'd been on it, Paris had sucked his dick until he was sobbing. "I know. But I can't stay. I have a couple things to finish up here and a ton of paperwork."

Max gave him a quick salute, then brushed past him and let Ben shut the door, testing to make sure it locked. "Uh. So..." He turned, rubbing the back of his neck. "I'm sure Paris told you about his birthday next week..."

Ben's eyes widened. "He didn't."

"Fuck," Max breathed out, then shook his head. "No, you know what, I'm not sorry. I only promised him one thing, and that was no surprise parties. And he's probably going to invite you."

Ben didn't want to assume. He didn't want to get his hopes up to have them crushed. "It's fine—"

"No, seriously," Max said, stepping closer. He reached out and grabbed Ben's upper arm. "You have no idea how much he likes you." His voice cracked, and he stopped, clearing his throat. "He said he told you, uh, some stuff. About when we were kids."

Ben nodded, trying not to let the pity show on his face. "Yeah. Some of it."

"Well, he doesn't do that. Ever. So him letting people celebrate his birthday is a huge thing, and I know for a fact he'll want you there." Max stopped and rubbed at the corners of his mouth with his finger and thumb. "I was thinking maybe you want to help me plan something." Max actually looked nervous, like Ben could possibly turn him down. He let out a small laugh and twisted his fingers together. "I don't actually know what the fuck I'm doing. I've never been to a birthday party before, so I could really use the help. And all the guys are, like, booze and barbeque, which is great, but we do that all the time. And—and I want this to be special, you know?"

Ben bit his lip, his heart aching. "Yeah," he said softly. "I know." Ideas were already starting to form, and he had to take in a small breath. "Can we talk later? I'll give it some thought and see what we can realistically put together in a week."

"Yeah?" Ben nodded. "Fuck yeah," Max said, his eyes shining with excitement. "You have no idea how long I've wanted to do something like this for him. God, I—" He stopped. "I'm sorry. I'm overexcited."

"I think you're sweet," Ben told him honestly. He dug into his pocket and pulled out his phone, opening his contacts. "Put your number in, and I'll text you. We'll come up with some fun stuff that'll only embarrass him a little."

Max laughed as he obeyed, and he handed the phone back. "I won't say anything to him yet. I don't want to jinx it. But I'm glad he met you, Ben. You have *no idea*."

Ben had no idea what to say to that, so he just nodded and watched Max walk away before hurrying back to his office so he could pretend to work and most definitely—not at all—plan a birthday party for the man he wanted to keep forever.

"You know, there was probably plenty to do on the islands," Paris said about half an hour into the drive. He was smiling, though, so Ben didn't think he was truly annoyed. "You could have taken me swimming with the jellyfish again."

Ben rolled his eyes and smacked him on the arm. "That was your own fault. I tried to protect you, but you wouldn't let me finish my sentence."

"I was nervous," Paris protested. "And anyway, if you'd told me that microscopic baby jellyfish were going to sting me in my fucking piss hole, I would have stopped interrupting you."

Ben laughed. "I was trying to get into your pants. That didn't seem like a good way to get you to spend the rest of the afternoon with me. I mean, that definitely isn't sexy."

Paris was quiet so long that Ben had to glance over at him, and he saw his ears tinged pink. "Everything you said and did that day was sexy," he eventually said. "I would have listened."

"Hearing people have a problem with that, I've noticed," Ben said, then winked as he stepped on the gas. Traffic was finally clearing, and he was feeling less anxious about the date. He'd worried at first that Paris was going to protest the long drive, and now all he had to do was hope that his lover didn't think he was a fucking moron for his choices.

The toy store was on the list, but so was a park, and ice cream, and lunch at his favorite hot dog cart. The guy who ran it was from Paris, and he made them French-style. They were spicy and thin, covered in hot mustard and tucked inside a warm baguette. They were a far cry from the fancy food that Paris could easily afford, but Ben had a feeling he wasn't the fine-dining type.

"You know, you're the only person I've ever let surprise me like this," Paris said after a beat. He drummed his fingers on his thigh, his gaze fixed out the window. "It's...not as uncomfortable as I thought it was going to be."

"Does that mean you're not mad about Max asking me to help plan your birthday party?" Ben chanced.

Paris had confronted him about it the night before, just after he'd gotten back to the motel. Ben had been half-asleep on his sofa and jolted awake when the room lights began to flash. Paris was there looking a little disgruntled, but after a few soothing kisses, he relented but made Ben swear there wouldn't be a petting zoo or any clowns.

Luckily for Paris, Ben couldn't have afforded anything that extravagant, so the promise was easy to make and easy to keep.

"Well, as long as you keep it chill," Paris groused.

Ben grinned, giving nothing away. He had several ideas, but he was feeling a little neurotic because this was Paris's first one since he was five, so it had to be good. His most favorite birthday memory was his thirteenth. It had been disco themed, but he wasn't sure Paris would appreciate that. He was leaning toward something with a giant cupcake table and maybe a face-painting station. He was pretty sure he could get Max and the other guys on board with that since they were all artists and loved to show off.

But he had time to figure it out. Not a lot, but enough that he could pin his ideas and put all of his focus into their date.

Reaching his hand out, Ben grinned when Paris linked their fingers together. He let out a happy sigh, settling back in his seat for the rest of the drive when his lover began to gently kiss the tip of each finger. Warmth cascaded up his arm and settled around his heart, and he wondered if it was possible to stay that happy.

After another half hour, the park's massive surface lot came into view, and he felt Paris's fingers stiffen in his before he pulled away. Ben's nerves began to fire up again, and he took a few calming breaths as he pulled into a spot under a couple of low-hanging trees. It was still early in the afternoon, and it was the middle of the week, which meant there weren't more than a handful of parents there with their toddlers.

The park spanned a good chunk of the acre it was sitting on, with a huge grassy field and playground equipment that had come straight out of Ben's childhood fantasies. There were plastic castles, seesaws, huge animal statues that were tucked in the Spanish-moss-covered trees, and even a little zipline that skirted nearly a quarter mile.

There was also a little lake, a place to rent paddleboards—which he didn't think Paris would be into—and a small snack shack with snow cones and Red Rope licorice. His parents used to take him and his brother there on weekends to play, and he remembered getting lost in the trees and pretending he was a jungle explorer.

Eventually, Levi would talk him into a jumping contest off the swings, and when he was eight, his brother broke his arm for the first time. Levi had laughed, Ben had cried, and their mother had threatened to ground Levi until he was eighteen. It was the strangest core memory, and it lived actively in his mind on afternoons like this.

"You're kidding me, right?" Paris asked when Ben turned the car off.

Ben's fingers twisted in his lap. "Um. No? But I can be if you hate it." He took a slow breath, then looked into Paris's eyes. "I kind of took a wild guess and assumed you didn't spend a lot of time playing on playgrounds."

"There was this shithole neighborhood park where I lived in La Mesa. We used to sit behind the tunnel slide and get high," Paris said, rubbing a hand across the back of his head. "We didn't have anything that looked like this, though."

Ben bit his lip and looked out the window at a pair of kids on the turtle-shaped seesaw. "Levi and I used to come here. It wasn't as nice back then. You know, super early nineties with the hot metal slides."

Paris snorted. "Brutal."

"Yeah. It was before my parents bought the motel and moved us to Key Largo. We don't have to do any of the playing stuff. But there's snacks. And a lake. And probably ducks."

Paris looked like he was torn, and then he squared his shoulders and turned, cupping Ben's face to kiss him. "Teach me to swing?" he murmured when he pulled away.

It took Ben a second to process what he said, and then he laughed. "You don't know how to swing?"

Paris looked slightly embarrassed as he ducked his head and shrugged. "I think I might have learned when I was really little. But I don't remember how anymore."

Ben was out of the car in a second, racing over to wrench Paris's door open, and he tugged him out. "We're rectifying that tragedy. Come on."

Paris snorted a laugh as Ben dragged him across the rubber mats that had replaced old sand—and eventually woodchips that had given the most fantastic splinters. Luckily, there were no kids around the swings as Ben shoved Paris onto one, then took his own.

"It's not hard. Just...follow my lead." Ben pushed himself back as far as he could, then let go and swung forward. "Legs out, lean back, legs in, lean forward," he instructed. "Use the force and weight of your body to get going."

Paris tried to copy him. "Dude. Why is this hard?"

Ben almost choked on his laugh. "I know you have better rhythm than that. Come on, baby. Just..." He demonstrated with exaggerated motions, going higher and higher.

After a bit, Paris seemed to catch on, and eventually, they were in sync, grinning at each other, and God, Ben wanted to jump off, tackle him to the ground, and kiss him. He just didn't want to deal with the moms who were very obviously watching a hulking tattooed man laughing like a lunatic as he learned to swing.

"...still...kids...?" Paris said, but Ben missed most of it since his head was turned away from him.

He twisted in the swing. "Repeat that?"

"So, does this still entertain kids these days?" Paris repeated.

Ben laughed. "I have no idea, but we always loved it. My brother and I used to see how far we could jump. He always won, but he was way more reckless than I was. Which was how he died."

Paris sobered a bit, and together, they started to slow. "Not to kill the mood, but can I ask what happened?"

Ben's gut twisted a little, but he wanted Paris to know. "He made a really, really terrible mistake. He started drinking, he thought he was fine...and he wasn't fine. He got on his bike, and he wasn't paying attention to how fast he was going. He hadn't bothered putting on any of his gear." He stopped with a quiet sigh.

Dragging their feet along the ground, their motion slowed, and Paris leaned on the swing chains, staring at Ben. "I'm so sorry."

"Yeah," Ben said. He swallowed past the lump in his throat that had never quite gone away. "I feel like there's this part of me that will always be angry at him for it. All he had to do was call a fucking Uber, you know? He just...he was the guy who always thought he would be okay. And usually, he was...until he wasn't."

Paris reached a hand out, brushing his knuckles over Ben's jaw. The touch was so soothing it almost startled him. "Want to buy me a snack? Since this is a date?"

Ben perked up, letting all the pain fall by the wayside to be picked up later. "Yes, I absolutely do."

Before Ben could get up, though, Paris was off his swing and standing in front of him. He clasped the chains, his fists brushing the tops of Ben's, and he leaned in. "Would it create a massive scandal if I kissed you here?"

Ben closed his eyes in a slow blink. "Maybe. But ask me if I give a shit."

Paris leaned in so close their lips were almost touching. "Do you give a shit?"

Ben answered him by closing the distance between them. The kiss was soft, sweet, almost chaste apart from the heat that raced through him, and he moaned softly as Paris pulled away. He blinked up and let out the smallest sigh. "I'm supposed to be wooing you right now."

Paris let go of the chain to brush knuckles over Ben's cheek again. "You already did." He took a step back to allow Ben to stand, and they linked fingers, Paris pulling him forward before turning to face the path that led to the lake.

13

Paris had a blue-stained tongue, a belly full of spicy hot dog and crusty baguette, and lips slightly plump from finding a spot behind a tree and making out with Ben until they were almost caught by a couple of kids.

Twice.

He was pretty goddamn sure that even if his life had been a bit more normal than it was and he'd been able to experience a semi-average dating life, that still would have been one of the best dates he'd ever been on. He knew people like Ben were the exception, not the rule. He just didn't know what he'd done to deserve him.

Ben clearly carried around the pain of loss and the pain of feeling like he didn't belong, but it didn't define him. It was not the sum of his parts, and Paris couldn't believe that someone like Ben would be so into someone like him.

Yet, there they were, Ben dragging Paris into a mall with their hands linked and swinging between them. His pulse ticked up when he saw where Ben was taking them. It was an old-school toy store tucked into the very corner of the mall. It had a retro, vintage vibe with a window display of eighties-style Care Bears and a cardboard cutout of the Ghostbusters.

"Ben," he said, tugging on his hand.

Ben just grinned and pulled until Paris's feet started moving again. "Come on, you're going to love this place. It used to be a K·Bs when Levi and I were kids, and some company rented out the space like a year ago. Amelia, Andrew, and I came here last year when we were shopping for their niece."

Paris rolled his eyes but let Ben tug him past the security monitors and into a space between brightly colored shelves. To the right was a massive display of old candy he remembered seeing in gas station racks when he was younger. He never had pocket change when he was growing up, but he remembered seeing ads on TV for them.

He recalled with an almost vicious clarity when he was ten and angry after watching his stepmom's new kid eating ice cream and being laughed at when he asked for some. Later that night, he swiped a Snickers off the shelf when his dad took him into the Texaco to pay for gas. He hoarded that little candy bar for months, taking tiny nibbles at a time and hiding it under his mattress.

By the end, he had to toss it after ants got into the house and their stepmom went on a rampage to figure out where they were coming from. But he could remember the taste of every bite, and he remembered the bitterness in the back of his throat when he'd see kids at school get whatever they wanted, whenever they wanted, without realizing how fucking lucky they were.

"Is this too much?" Ben asked, holding one of the small rolling carts in one hand.

Paris realized he'd been standing still and quiet for way too long, and he forced a smile, though he knew Ben would see through it. "I, uh. I just don't know where to start."

Ben bit his lip, then pulled Paris away from the candy and into the action figures. "Transformers," he said, pointing at the shelf. "I used to get one figurine a year, on my birthday."

“Not Christmas?” Paris asked with a tiny smile.

Ben rolled his eyes. “We’re Jewish, so no. We got really small stuff on Chanukah just so we could go back to school and not feel like shit when all the other kids were bragging about their Santa haul.”

Paris grimaced, feeling oddly guilty in spite of the fact that Santa hadn’t visited him since he was five. “Shit. Sorry.”

Ben waved him off, then tapped his thumb on his chest. ‘It’s fine.’

‘Okay,’ Paris signed back, loving the way it made Ben go all bright and happy to see his language on Paris’s hands. ‘Your favorite?’

Ben tapped his chin, then shrugged. “I don’t think I had one. I grew out of them before I was able to collect enough to make any of the really cool shit.”

Paris snorted and stroked his thumb over Ben’s wrist. “What was the best birthday present you ever got?”

“Moon shoes,” Ben answered immediately.

Paris’s eyes went wide as an old, atrophied memory clawed its way to the surface. It was some TV ad with the happiest kids on the planet on a suburban street that looked nothing like the place where he grew up. “Bouncy things, right?”

Ben laughed. “Yeah. My parents were dead set against them, but I begged my grandparents, and they got them for me for my twelfth birthday. Levi was ten.”

“The second time he broke his arm?” Paris chanced.

Ben looked both happy and sad at the same time. “They made me put them in the closet and leave them there. I snuck them out a couple of times at like two in the morning and took them out to the grass so they couldn’t hear me.”

They started walking again, and Paris tugged on Ben’s hand. “Why was that the best gift?”

Ben shrugged. “My grandparents didn’t get to spoil us much. They grew up dirt-poor, and my parents were mostly taking care of them. My great-aunt died that year and left them a little bit of money. It was the first time my bubbe was able to do something like that."

Paris lifted his hand and kissed his wrist, watching the way it made Ben shiver all over. He was starting to see how the bits and pieces of Ben's past made him the man he was today. "Do you still have them?"

Ben blinked, then laughed. "I bet my parents do. My mom's a compulsive hoarder when it comes to shit like that. My dad makes her go through her closets once a year and get rid of ten percent. He finally convinced her that I'm not going to have a bunch of kids for her to pass all her crap down to."

Paris felt a chill crawl up his spine as they came to a massive wall of board games, because Jesus, they hadn't come close to talking about shit like that, and maybe they should. "You...uh. Do you want kids?"

Ben swallowed heavily and turned slightly to face Paris. "No. I don't. You?"

"Fuck no," Paris breathed out, feeling an odd punch of relief. "Sorry, I don't mean to sound like an ass, and I know I'd raise a kid better than Max and I were raised, but I barely trust myself with my own care."

Ben let out a laughing breath through his nose. "You're doing better than you think you are."

"Yeah, but that's new," Paris said with a half grin, pulling Ben over to the kiddie games. He stared at the one with the mouse on the box and had another vague memory of his stepsiblings playing it. There was play dough involved, he was pretty sure. "You ever have these?"

"Most of them. My grandparents always stocked up on this stuff so when we spent Shabbat at their place, we had something to do. Levi was hard to keep distracted when he wasn't allowed to turn on the TV." Ben stepped close to the shelf and ran the tips of his fingers over the boxes until he stopped at one with a giant shark on the box. "He got brutal when he played this one."

Paris scanned the brightly colored games and grinned. "I feel like Max and I would have killed each other."

Ben turned with a tiny smirk. "Pick some."

"Um. What?"

"Pick a couple games. For date night," Ben clarified, and Paris felt his stomach do summersaults.

"Kids games?"

Ben gave him a slightly dark smile. "They don't have to be kids games. We could play strip Sorry if you want to."

Paris swallowed heavily. The thought should have been absurd. Comical. But he pictured Ben smiling across the table at him while peeling away his shirt, and...

Ben interrupted his thought spiral by pulling the shark game from the rack, then the mouse one, and stacking them in his arms. "If you don't pick, I'm going to pick for you, and I have to tell you, I'm not nice when I compete."

Paris couldn't help a small laugh when he saw Ben's eyes narrowed in determination. "Is that seriously what we're doing here?"

"No," Ben said. "We're going on a shopping spree. We're going to get a bunch of crap, take it home, and play with it like we're kids." He dumped the games into a cart, then turned toward an end shelf that was stocked with packets of gooey sticky hands and grabbed four. "Test me, Paris. I dare you."

Paris's stomach burned hotly with a feeling very close to need, though it wasn't sexual this time. It was something else. He rubbed the back of his neck and then turned toward the game shelf, blindly grabbing at one and tossing it into the cart.

"There you go," Ben said quietly. He moved closer. "Are you okay?"

Paris nodded, his throat tight. "Yeah. I...yes."

"You're going on a face journey, but I have no idea what kind."

Paris let out a strained laugh. "It feels like...I'm horny, but like, with my emotions."

Ben stared, then burst into laughter, pushing Paris against the shelf. He let out a quiet huff when Ben's body collided with his, and then he was kissed. This time, it was hot and most definitely not chaste. "Well, I'm regular horny for you, so let's hurry the fuck up so we can get home."

Home, Paris thought. He let Ben take his hand and drag him down several more aisles, and in the end, Ben banished him from the store so he couldn't see the total. Paris tried to put up a protest, but he could tell his lover wouldn't be moved, so he quietly made a mental note to get him back.

Tenfold.

Once he got the chance, he was going to spoil the absolute fuck out of Ben. The little shit would never see it coming.

"Okay," Paris said, staring at his poorly done turtle sculpture that was made out of some kind of slime material and tiny foam balls. "Please explain this shit to me again. What's the point? Do you glaze and bake it?"

"You smash it," Ben said, then took his fist and squashed the turtle unrecognizable as Paris let out a cry of protest. "Then you make a new one."

Paris ran a hand down his face and groaned. "I don't get it. It's like, you don't even keep it or finish it. You just shove it back into the little bottle."

Ben snorted, rolling his eyes as he scooped up the floam and shoved it back into the jar. Capping the lid, he turned toward Paris, and Paris resisted the urge to pull him close. They were sitting on his couch, surrounded by a sea of toys, games, and old-school candy, but he only wanted one thing, and Ben was making him wait for it.

"That is the point, sweetheart. You don't need to accomplish anything with it. There's nothing to finish. You just...have fun."

Paris grumbled, but his hands reached out, grabbing at Ben and pulling him until he gave up resisting and straddled him. Paris spread his legs slightly and curled his hands around Ben's hips. "There's nothing wrong with finishing something."

Ben's ears went a little pink, and he rocked his hips forward. "I might see your point."

'Yes?' Paris signed.

Ben sucked in a breath, and Paris could feel him harden. 'Yes.'

'Want me?' Paris asked. He wasn't sure that was the right sign.

There was probably some colloquial way of saying it in ASL, but Ben clearly got his message because his lips parted gently, and he lifted a C-shaped hand to his throat, running it up and down.

"Hungry?" Paris asked in a near whisper.

Ben's grin widened, his eyes going darker. "Horny."

Paris repeated the sign, and before he could move his hand down, Ben was kissing him. His lips forced Paris's to part, his tongue darting in to taste him. He took Paris's bottom lip between his teeth and bit down hard, letting go with a wet pop.

"Did you get condoms?"

'Yes,' Paris signed back. 'Yesterday.'

"Fuck, you're getting better at that. I never had a hand fetish, but yours are so..." Ben trailed off as he reached for Paris's wrist and took his first finger into his mouth. Paris watched as his ink disappeared behind Ben's plush lips, then reappeared again as he slowly slid it out. "Can we take this to your room?"

'Yes,' Paris signed again when he had his hand free. His vocabulary was tiny, but it was working just fine for him in that moment. He eased his grip on Ben, waiting for him to slide off, and then he stood up and started toward his room.

He was just about to reach for the door handle when a warm arm snaked around his waist, and he froze, pressing one palm to the wall beside the doorjamb. "Ben," he warned, hoping he was speaking loudly enough.

Ben let out a small moan, pressing his front against Paris's back.

With a small roll of his hips, Ben's stiff cock rubbed against Paris's ass, and heat rushed through him.

"Ben," he warned again. "I'm about two seconds away from fucking you against the wall."

"You say that like it's supposed to deter me," Ben answered back, his voice a low growl.

Paris's control snapped. He'd never been like this with his lovers. Sex had been perfunctory—scratching an itch. He was rarely sober when it happened and rarely gave a shit if the other person got off. Now, all he wanted in the world was to hold Ben and watch him completely fall apart.

Gritting his teeth, Paris spun, gripping Ben by the back of the neck with one hand while the other reached behind him to get the bedroom door open. He stumbled a bit as he took a step backward while pulling Ben close, but he managed to keep them from tumbling to the ground.

Their lips met in a frantic kiss as Paris began to walk them toward the bed, and he stopped just before they reached the nightstand, but only because Ben broke away and sank to his knees.

Paris's vision was foggy with lust, and his hands moved to Ben's hair without being consciously aware of it. They tangled in his curls, knocking against the processors enough that Ben pulled away with a soft grunt.

"This is stop," Ben said, showing him a sign Paris already knew. "More. Again. Harder. Fuck me. Kiss me." Ben's fingers were trembling like he had to force himself to go slow.

Paris swallowed thickly. "I think I got it."

Ben met his gaze for a lingering moment, and Paris was almost lost to the open look of want on his face and the way he was just kneeling there at his feet. Christ, he was going to blow his load in ten seconds if he couldn't get himself under control.

Dragging his tongue over his bottom lip, Ben eventually reached up and pulled his processors off, placing them on the nightstand. Their gazes locked once more, and then Ben's clever, gorgeous fingers went right for Paris's jeans and within seconds had the button popped, the zipper down, and his cock out.

Ben's eyes went heated, lids heavy as he stared. He ran a reverent hand over the length before leaning in, and Paris damn near lost his breath at the feel of a metal barbell dragging over his skin.

"Shit," he gasped, forgetting Ben couldn't hear him now. "Shit. Shit."

Ben suckled at the head, then pressed the barbell into Paris's slit, making him stumble back. Ben caught him around the backs of his thighs to steady him, then—without letting go—urged Paris to grip his hair again.

He did, giving an experimental tug, and Ben let out a low groan before sinking low, then pulling back to swirl his tongue around the tip.

Paris's knees began to shake after just a few seconds of that attention, and he carefully tapped Ben on the cheek. 'Stop.'

Ben looked worried for a second as he pulled away with a wet pop, but Paris quickly shook his head, then leaned to the side and opened his nightstand drawer. There were condoms there and a bottle of lube—freshly opened and unused. He pulled them out and set them on the top, then looked back down at his lover.

'I want,' he started, struggling to remember.

'Fuck me?' Ben offered, mouthing the words.

Paris nodded so hard he got dizzy, and he grunted hard when Ben was suddenly on his feet and taking him by the front of his shirt. 'Please,' he managed, circling his palm on his chest between them.

Ben's fingers flew through signs he couldn't keep up with, but he caught enough of them to understand that Ben wanted it too. And he was willing to beg. He crashed their mouths together as Paris fumbled with their clothes, and only breaking the kiss twice to remove their shirts, he managed to get them undressed before walking Ben against the wall and pressing him there.

'Here?' Ben asked.

Paris nodded his fist. 'Yes.'

Ben reached over and grabbed the lube, slapping it against Paris's palm before turning around and bracing himself against the plaster. Paris's entire body felt like it was on fire, but instinct had taken over. He dropped to his knees, the floor unforgiving against his aging skin, but he didn't give a single shit as he dropped the lube so he could spread Ben's cheeks wide.

He heard Ben grunt as he nosed along his crack, and Ben let out a shattered groan when Paris applied his tongue in small kitten licks. He was salty and musky and somehow absolutely perfect. Paris had never done this before—never considered it. He dug fingers into Ben's hip, holding him still as he took him close to the edge.

He ran his free hand along the inside of Ben's thigh, urging his legs wider, then cupped his balls and rolled them gently against his palm. Ben let out another sob, his forehead thudding softly against the wall, and his legs were starting to tremble.

"Please," Ben said. "Please, please." The word was spoken with a thick tongue, and Paris damn near lost his head at how close Ben sounded to losing himself.

Wanting to make it last, Paris pulled back, then grabbed the lube from the floor and flicked the top open. He pressed a hot, open-mouthed kiss to each one of Ben's ass cheeks, then climbed to his feet and rubbed two fingers around his lover's hole before pressing down.

Ben grunted, pushing back against Paris's hand, and it only took a second for him to slip inside. He was warm and pulsing around Paris's digits, and his breath was coming so quickly Paris worried he might pass out.

"Easy," he murmured, then kissed the side of Ben's face until he turned his head to look at him. 'Easy,' he spelled. 'Breathe.'

Ben nodded, his eyes dilated and wild. He licked his lips. "Kiss me."

Paris didn't hesitate. He pressed their mouths together, the angle awkward but somehow perfect, and he spread his fingers carefully and thrust in until the heel of his palm was meeting Ben's soft skin.

"Fuck," Ben groaned. "I'm ready."

Paris nodded, then slipped his fingers out and reached for the condom. He rolled it over his dick, then added more lube before grabbing Ben by the hips and hitching him up onto his toes. Ben's back arched, the perfect angle for Paris, who gently spread Ben's cheeks and pressed the head of his cock to the slick, waiting hole.

Ben's fist knocked against the wall, then lifted up. 'Ready. Now.'

Paris clenched his jaw, trying to maintain his restraint as he gave a single thrust forward. There was a little resistance, but on the edge of Ben's sharp grunt, Paris breached him. He slid in a single inch before stopping, and Ben moaned in protest, his hips thrusting back.

'Slow,' Paris signed, using his hand on Ben's arm. 'Slow.'

"Fuck me," Ben countered loudly, then arched his back more.

Paris was about to lose his mind at the sight of Ben presenting his ass like it was his job to get fucked. His legs were spread, and his hands were braced against the wall, and Paris knew he didn't need to be careful. Ben was precious—he was a damn treasure—but he wasn't fragile.

He dug his fingers into Ben's fleshy side, then gave a hard thrust forward.

Ben's body hit the wall as Paris slid all the way in, their skin slapping like a goddamn gunshot. Paris bowed his head against the back of Ben's neck, and then he bit down with sharp teeth as he rolled his hips, forcing Ben harder against the plaster with his shallow thrusts.

Ben grunted again, the noise primal and desperate, and Paris felt like he could listen to that all day, every day, and never, ever get tired of it. He rolled his hips again, his fingers dragging lines from Ben's thighs to his ribs, and he felt the tremor rush through Ben's body.

He was clearly struggling with his control, just like Paris was, and Paris didn't know if he wanted to speed things up or slow them down. He wanted this to last forever, but he also wanted to believe he could keep this for a lifetime.

He took a step back so he could get more purchase as he began to rapidly thrust into Ben's ass and laid soft kisses along the back of his shoulders. The contrast of rough and gentle had Ben groaning, his fingers scraping at the wall as he tried and failed to meet Paris thrust for thrust.

Somewhere in the heavy breathing, Paris heard a soft noise, and he realized it was Ben begging. "Please. Please...fuck, please."

Paris latched an arm around Ben's waist, pulling him back so his arms were stretched out, his palms flat, skin tan against hotel-white paint. Ben had to go further up onto his toes, and Paris began to fuck him harder, faster, as his hand searched out Ben's throbbing cock.

He was leaking a steady stream of precome, and Paris gathered some on his fingers before gripping Ben tight and stroking him in time with his hips.

"Fuck," Ben gasped. His nails were leaving marks on the wall. "Just like that. Just like that. Squeeze my cock, sweetheart. Choke it with your hand."

Paris's head spun at the filthy request, and he tightened his grip hard enough it should have hurt, but Ben began to writhe like it was the best thing he'd ever felt. When his knees started to buckle, Paris gripped his waist harder and held him up as he pounded into Ben's ass, his arm flying so fast he was pretty sure he was going to pull a fucking muscle.

But he didn't care.

He could feel Ben's orgasm cresting, and he was only just holding off his own. His face was hot, and his balls were pulled tight, and he said a small prayer because he wasn't going to last.

The universe took pity on him a second later because Ben let out a rough, ragged grunt as he fell forward, his elbows collapsing, and he spilled hot ropes over Paris's fist. Paris stroked him until Ben started to whine, and then he pulled his hand back, and his body lost rhythm as he rutted into Ben, lifting him back on his toes as he came.

He felt himself fill the condom, and he only just managed not to go full limp noodle as all of his strength left him. He pulled out of Ben's ass far too soon, and the pair of them stumbled to the bed, falling onto the duvet in a heap of limbs.

Paris grimaced as the condom started to shift, and he let out a noise of protest when Ben reached for it and gently pried it away. Paris watched with a heated gaze as Ben tied it off and dropped it into the little trash can beside the bed, and then he snagged one of his processors and attached it before curling back up against Paris's side.

"That was," Ben said, then lost the rest of his words.

Paris laughed, but the sound was far-off, and he felt sluggish. The corners of his vision started to go dark. He'd never, ever passed out after sex before, but he wasn't sure he could stay conscious. "Babe." His voice was shaking like he was freezing cold. "Babe, I..."

"It's okay," Ben murmured softly. He shifted so Paris could turn on his side and take Ben in his arms, holding him tight against his chest to combat the fear that this was all some dream and he was going to wake up back in LA, alone and miserable. "I'm here. I've got you. I'm not going anywhere."

"Just," Paris slurred, "need a minute."

"Take as many as you need," Ben said. His voice went with Paris as he drifted. "I'm here. I'll always be here."

14

Paris woke from his light doze to a gentle touch over his brow. He struggled to open his eyes and eventually gave up, leaning over and searching until soft lips met his own. The taste of Ben was familiar on his tongue as Ben's slid against his own, and he groaned softly before pulling back and scrubbing at his eyelids until they finally gave in.

His vision was blurry, but he could see Ben well enough as he hovered over Paris's body, leaning with his head propped up on his hand.

"How long was I out?" Paris asked, then hesitated because he had no idea if Ben could hear him or not. He lifted one hand to try and sign it, but Ben answered him before he could.

"Ten minutes. Fucked your own brains out, didn't you?"

Paris scoffed and rolled onto his side, shoving Ben onto his back and making him laugh. "You were louder with me than you were with your, uh...*friend*. So I'm calling it a win."

Ben pressed his elbows into the mattress and leaned up. "Were you competing with Theo?"

Paris felt his ears get hot as he shrugged and looked away. "I wasn't competing. I was just...aware of the differences."

"You're such a goddamn nerd," Ben cried, then rolled over and pinned Paris to the bed, swinging his legs over his hips and kissing him softly until Paris's entire body went lax. When he pulled back, Ben rested his forearms against Paris's chest. "I like you more than I have ever liked Theo. Does that help?"

Paris swallowed heavily and tried to shrug as best he could with Ben lying on top of him. "I don't actually know how to manage all this stuff I'm feeling." He lifted one hand to rub at his temple where his head was starting to ache. "I like you so fucking much, and I don't know how to go forward without fucking it all up."

Ben sighed very softly and lifted the tips of his fingers to Paris's lips, tracing a touch around them. They felt a little sore but in the best way. "You're doing a really good job so far."

"I know. I just..." Paris felt something uncomfortable and tight in his chest. There were words he wanted to say, but they scared the shit out of him. He let out a long, slow breath. "Never mind. I'm sorry."

Ben pushed forward, kissing his chin first, then the corners of his mouth, then his cheeks. He laid a delicate press of lips to his closed eyelids, then settled back down to take a proper, deep kiss. "You might be overthinking this."

"I might be a neurotic fucking mess because you're the last person who deserves to get hurt with my bullshit," Paris countered, but he couldn't put any venom in his voice. He was just resigned to the knowledge that he was probably going to mess this whole thing up, but reward far outweighed the risk.

"So, is it insensitive of me to ask if your dog died or some shit?"

Paris blinked and realized he'd been staring at his beer bottle for so long it no longer looked real. Turning his head, he saw Miguel standing a few feet away, leaning against the balcony railing. Paris stood up straight and rocked himself from left to right, trying to shake the tension from his muscles.

"I've never had a dog," he said, realizing too many seconds had passed for it not to be awkward.

Miguel chuckled under his breath. "Hamster?"

Paris snorted. "No one died."

"He's just missing his boyfriend," came Max's voice from behind him, and Paris braced himself for the arm that was slung around his shoulder. "Who knew you'd turn into a thirteen-year-old emo kid with the first person you decided to date."

"Eat a dick," Paris muttered.

"I would, but it's clearly not working for you," Max replied way too cheerfully. He let Paris go and took a step back, turning his attention to Miguel. "We should just be thankful Paris even showed up tonight." And with that, he headed down the steps to the long benches that were set up for the barbeque that Tony was cooking.

"Y'all are related, right?" Miguel asked. "Brothers?"

Paris rolled his eyes as he settled back against the railing. "Yeah. I think he's a little too happy that I'm seeing someone."

Miguel laughed quietly and shuffled a bit closer. "I feel that. I mean, there wasn't anyone who gave two fucks about my mood change after I started dating Amit, but I think I've been where you are."

Paris raised a brow. "The filling in a shit sandwich?"

"Something like that. I had a bastard old man who made my life a living hell, and I wasn't sure I would ever be good for anyone."

Paris winced. "Yeah. Is your old man the one who..." He trailed off and made a vague gesture toward Miguel's scars.

Miguel shrugged. "Not directly, but close enough. I thought I was gonna live and die in his good-for-nothing club. Even when I was on my tattoo journey, I didn't think I was gonna settle anywhere."

"Then Tony happened?"

Miguel chuckled and bowed his head. "Yeah. Fucker hugged me like he was a goddamn Care Bear, and I realized I wasn't going anywhere. Then Amit came along and took a chance on a bitter piece of shit who definitely didn't deserve it."

Paris's gaze scanned the small crowd, and he found Amit sitting at the table, using ASL with Felix and Harley. "Did you sign before you met him?"

"Nah," Miguel said. "I didn't think I could with just the one hand, but we eventually figured it out."

"And he's okay with...with talking, and...?"

Miguel frowned for a second, and then his eyes widened. "Oh shit. You're dating that Deaf guy, right? Cute one with the dimple?"

Paris felt a rush of possessiveness before reminding himself that Miguel was happily married and that Ben deserved the praise. He took a slow breath, then nodded. "Yeah. I guess. I mean, we haven't defined it or anything. But, uh...yeah. I'm taking that online class with those guys, and I feel like it's never going to stick." He trailed off, picking at the label on his bottle until it was in shreds.

"He'll only care if you give up," Miguel said. "You know that, right?"

Paris laughed, but the sound was hollow. "Yeah, I do. I just...fuck, man. He's so *good*. He's spent the last two weeks taking me on all these dates, and I..." He dragged a hand down his face with a soft groan. "I don't know. There's no way I can match that. I don't know what the fuck I'm doing."

Miguel stared at him for a long time. "Does he seem unhappy with what you give him back?"

"No."

Biting his lip, Miguel looked like he was trying not to smile. "For what it's worth, especially since I don't really know that guy, you should trust that he'll tell you if there's something more he needs. Amit was way more put together than me. I almost ruined everything because I got too far in my head instead of just talking to him."

Paris twisted the bottle in his hands and stared at the ink on his finger. He had a vivid memory of that digit disappearing between Ben's plush lips, and he quickly shoved it away. "We're not there yet, but I'm afraid we will be. I don't know how to keep myself from fucking it all up."

"Time. And you got plenty of that." Miguel clapped him on the shoulder. "Show yourself a little grace."

Paris laughed. That was a hell of a lot easier said than done. He nodded his thanks, then clapped Miguel on the shoulder before someone across the room called his name.

As Miguel disappeared into the small crowd, Paris turned to follow him when the back door opened and Zeke stepped out. Paris hadn't seen much of him since the move. He'd helped get the shop set up, then headed back to Colorado for management training.

"Hey!" Zeke said when his gaze landed on Paris. "Fuck, man, I was hoping you'd be here."

Zeke was one of the few people Paris had let himself get close to just before Zeke's apprenticeship ended, and he felt that sentiment in his chest. He took a step closer, and Zeke pulled him into a hug.

"Glad you're back. I was beginning to think you were gonna stay in Denver forever."

"Fuck no. You couldn't keep me from the ocean," Zeke said. His gaze scanned the crowd for a long second. "How's it been?"

Paris shrugged. "Same shit, different day. I, uh...I think I might be seeing a guy, but that's not—"

"Shut the fuck up," Zeke said. "Are you lying to me right now?"

Paris scoffed. "No. Trust me, I wouldn't lie about that. But I really don't want to talk about it, so please tell me you've got stories."

Zeke swallowed heavily, then said, "Yeah. I, uh...I ran into this guy I used to know back in high school, and we had a thing. Uh...and it turns out he's kind of fucking famous."

Paris's eyes went wide. "Seriously?"

"Yeah. I'm shitting myself, man. This might be an actual crisis." Zeke dragged a trembling hand down his face. "Is Linc here? He knows who I'm talking about."

Paris nodded. "Yep."

"Grab him and meet me in the garage so you fuckers can talk me down? I think I'm having an actual panic attack."

Paris grabbed him by both shoulders. "You're fine. We'll see you in a second."

Zeke gave an almost frantic nod before turning on his heel and rushing back into the house, and Paris turned to the stairs and headed toward the table where Linc was sitting with his head on Ryder's shoulder. He approached with some hesitation, hating himself for interrupting, but he offered an apologetic smile when Linc glanced up at him.

"Emergency crisis in the garage."

Linc snorted. "Does this have anything to do with the fifteen grimace emoji texts Zeke has been sending me since Tuesday?"

"I'm going to say yes," Paris told him.

Linc grinned wider, then hooked his finger under Ryder's chin and kissed him. "Good here? All quiet upstairs?"

"Super quiet," Ryder said.

Paris didn't know what that meant, but he wasn't going to ask. He just waited off to the side for Linc to join him, both hands shoved in his pockets. "Did he tell you what this is about?"

"Yeah," Paris said. "He apparently hooked up with someone on the road, and the guy's famous? He also said he knows him from high school."

"Fuck me," Linc said. He yanked one hand out of his jeans and gripped Paris's shoulder tightly with his finger and thumb. "I know who he's talking about. This is..."

"Not good?" Paris asked.

"He definitely could have chosen better," Linc said. He frowned at Paris and quickly pulled his hand away. "Sorry. I know my fingers are freaky..."

Paris realized Linc assumed it was his hand that was bothering him, so he nudged Linc with his elbow and stayed in close. "Dude, no. No. I'm having my own crisis, but I'd rather deal with this right now."

Linc immediately relaxed and dropped his hand back to Paris's shoulder. "Yeah. If it's who I think it is, he and this guy fucking hated each other back in school. This could either end amazing or a damn disaster."

"I couldn't tell if he needs us to praise him or smack him upside the head," Paris admitted as they came around the corner and headed toward the open garage.

Linc bit his lip. "The guy's name is Hendrix, and he went super viral on YouTube a couple years back. Now he's got a record deal. He was kind of an obnoxious attention seeker in high school, and he never wanted to leave Zeke alone. His cronies fucking tormented him."

Paris scowled. "And now he's fucking him?"

"Well, he was kind of in love with him in spite of all the bullshit," Zeke admitted.

Paris hummed in thought. "I mean, if this guy makes him happy, then I don't see what the big deal is. People change, right? So maybe Hendrix is less of a dick now."

Linc gave him a skeptical look. "Maybe. I mean, all the interviews I've seen, he seems pretty down-to-earth, but you know how celebrities are in front of a camera."

Paris didn't actually know that. He'd never paid attention to that sort of thing. "Well, look, the only thing that matters is that we've got his back."

"Yeah," Linc whispered as they got closer to the garage. "You're right."

"We want him to be happy, so we figure out what makes him happy."

Linc gave him a firm nod, then linked their arms together before tugging Paris through the side door and into the nearly empty space.

They found Zeke with his hands over his face, sitting on an old, rusted riding mower that Paris was pretty sure had come with the house. He couldn't picture Felix having shopped for something like that—or using it, considering he didn't actually have any grass to cut. The thing looked like a tetanus hazard, and Paris wasn't brave enough to get too close.

"Bud?" Linc asked like he was talking to a terrified five-year-old. "You with us?"

"I fucked him," Zeke said, his voice thready and soft. "He was stranded on the side of the road, and we went to some bed-and-breakfast, and I fucked him." He lifted his head and took a breath. "It was Hendrix."

Paris and Linc exchanged a look before Paris took a step closer. "Okay," Linc said, his tone still careful. "And how are we feeling about this."

Zeke's laugh was high and tight. "I don't know." He took in a short breath, then looked over at Paris. "So, there was this guy..."

"It's okay," Paris said, taking a step closer. "Linc filled me in."

Zeke's shoulders sank. "Thank God." He rubbed both hands down his face, then squared his shoulders and hopped off the riding mower, pacing a few feet in front of it. "It was like my worst nightmare and my high school fantasy all rolled into one."

Linc walked over to a dilapidated workbench and leaned his hips against it, crossing his arms. "Was he a dick about it?"

Zeke laughed, the sound just as hysterical as before. "No? Yes? I don't...it was weird. Apparently, he was riding with his manager, who tried to, like, dirty touch him or some shit, and then left him in the middle of fucking nowhere with a massive storm on the way. And I'm not a total asshole, so I offered to drive him, and he fucking pretended like he didn't know me."

Linc pulled a face, and Paris winced. "Not cool."

Zeke shrugged. "I mean, I kind of wanted to do the same. It was so awkward. But shit...he was also shaking and totally freaked-out, and I couldn't just leave him. The bed-and-breakfast was booked, so I told him he could chill in my room until he could get ahold of someone. Then we lost power, and..." His arms flopped to his sides.

"And you fucked," Linc said.

Zeke gave him a flat look. "It was a little more complicated than that...but yeah. We fucked. His ride showed up in the morning after the storm passed, and now he's on tour, and I'm here."

"Did you get his number?" Linc asked.

Zeke bit his lip as he nodded. "Yeah, but I haven't been brave enough to text him. Did you know he's like rich and famous now? He played a goddamn sold-out concert in Orlando last week."

Linc grimaced and exchanged a look with Paris before nodding. "Yeah. I did."

"Even if he's done being an epic asshole on his life journey, he's not going to want some random tattoo artist."

Paris heard the pain in his voice and the want. He understood it a little too well. Ben wasn't rich or famous, but he was a much more deserving person than Paris would ever be. And yet, he was there. "Don't write him off so easily," Paris said.

Zeke gave him a surprised look, but he said nothing.

"Rich and famous doesn't get you anything meaningful, and I doubt he slept with you because he was bored," he went on.

Zeke chewed on his cheek for a long second before answering. "Maybe he was just grateful."

"Did it feel like he was just grateful?" Paris pressed.

Swallowing thickly, Zeke rolled his eyes up toward the ceiling and took a breath. "No. It...fuck. Don't shun me for this sappy shit, but it felt like making love, okay? It felt ten times better than I ever thought it could."

Linc let out a slow breath, then walked up to Zeke and laid his hands on his shoulders. "Text him. Call him. Email him. There's no way it didn't feel the same for him, and he's probably afraid to make the first move."

"Why the fuck would he be afraid?" Zeke demanded.

Paris couldn't see Linc's face from that angle, but he could picture his frown. "Because he was the one who tormented you all those years ago. He has a lot to make up for, and you have to be the one who tells him he's got the chance to do it."

"Fuck," Zeke breathed out. He took a step back and rubbed his eyes tiredly. "That's gonna suck."

"Yep," Paris chimed in. "It's really gonna suck. But it's also going to be worth it."

Zeke dropped his hands and stared at Paris. "Who even are you?"

Paris thought maybe he should be offended, but he couldn't bring himself to be. Not when he knew damn well he would have been the last person in the world to say something like that not even six weeks before. "I'm a guy who might be starting to understand the way you feel right now."

"Fuck! I'm gone for three weeks, and hell's frozen over. Who is this guy?" Zeke demanded, shifting to the edge of the mower.

Linc's eyes went shiny. "God, to think I almost decided not to move out here."

Paris lifted a brow at him. "Seriously?"

"I liked the other shop," Linc told him quietly. "I fit in."

Paris felt his stomach twist. "Hey, if we're making you feel like—"

"No," Linc said in a rush. "Fuck that. Y'all are amazing. I just get insecure, and I miss my band and shit. But this makes it worth it." He curled his finger and thumb around Zeke's wrist, then tugged him into a back-slapping hug.

When Linc let him go, Zeke took another deep breath. "What if he tells me to fuck off?"

"There's no chance in hell," Linc said.

"Yeah?" Zeke pressed.

Both men nodded, and Zeke let out a shaking breath. "Okay. Cool. So I'm just gonna call him and ask if I can see him. That's...no big deal. Cool, cool, cool."

"Again, breathe," Paris told him.

Zeke nodded, then turned and narrowed his eyes. "I'm breathing.

And now it's time to fucking spill on this new guy. I want foot size, dick size, hair color..."

"Brown, and the rest, fuck off," Paris said.

Linc laughed and nudged Zeke with his elbow. "Don't worry, man. You'll get to meet him next Friday. At Paris's motherfucking *birthday party*."

15

"LIKE THAT. LIKE, *HNNG*—RIGHT THERE, RIGHT THERE!" BEN ARCHED HIS back, his hands pressed against the top of the bathroom counter as Paris's fingers dug into his hips. He was up on his toes, his calves burning, but none of that mattered with the way he was stretched around Paris's cock.

The angle was so perfect he felt like he was going to lose his fucking mind with how Paris railed his prostate with every thrust. The edges of his vision went white as his orgasm started to build.

"Baby," Paris grunted. He yanked Ben back away from the counter, wrapping one hand around his throat, the other around his hips.

Ben's eyes slammed shut as the back of his head hit Paris's shoulder. "Oh fuck. Oh, sweetheart."

"Yeah," Paris rumbled against the side of his head. "You fucking love that, don't you. You love the way I fuck you."

Ben trembled with need, with want, with the words in his chest he was so desperate to say. He kept them at bay—just barely, because it was way too fucking soon for a man like Paris, and he knew three tiny syllables would send him running for the other side of the country.

But it was true. There was no denying it.

It wasn't just the way Paris fucked him or the way he held Ben after. It wasn't the way he curled up in bed next to him and stared at him like the sun rose and set on his command.

It was the way Paris was raw and honest and open. It was the way he brought to life every fantasy Ben ever had about what it would be like to be truly loved. He was being given a gift, and he was terrified because it was so damn fragile. The wrong move, the wrong word, would shatter everything, and he didn't want to think about what life would be like without Paris.

It would be a new kind of grief—like a death, except that Paris would still be alive. Ben wouldn't be allowed to have him, to touch him, or hold him, as though he were a ghost. Only he wouldn't be. And one day, Ben would have to watch him give all of this to someone else.

It would ruin him.

A small sob escaped him as Paris thrust in, a slow roll of his hips. His eyes moved to the mirror, and he was startled by the reflection there staring back at him. His hair was a mess of sweaty curls, his face splotchy and pink, his eyes half-lidded. Paris was just above his shoulder, looking like a wild Greek god with his olive skin and gorgeous ink decorating it.

It was too much.

"I...please. Please, sweetheart," Ben begged.

Paris dipped his head and latched his teeth to the tendon in Ben's neck with a gentle bite. When Ben sucked in a trembling breath, Paris fucked forward—almost hard enough to send Ben crashing into the counter. Only Paris's hands kept him in place. His fingers grazed the hair on Ben's stomach, and just when Ben felt like he was going to truly lose his mind, Paris picked up the pace again and wrapped his fingers around Ben's cock.

He stroked, a furious rhythm that sent Ben spiraling. The whole world whited out as his body bowed forward, and he was barely aware of his hands hitting the counter and his ass thrusting backward to try and get as much friction as he could while he came.

Paris continued to stroke him until his own hips started to stutter, and Ben was just coming down from his high as he felt Paris spill inside him, filling the condom with hot, throbbing pulses.

"Holy fucking shit," Ben gasped.

Paris laughed, the sound a little strained as he pressed one hand to the small of Ben's back and trailed a line of kisses up his spine. "You're fucking amazing."

Ben winced as Paris pulled out, and he waited until he saw the condom fly toward the little trash bin before he spun around. Paris crowded him back against the counter and cradled his face, kissing him sweet and slow.

"You're gonna have to decommission the rooms next to ours pretty soon, or people are gonna start mentioning this shit on Yelp," he said when he pulled back.

Ben's eyes widened, and then he laughed. "Oh God. I'm surprised it hasn't happened already."

Paris gave him a wicked grin as he stole a last kiss before stepping back to give him room to stand. "Then again, I'll have my own place soon, so you won't lose out on too much business."

Ben smiled, but there was a sudden ache in his chest, which was absolutely ridiculous, considering he knew damn well Paris wasn't planning on living at the hotel forever. Not only was it absurdly expensive compared to rent, but it was a motel. *He* wouldn't live there if he had another option—or the will to move somewhere else.

But the feeling inside him still felt a little twisted and ugly. It had no place there between them that day, though. It was Paris's birthday, and Ben had plans. Big plans. Not just the party, though he'd worked his ass off on it with the guys at the shop, so he felt a bit like a kid waiting to go to Chuck E. Cheese or some shit.

The morning sex had been a more spontaneous thing, anyway. He was going to take Paris to breakfast before his first appointment, and then he was going to bring him lunch and hopefully give him a birthday blowjob before the party.

"We need to get dressed," Ben said as he pushed his way past Paris, who was still hovering in the bathroom doorway. "I want to make sure we can get a table before you have to be at the shop."

He started toward the bedroom when Paris caught his arm and spun him around. There was something in his eyes that Ben could read, but he was too petrified to hope. "Hey."

"Hey." Ben swallowed heavily. "Happy birthday, sweetheart."

Paris softened further, walking Ben backward until he hit the wall. He dipped his head, kissing him deeply—his tongue slightly minty and warm. When he pulled back, he knocked his forehead against Ben's and took a deep breath. "You've made this the best birthday I've ever had. I don't know how to thank you."

"Please don't thank me," Ben told him. He cupped Paris's cheek and urged him back so he could look at him. "You deserved better your whole life. Now you have a huge family who loves you. So just... bask in it, okay? That's all I want."

Paris shook his head, his mouth dropping open before it shut again, and he stole a swift kiss before moving away. Ben felt his stomach sink in disappointment because if Paris said it first, he could unleash the raging storm of obsession and love he was feeling for that stubborn fucker, but every time he thought Paris was going to say it, he didn't.

And while Ben understood why, he was starting to feel like maybe Paris would shy away from the words forever. He could tell Ben a thousand times a day in a thousand ways he loved him without using the words, but Ben didn't know how he'd handle being muted for the rest of their lives.

They had brunch on the water, a little restaurant Ben picked out on Islamorada, which gave them enough time to enjoy their food and then get Paris to the shop before his first appointment. They had spare time, which Paris used by dragging Ben into the drawing room and kissing him until a hulking man Ben was pretty sure was named Harley came in and yelled at them for soiling their sacred space.

"No getting jizz in common areas," he demanded.

Ben felt a twinge of fear in his gut until Paris laughed and flipped him off before dragging Ben out the back door and into the side parking lot.

"Is he actually mad?"

Paris scoffed. "No. He just has a loud bark." He stroked his knuckles down Ben's cheek. "Remind me why I can't just cancel everything today and take you back to bed."

Ben swallowed heavily. "Remind me why I should remind you."

Paris groaned and dropped his forehead to Ben's collarbone. "You're not making this very easy."

Snorting a laugh, Ben tipped Paris's head up by the chin. "I'll be easy for you tonight. Now, kiss me and tell me to fuck off."

Paris did exactly that. The kiss was deep, but it didn't linger too long. 'See you later tonight,' he signed.

Ben softened and nodded his fist. 'Yes. See you soon.' He backed away and watched Paris turn and head back into the building before forcing himself to head to his car. He'd never felt this way before. Ever. He didn't even know he could.

The day was going to drag ass to the point he knew he'd start to feel a little bit like he was losing his mind. He had a ton of paperwork to do, rooms to clean, and all of that before Max was supposed to pick him up so he could pick up the cake, food, and set up for the party.

His only saving grace was that Paris knew the party was coming, so he didn't have to keep any of it quiet. He wasn't sure he'd survive if he had to act aloof and tight-lipped because being with Paris made him want to flay himself open and spill every secret he'd ever kept.

It was halfway into his lunch break—which was a sandwich at his desk as he tried to make sense of Callisto's accounting notes—

when his phone began to buzz with a FaceTime. He looked down to see Theo's name on the screen, and he picked up.

'Hey.'

Theo was signing, but the connection was shitty, and the glitch was making him look like he was signing through a broken strobe light.

'Can't understand,' Ben signed quickly. 'Where are you?'

'...around...tonight...important.'

Ben ended the call and switched to text.

Ben: Your connection is fucked.

Theo: Sorry. Getting ready to take off. I need to talk to you. Will you be around tonight?

Ben: It's Paris's birthday party. Can it wait?

Theo: Sorry, no. Where can I meet you?

Feeling a wave of apprehension—like maybe this was the shoe dropping—Ben gave him Felix and Max's address and said he'd be around. He didn't make Theo promise anything because he knew his friend wouldn't do this if it wasn't practically life-or-death. And Jesus, he hoped it wasn't that serious.

He took a breath and started to go back to the books when the icon on his computer lit up with a Skype request.

"Fuck's sake," he muttered to himself. He knew it was his dad because he was the only person who used Skype anymore, so he fumbled around for his processors and got them on just before the call ended.

It took a second, but eventually, his dad's face filled the screen, and Ben felt a small pulse in his chest because Levi had looked so much like him, and sometimes it hurt to see it. But he smiled anyway.

"Hey."

"I hope I'm not interrupting," he said.

Ben's gaze followed the captions since the audio was always shitty, and his dad's laptop was at least a decade old. "Nah. You're saving me from accounting."

Abe pulled a face. "Always was my least favorite part of the job."

Ben gave him a smile, but he was still irritated at the interruption. "Is everything okay? I'm kind of on a tight timeline today."

"I just wanted to check in. Your mom said she saw a post on that Instagram thing you do. Said you were with a boy."

Ben's entire body went tense. His parents loved and accepted him as their son, but his life wasn't what they'd envisioned, and his mom had sort of doubled down after Levi died and made Ben solely responsible for providing grandkids. Which was not happening.

"So she's internet stalking me now?"

Abe sighed. "She doesn't mean anything by it. It's just almost the yahrzeit, and..."

"I know," Ben said, rubbing at his eyes. "I know." And he did. He hadn't forgotten the anniversary of his brother's death. That would be impossible. He just didn't like thinking about it until the day was on him. And he knew it would be like that for the rest of his life. "I've had a lot going on, and I really don't want to talk about marriage and kids with her. You know that's...that's not my path."

Abe nodded, and while he looked sad, he didn't look as intense as he usually did. "She's coming around."

Ben snorted. "Sure."

"She just misses you. You're all she has left," Abe said.

"I get that, but that's a lot of pressure to put on me," Ben told his dad, hoping he didn't sound as frustrated as he felt. "I can't be all the things she wants me to be. I'm not going to live any life but my own."

Abe was quiet for a long time, his face still, and Ben hated it because he wished his parents could sign. He wished they were more expressive and met him halfway. "Will we get to meet him?"

Ben squeezed his eyes shut for a long second. "I hope so. It's new, and I'm...I'm not ready to talk about it right now."

"I understand. But please know you can bring him home. We won't embarrass you any worse than we usually do."

Unable to help a small laugh, Ben leaned back in his chair. "I think you'll like him. He's learning ASL for me."

There was a flicker of pain in his dad's face, and once upon a time, that would have made him feel guilty. He told himself growing up that his parents had done the best they could. He told himself that he couldn't expect someone to learn a whole new language for him.

But a friend in college asked him, "If your brother got a brain injury and woke up from a coma only being able to speak Spanish, and the doctors told your parents he will only ever be able to speak Spanish, would they learn for him?"

It was a harsh wake-up call, and it forced him to confront the way his parents saw him and the value they put on his natural language.

He had no plans to try and change them, but he was done apologizing for who he was.

"Actually, all of the guys at his work are leaning it. It's been nice."

"I'm happy for you," Abe said.

Ben's stomach twisted again, wishing his dad would give him something more than that. But he'd long since stopped wishing for miracles. "Anyway, I should go, but I'll be in touch soon."

"You promise?"

Ben smiled a little and lifted his finger to his lips to sign, 'I promise.'

'Thanks,' his dad signed back—one of the dozen signs he knew.

Ben ended the call and couldn't help but wonder if the talk with his dad and the message from Theo was the precursor to a total disaster instead of the birthday celebration he'd been so desperate to throw.

16

Paris had spent the entire day rethinking his stance on surprise parties. Even the fact that the shop had been so busy no one had time to breathe since they opened didn't stop him from being consumed with anticipation.

He trusted the guys enough to know they weren't going to spring some shit on him, but every time they clapped him on the shoulder to wish him a happy birthday or gave him a knowing little smile, his heart rate picked up.

He had a slight reprieve for lunch, which only lasted as long as it took for Max and Jamie to walk in with huge bags of Greek food, which they spread out on the drawing room table buffet-style. Paris appreciated that there wasn't some big to-do where he was the center of attention, but when he went to fill his plate in the short space between clients, Max was waiting for him with a gift in his hands.

"Why did you go all the way over there?" Paris asked, staring at the food. "Midnight Snack is next door."

Max bristled, and it wasn't the first time Paris had seen his brother get weird about the innuendo restaurant. He tried to bring it up once, but Max bit his head off, so he'd let it go. "Uh. I thought this might be better. Does it matter?"

Paris shook his head and let it go, squeezing the back of Max's neck. "No. This is great. Thank you."

"You never let me do this before," Max said quietly.

Paris bowed his head. "I know. How about instead of getting me a gift, I let you tell me what a piece-of-shit brother I've been for twenty years, and I won't punch you for it."

Max laughed, elbowing Paris gently. "Shut up and take it, dick-head. It took me a hundred years to find it."

His fingers felt oddly weak as he took the poorly wrapped lump from his brother and felt around it. There was weight to it, and he suddenly didn't want to do this there in front of him. "Can I save it?"

Max let out a sharp laugh. "Fuck. Yes, please. I thought I was about to have a goddamn heart attack watching you open it. How the hell do people do this all of their lives?"

Paris grinned as he walked to his cubby and gently put the gift inside. "Yeah, and they think we're the weird ones."

Max was quiet for so long Paris looked over his shoulder at him and saw his face was drawn and troubled. When he realized he was caught, Max laughed and rubbed the back of his head. "We are the weird ones, though, aren't we? We're the kind of guys that people fuck and then sneak out on in the morning."

Paris dropped into a chair and pulled his plate close, frowning at his brother. "Aside from Ben, pretty much, yeah. I mean, we lived it, so it doesn't feel as fucked-up as it probably should, but it's been harder to ignore lately."

"But Ben is different, isn't he?" Max asked, sounding honestly worried.

Paris kicked a chair out so his brother could sit. "He took me to the park for one of our dates. Like, kid shit, you know?"

"Swings and seesaws?" Max asked with a grin, then took a huge bite of pita.

Paris laughed. "Yeah, dude. Literally. There were kids running around, and we ate snow cones and hot dogs. And I...fuck, man, I had fun. We went to a goddamn toy store afterward, and he made me buy a bunch of junk."

Max's eyes widened. "Is that where all that slime crap came from?"

Paris rolled his eyes as he swallowed down some of his chicken. "Yeah. He got board games and Transformers toys, and, like, I don't know if it was supposed to be romantic..."

"Dude. He's spent three weeks trying to fill those fuckin' swiss-cheese holes you got inside you," Max pointed out. "Toys or not, that's the most romantic goddamn thing anyone has ever done."

Paris swallowed thickly. "Hah, yeah. And what do I do for him?"

Max started to laugh, but then he sobered and set his plate down, leaning over his knees. "Wait, you're serious?"

Paris let out a slightly hysterical laugh. "Yeah, I'm serious! I'm this anxious mess who can't even tell him how I feel, so I just try to distract him with—" He stopped abruptly, and Max grinned.

"Dick?"

"Shut up. But yes," Paris said. "I don't even know the words for how he makes me feel. And lately, I've been so goddamn angry about Dad and the Witch and what they did. And at my fuckin' self for not saying anything about it for all those years. I just rolled over and took it. I didn't even protect you—"

"Stop," Max said, and the tone of his voice had Paris's jaw snapping shut. "You don't get to blame a six-year-old *child* for not doing something about his abusive stepmom and his good-for-nothing dad."

Paris bit the inside of his cheek until it stung, and only then could he breathe again. "I just..."

"No," Max said. "You sacrificed everything, Paris. You gave up your childhood, your teenage years, your adult life, all to make sure I didn't have to spend more time in that hellhole. So we fucked up Christmases and birthdays. So we didn't eat snow cones or go to the zoo or whatever. You never let me go a single day without showing me you love me."

Paris wanted to run. He didn't want to have this conversation. It was too fucking raw, and even though Max was right, and even though it was validating to him that Max understood all the years of Paris's stunted emotional growth, it was overwhelming.

"Now, we don't need to do this shit on your birthday," Max went on, and Paris let out a breath. "But I want you to at least stop second-guessing this thing with Ben. I don't know if it'll last. I don't pretend to understand how normal relationships work. But I do know that you deserve someone to love you the way Ben loves you."

"He doesn't," Paris said quietly.

Max laughed and shook his head. "Yeah, he fuckin' does. So get over it. Accept it. Enjoy it. And eat your food so you don't pass out on your next client." With that, he stood up and clapped Paris on the shoulder once before disappearing.

Paris hadn't expected to be viciously run over by his feelings, but he let some of Max's words stay with him as he sat there and finished his plate. Mainly that while he wasn't sure he could ever truly feel like he deserved someone as good as Ben, he was maybe ready to let himself try.

The rest of the afternoon passed almost in slow motion. Paris had three more clients before they were ready to close up shop, and as he was packing his shit away, he could hear Tony and Miguel at the front, arguing with a group of not-quite-sober tourists who were pissed that the shop was closing up early.

"Your website hours say you're open until two a.m.," a woman's voice said, gently slurred. "It's only seven. This is *bullshit.*"

"We have a special event happening tonight," Tony said, and his patience was far beyond what Paris was capable of.

“Yeah. You Disney Princess fuckers should be used to that special-event shit,” Miguel chimed in.

Paris covered his laugh and glanced over at Linc and Zeke, who were leaning against the partitions. ‘We’re never getting out of here now,’ he mouthed.

Zeke just shrugged as the woman shrieked, “I want to speak to a manager right now!”

“That would be him.”

Zeke blinked when he realized Tony was talking about him. “Oh, come on.”

“Sorry, bud,” Linc said, giving Zeke a shove. “This is what you signed up for.”

Zeke rolled his eyes as he stood up straight and walked over. “Hello, ma’am. How can I help?”

“Did you hear the way your employee just spoke to me? Do you have any idea where we’re from? One word and I can ruin this place.”

Paris shifted closer to Linc and tipped his head low to murmur, “I know a guy back in LA who would have invited her in and tattooed a dick on her forehead.”

Linc choked on a laugh. “Introduce me if we ever go back.”

Paris grinned as the woman continued ranting. He was mostly packed up and ready to go, but he had no idea how long this was going to drag out, so he pulled out his phone and took a quick photo before texting it to Ben.

Paris: Our first Key Largo Karen. We might be a while.

Ben: Fantastic. It’s been a fucking day for me too. I’m already with your brother and a few of the other guys, so just get here when you can. I miss your face.

Paris: I miss you too, babe.

He tucked his phone away and looked over at Linc, who was

making a heart with his fingers and thumbs. "I'm pissed I can do this, but I don't have middle fingers to flip anyone off with," he said, dropping his hands.

"I'm pretty sure you mastered 'fuck you' with your face," Paris told him, patting him on the shoulder.

Linc grinned. "Many hours in front of a mirror, my friend." He glanced over again, then sighed. "Should we bail and leave them to the she-wolves?"

"I feel like that's an insult to wolves, but yeah. It's my birthday, right? I get a special pass."

Linc nodded. "Fuck yeah. And I'm driving you, so I do too." He pushed away from the partition and leaned over the desk. "Yo, Zeke. Have fun with that shit. Paris and I are gonna take off before they close down the pony rides."

"*Excuse* me?" the woman demanded.

Linc cackled, then turned and grabbed Paris's arm, hauling him through the side door and out the back. Paris tugged on his arm as they headed for Linc's car.

"Please tell me there's not actually pony rides," he said as he reached for the door handle.

Linc laughed again. "I tried, bud, but Max put his foot down about the budget."

"Remind me to send him a damn muffin basket," Paris muttered as Linc started the car and took off down the street.

The drive to Felix and Max's place didn't take long, but Paris was already feeling a little antsy. He was nearly an hour late to his own party, and he didn't want Ben to think he was trying to avoid him. He wasn't exactly looking forward to having his first birthday celebration since he was a little kid, but that was mostly the unknown factor.

But he knew everyone had worked their asses off for this, and the least he could do was seem grateful.

Tapping his fingers on his thigh, he listened to Linc drone on about the new place he and Ryder had moved into, half contemplating his own move because it was about time he started looking beyond the motel. He knew it was bothering Ben, but it would be nice for him to have a place that was apart from Ben's work and all the other obligations that rested on his tired shoulders.

Paris wanted a place he could spoil his boyfriend without other people looking over their shoulders at them. He wanted to navigate this new, fragile thing he didn't quite understand and figure it out without worrying about who was judging him.

His anxiety got a little worse as they pulled into the driveway and he saw the sheer number of cars and bikes parked along the road, but he told himself it was for the best. The more people that were there, the less likely they would pay attention to one single guy most of them barely knew.

"Ready?" Linc asked, his voice cutting into Paris's thoughts.

Paris looked over at him. "No surprises?"

Linc softened and squeezed the back of Paris's neck with his finger and thumb. "No surprises, bud. We got your back."

Paris nodded, then let himself out of the car and walked with Linc a few steps behind as he made his way in. There was music thumping from outside, and there were several people milling around the front room that Paris didn't recognize. He eventually spotted Max, who was talking to a massive guy with broad shoulders, a neck tattoo, and a missing left arm with a scarred stump that ended just below the shoulder.

He was wearing a tank top and dog tags, which told Paris that he was military, and he looked friendly—he had a booming laugh that Paris could hear from across the room. When he caught his brother's eye, Max jerked his head for him to come over.

Paris gave an internal sigh, but he shoved one hand into the pocket of his jeans as he made his way through the small crowd.

"The man of the goddamn hour," Max said, grabbing Paris's arm and hauling him close. "This is my brother, Paris. Paris, this is Deimos. He lives with his sister like three houses down from here, and he's going to let me dog sit!"

Max sounded like a kid, and it made Paris smile as he extended his hand to the guy. "Well, you clearly found the way to his heart. It's nice to meet you, Deimos."

The guy laughed, squeezing Paris's hand lightly. "Call me Dei. And anyone who loves Millie as much as I do is a friend of mine. And happy birthday, by the way. I have gotta ask..."

Paris braced himself.

"Your dad fuck a demigoddess or some shit because you two are way too pretty to be real."

Paris's eyes widened, and he glanced at Max, who was cackling. "He's not hitting on you."

"Nah. I'm not on the market," Dei told him with a wink. "But that was a serious question."

"Well, I think we're fucked up enough to be considered Greek gods," Max said and nudged Paris with his elbow. "Anyway, Paris, you should go mingle. It's your party."

Paris tried for a smile, though it failed. "Have, uh...have you seen Ben?"

At that, Max's face fell just a fraction—just enough to make Paris antsy. "Yeah. His buddy showed up. The Deaf one. They went to find a place to talk."

Paris felt his face start to go a little numb. "Cool," he heard himself say. "You see where?"

Max shook his head and gave him another worried look, but he didn't try to stop Paris as he turned and headed for the back door. Outside was a little more chaotic than in with the loud music and people milling around tables full of food. Out of the corner of his eye, Paris caught another table loaded with gifts, and his stomach twisted.

He still hadn't opened the one that his brother had gotten him, and he couldn't stand the thought of being expected to open all of these in front of a damn audience. Fuck, he wanted Ben. He needed him. He *needed* to curl up in his arms and catch his breath.

Moving into the grass, he nodded a few hellos to a couple of guys from the shop and their friends he didn't recognize. He spotted Andrew and Amelia talking with a few strange faces, but Ben wasn't with them, and his panic started to get a little more intense.

Pulling out his phone, he walked to the side of the house and leaned against the brick wall. He started to open his messages when he heard a soft noise, then what sounded like hands slapping together, and he knew what it was.

Unable to stop himself, Paris peered around the corner into the little area where Felix and Max kept their trash bins, and he saw them.

There was a faint light coming from the side of the house, and it illuminated Ben, with his curls wild from humidity, his face drawn, hands up as he signed at a speed Paris was pretty sure he'd never follow. The other guy—Theo—was as good-looking as Paris remembered seeing once or twice in the parking lot.

He was tall, dark-haired, with chiseled features. He was the perfect complement to Ben, and it made him want to scream.

Instead, he watched in silence as Ben's hands lifted, cupping Theo's face, and then he pulled him close. It was all Paris could stand. He turned on his heel and hurried through the house. He caught sight of Max and rushed over, yanking on his elbow and pulling him close.

"I need to leave. Give me your keys."

Max stared with wide eyes. "What?"

"I need to leave. If I don't get out of here right now, I'm going to fucking lose it."

Max dug his hand into his pocket and pressed the keys against Paris's palm, but he didn't let him go. "What happened?"

"Ben's getting back together with his ex."

Max shook his head. "There's no way."

Paris let out a dry, humorless laugh and tried not to feel all the pain all at once. "Unless you have another reason why the two of them were holding each other and kissing behind the house, then

I'm gonna go with yeah. It's happening. And I need to leave before I lose my shit."

Max nodded. "Okay. Go. I'll come by in a bit."

Paris shook his head as he stepped back. "Don't. I need some space, but just...fuck. Tell everyone I'm sorry and I'll make it up to them, okay?"

He didn't wait for an answer. He just got the fuck out of the house and scanned the driveway until he found Max's bike. It had been a while since he'd driven one, but it didn't take him long to get his bearings, and as he approached the motel, he felt his stomach sink.

Ben wasn't there, of course. No, he was busy making out with his goddamn ex at Paris's birthday party. He found himself laughing, a high, hysterical sound as he rolled to a stop and killed the engine. Bowing over the handlebars, Paris let a tremor of frustrated irony roll through him.

Of *course* Ben would do this at his birthday. Of *course* Paris would be cosmically punished for letting himself experience a single moment of true happiness. He was fucking cursed. There was no other explanation for it.

Pocketing his keys, he fumbled in his pockets and almost panicked when he couldn't find the key card, but eventually, his fingers touched the edge, and he pulled it out. As he opened the door, his heart ached. It smelled a bit like Ben's cologne—soft and sort of woodsy. It was the remnants of their early morning together. One of his shirts was lying on the sofa, one of his socks near the kitchen table.

He wanted to put his fist through the wall, but instead, he just pulled out his phone, pulled up the hotel app, and found a room nearby. It was expensive as fuck, but it was on the other side of the road and tucked in a little cove. It was obviously for families with the fancy-ass pool and dockside entertainment, but he didn't care.

He threw in his credit card number to reserve a room, then darted into his room to throw shit into a bag. There was no way in hell he could keep staying at Ben's motel after this, but he needed a few days to get his head together because, looking around, the place was fucking lived-in. Yeah, none of it was his, but he'd unpacked. He'd settled.

He'd been...

Fuck, he'd been happy.

His throat burned as he started to pull socks out of the little dresser, and he was so busy with trying to remember what else he'd need that he didn't hear the knocking. Or his door opening. He didn't hear anything but the sound of his own heavy breathing until a fist tapped on the wall.

Paris spun and felt his heart threaten to beat out of his chest when he laid eyes on Ben. His eyes were red, and his mouth was drawn.

"Going somewhere?"

Paris let out a humorless laugh. "Why the fuck do you care?"

Ben dragged a hand down his face. "Look, I know what you think you saw—"

"So you knew I was there," Paris shot back.

Curling his hands into fists, Ben looked like he wanted to hit something, and God, did Paris know the feeling. 'Yes, I knew,' he signed almost too fast for Paris to follow.

Paris's fingers were trembling, but he lifted his hand to the side of his head anyway. 'Why?'

Ben's whole body was still for a long time, and just when Paris thought he wasn't going to answer, he dropped his hands to his sides. "It's complicated."

"Yeah. Making out with your ex at my birthday party sounds really goddamn complicated." Ben's mouth dropped open, but Paris held up a hand to silence him. "I can't do this right now, okay? I just...I need to leave."

"Fine," Ben said from behind a sigh.

For some reason, that gutted him worse than anything he'd seen that night. The fact that Ben was just resigned to it—that he had no fight, no explanation.

That it was over.

Turning away, Paris went back to packing, and when he turned back around, Ben was gone.

His heart stayed firmly lodged in his throat when he got back on the bike, his backpack straps tight against his shoulders. Leaving felt like an ending, but this time—unlike when he left LA—there wasn't a bright, welcoming sunrise on the horizon.

17

PARIS MADE IT TO HIS NEW HOTEL BEFORE HE COMPLETELY FELL APART. HE pulled into the check-in parking spot, then curled up over the handlebars of the bike and pressed his hands over his face. He fought the urge to scream and instead let out a few dry sobs before forcing himself to stand. He tried to ignore the way his legs were shaking as he took a few steps away from the bike.

He hitched his bag over his shoulder, and he made it as far as the stairs to the lobby when he just turned around and sat, unable to go any further. How the hell had it come to this? How had he gone from absolute and utter bliss to so fucking bleak he wasn't sure he'd survive it?

He hated himself for thinking he could ever have something good. That he could have kindness and love and affection in his life without some kind of cosmic price.

He closed his eyes and immediately pictured Ben and Theo together, locked in an intimate embrace, and he wanted to be sick. He wondered if Ben had texted Theo to come over the second he was gone. Maybe they were already in bed together. Maybe they were...

"Sir? Do you need help?"

Paris's head snapped up, and he saw a man with an impressively large torso moving toward him in a sleek wheelchair. He had light olive skin and curly hair worn in a sharp undercut, and his smile was cautious. He didn't have a badge pinned to his shirt, but he had an air of authority about him, so he was probably with the concierge service.

"If you're intoxicated, I can call someone to help you to your room," the guy went on.

Paris let out a bitter laugh and shook his head. "I fucking wish." He stopped and slapped a hand over his face. "Shit. Sorry. I've had a bad night."

The guy came to a stop near the side of his foot. "You're the one who booked the suite a few minutes ago, right?"

Paris grimaced. "Let me guess. I'm the only pathetic loser who had to change hotels at nine p.m. because their boyfriend..." He stopped abruptly.

The guy grimaced in sympathy. "Tonight you are, but it's way more common than you think. You'd be surprised how many people come here to fix something in their relationship only to learn that the tropics are good for food and drinks, and even some decent snorkeling, but it's not therapy."

Paris scoffed. "Yeah. I actually live here, though. I work at the new tattoo shop..."

"Irons and Works," the guy said, sounding almost excited. When Paris lifted a brow at him, he gave him a slightly sheepish smile. "I know about those guys. I follow a guy from the Colorado shop on Instagram. He does wheelchair fitness."

"Sam," Paris said absently. "We've only talked a couple of times, but he's a good dude. He's supposed to be coming out here sometime soon to check out the new place."

"Well, I hope I get to meet him." The guy's hand did something by the side of his wheel before he offered it to Paris. "I'm Eli Steiner, by the way."

"Paris Marin," he offered back, shaking the guy's hand. It was calloused, and his skin felt rough and thin, but it was the most comforting touch he'd had since before the party. "I promise I'm not gonna be loitering long. I just...um." He huffed a quiet breath. "I think I caught my boyfriend cheating, and I've never actually been in this situation before. And now, apparently, I'm telling a total stranger about it."

Eli laughed, the sound low and almost melodic. "Mind if I have a seat next to you?"

Paris shifted over, and the guy pressed his hands to his chair seat, then hoisted his body off and to the side. Once he was out, Paris could see his legs were very small and stiff. He moved on his hands like he'd been doing it that way his whole life, though, and he offered Paris a quick wink before pulling his chair close and digging into the bag that was hanging off the back.

"Normally, I don't advocate getting wasted during heartbreak. I tried it once, and it was a mistake. But I don't think a couple shots will hurt." He produced four tiny airplane bottles of Jim Beam, and Paris laughed.

"I accept." He took two of the bottles, twisted the cap off one, then tapped it against the one Eli was holding out before letting it drain into his mouth. The burn was sweet, though he had a feeling it wasn't going to help matters. "Tonight's my birthday."

"Oh, shit," Eli said. "Seriously?"

Paris let out another laugh, though it didn't sound as bitter this time. He was mostly resigned to the fact that nothing would ever be soft for him. Or kind. "Yeah. I've never celebrated my birthday before. I mean, not since I was a real little kid. Uh, and my friends talked me into it."

"Is that where you found out your boy was sleeping around?"

Paris tried to swallow, but there was a lump in his throat, so he tried to chase it with the other bottle of Jim Beam before he spoke again. It didn't work, but it was a little easier to breathe. "I saw him with his ex. Or...I don't know. Whatever the guy is to him. And I hate that I'm not even surprised. They're a way better match than he and I are."

Eli cocked his head to the side, leaning back on his elbow. "How do you figure?"

"Well, apart from the fact that he's got his shit together better than I do," Paris said with a wry grin, "they also kind of...I don't know. Share the same experience. They're both Deaf, and this guy's a fuckin' pilot, and..."

"You're talking about Theo," Eli said very quietly.

Paris wanted to scream. He should have figured everyone on this fucking island the size of a thimble would know everyone else. The alcohol in his gut soured. "You two friends?"

Eli bit the inside of his cheek, then nodded. "Yeah, actually. We are. And I'm also going to assume you're talking about him and Ben, and trust me, they're not a good match. Being Deaf is about the only thing they have in common."

Paris snorted. "If you say so."

"I'm serious. Ben wants things Theo can never give him. It's always been like that, and the two of them..." Eli trailed off for a second, playing with the second bottle in his hands. "Let's just say that Theo has broken more than a few hearts without meaning to. He was better at setting expectations with Ben, but that didn't mean it was a good situation. And not to defend him because I don't know what you saw tonight, but I don't think Ben would do that to someone he cares about."

"That's what I thought too," Paris said, the misery rising in his chest again. "But I *saw* them. Ben was holding him. It was...it was fuckin' intimate, man."

Eli rolled his eyes toward the sky as he let out a long, ragged breath. "Yeah. Yeah, that was... Look." Eli paused for a long second. "Did you talk to Ben about all this?"

Paris shrugged. "Not really. It was too much. He was my first—" His voice cracked, and he had to stop himself from falling apart again because clearly, this guy was going to take Ben and Theo's side no matter what. And as much as Paris was desperate to believe that Eli was right and Ben hadn't betrayed him, he couldn't trust fate. "He's my first everything. I'm sorry."

Eli quickly shook his head and laid his hand on Paris's shoulder, giving him a gentle squeeze. "Do me one favor, okay?"

Paris nodded, staring down at his hands because he was too afraid to face the kindness in Eli.

"Talk to Ben tomorrow. I'm not going to sit here and say there's no possible way the worst didn't happen. But I'm saying that some shit went down tonight, and it's probably not what you think."

Paris scoffed. "Sure."

"Listen, I've been there, okay? It took me years to get my first serious relationship, and that ended in flames. Like the kind of flames that leave scars." Paris looked over and saw the truth on Eli's face. "I don't say this lightly as someone who's been where you are. But the one thing I do trust is that Ben will tell you the truth. So go upstairs, sleep on it, take some time, then talk to him."

It was fair. Ben deserved at least that much—for now. And if it turned out that Eli was wrong and Ben had done the unthinkable, well, he'd only lose a few minutes of his time. And the last few weeks.

But even now, with all this hurt, he wasn't sure he was going to ever regret Ben.

Not completely, anyway.

"I'm going to send some comfort food up to your room," Eli said as he reached for his chair. He transferred back into his seat with rippling biceps moving smoothly like flowing water. Rolling his shoulders back, he tucked the empty bottles into his backpack, then offered his hand again, squeezing Paris's lightly. "I'm also gonna comp your room."

"Oh, dude. No. Trust me, I can afford it."

"Yeah, but it's also your birthday, and it seems like it went as badly as any birthday can go."

Paris deflated, no idea what to do with all this sudden kindness from a total stranger. Part of him wanted to fight Eli, not quite sure why he'd even deserve it. But the bigger part of him said he was allowed to have this.

"Thanks," he finally said.

Eli chuckled. "Thought I was gonna have a bigger fight on my hands. You take care, okay? And listen, I live on property, so if you feel like things are really bad, call the front desk and tell them to send me an SOS. I'll be right over with more tiny booze bottles and maybe a rom-com or two."

Paris pushed himself up to stand, rubbing the back of his neck. "Would it be really fuckin' weird if I hugged you? I haven't had a lot of people be nice to me in my life, and—"

His words were cut off when Eli seized his wrist and tugged. Hard. Paris bent over at the waist and let his head fall against the top of Eli's shoulder. "You'll figure out we take care of our own, Paris. And living here makes you just that. Got it?"

Paris sniffed against a wave of heat in his eyes, but luckily, no tears fell. "Thanks," he whispered.

Eli squeezed him once more before leaning back and giving his arm a pat. "Try to get some rest."

"I will." Paris walked up one step, then froze and turned back around. "If you want some ink, come see me. I'm really good at what I do."

Eli beamed at him. "I'm gonna take you up on that. See you soon."

Paris gave him a quick salute before adjusting his bag on his shoulder, then finishing the climb to the lobby with the hope that, if anything, he'd be able to get a little rest so he'd have the courage to face Ben in the morning.

18

Ben didn't cry. He wanted to, more than anything. He wanted to bury his face in his pillow and scream until his vocal cords gave out. But his emotions seemed locked behind a wall, and all he could do was sit on his sofa and stare at the wall.

That was not how the night was supposed to go. He'd worked his ass off to make it perfect, and it wasn't like he hated Theo for showing up and dropping a bomb on him, but he was starting to wonder if God had it out for him with the way it all happened.

When Ben first saw him, he could tell Theo was shaken. No, he was more than shaken. He was pale, and his eyes were surrounded by dark circles like he hadn't slept in a week. His hands were trembling when he asked Ben to talk with him outside, and when he confessed what he was holding in, he looked like he was going to collapse.

And Ben's entire world was shattered.

'My test came back positive.'

Ben didn't need to ask what test. He'd been sexually active for too fucking long—taken too goddamn many of those tests—to not know. His throat felt like it was going to close up, although logic had told him that he and Theo had always taken every precaution, and he'd been on PrEP for a decade.

But so had Theo.

'How? Who?' was all Ben managed to ask.

Theo's chin trembled a bit. 'A guy in Jersey that I've been sleeping with for a few years. We only see each other a couple times a year, but he called me last week. I went in that day.'

Ben dragged his hands down his face and took a deep breath. 'Your numbers...'

'Fine for now,' Theo said, his hands shaking harder. 'Already saw my doctor, and he said my chances are good. But I'm...I'm...' Theo swiped his palms over his jeans. 'I'm scared.'

Ben was too. He was ready to piss his fucking pants because not only did he have to worry about himself, but he had to worry about Paris. They hadn't fucked without protection, but that wasn't the only thing they'd done. Paris had swallowed plenty of his come, and it didn't matter how low the risk was.

There still was one.

All the same, he couldn't stand the expression Theo wore and the fear in his eyes. His life was effectively changed, and there was nothing he could do about it. So Ben took Theo's face between his hands and gave him a single nod before pulling him close to hold him.

They hadn't stood there long. Ben resolved to get back to the party and talk to Paris about it once they were alone. After all, they'd both need to get tested and figure out where the hell to go from there if the worst happened.

When Ben told him that, Theo promised he was going to be okay. He was heading to his brother's house so he wouldn't be alone. Ben walked him to the door, and when he turned back around, he saw Max and another massive guy with one arm glaring daggers at him.

It only took him a second to understand what happened. Paris had seen him and Theo. There was no chance he had understood what they'd been signing to each other, but Ben didn't need to be in his right mind to know what it looked like. He didn't bother to stay and explain himself. It wasn't really his story to tell. Not yet, anyway.

He felt like he was driving in a fog on the way back to the motel, and then when he came face-to-face with Paris, he realized that he wouldn't be allowed to explain himself that night. Paris's trauma from his past was too deep, and nothing Ben said would make it better. Not right then.

So he let him go.

Once Paris had time to calm down and breathe and maybe think about whether or not he trusted Ben to be better than all the people in his past who had tried to hurt him, then Ben could unload everything on him. But there was every chance Paris wouldn't want him after this. His own life might be completely upside down now, reality shifted, nothing ever the same again.

Or it might be just a scare.

He had no idea how long he sat there, but he jolted back to himself when his doorbell began to flash, and he jumped up, saying a small prayer that Paris had changed his mind. Throwing open the door, he blinked in surprise at the sight of Callisto and Andrew. The last he'd seen Andrew was at the party, and Callisto rarely left his house once his work shift was over.

A part of Ben wanted to turn them away. He was in no mood to entertain, and the last thing he wanted to do was talk about anything that had happened that night. But he could see the concern on their faces, so he stepped aside to let them in.

"I don't have my processors on," he said aloud, hating that he'd have to let sound back into his head. The only peace he'd gotten since Paris left was the silence.

Callisto quickly shook his head and tapped his thumb on his chest. 'It's fine.'

Ben almost laughed because it wasn't exactly fine. The only person with fluency had just dropped an atom bomb on his life and then left. The idea of hearing anything right then was bad, but trying to figure out how to communicate with his friends was worse.

"Just give me a second," he said, then walked into his room and pressed his back to the wall, forcing himself to take several breaths before he snatched his processors off the nightstand and put them on. The apartment was relatively quiet, which helped, but even the sound of his friends shuffling around threatened to send him over the edge. He stood in his bedroom doorway and wrung his hands together. "Look, not to be a bad host, but—"

"Andrew told me what happened," Callisto said quietly.

Ben's gaze snapped over to Andrew, who threw his hands up in surrender. "I don't know the details. I just know that after you and Paris left, Max and Amelia got into a huge fight."

Ben's stomach sank. "What the hell for?"

"Max said you were cheating. Amelia said that you'd sooner cut your own face off than do something like that," Andrew explained. "I agreed with her, but things got heated, so we took off."

Ben dragged a hand down his face and groaned. "Paris saw me comforting Theo and came to the wrong conclusion, but he wouldn't let me explain."

"You know he's—" Andrew started, and Ben quickly shook his head.

"Trust me, I know. I'm letting him cool off right now because he's not going to hear me while he's this worked up." Ben shuffled over to the armchair and sank down. "And when I tell him what really happened, it's probably going to end things anyway."

He braced himself for the guys to ask, but instead, Callisto just reached over and squeezed his knee. "What can we do? Do you want us to stay, or do you want to wallow? There's no judgment either way."

Ben let out a tense laugh, then stood up. "Fuck it. Beers on the boat?"

Callisto grinned and followed suit, pulling Andrew up from the cushion. "Come on. Beers on the boat."

Two hours later, Ben was buzzed, which was the worst state of mind he could be in because all he wanted was Paris. He wanted to curl up in his arms and let Paris hold him through the fear of what might be coming. And he knew damn well it wasn't his fault that Paris had seen him and Theo and gotten the wrong idea. Ben wasn't sorry for comforting his friend or himself, really.

He was slightly irritated that Paris had jumped to conclusions and wouldn't give him even a scrap of trust that he wasn't the kind of man who would hurt him so cruelly. He understood Paris's issues, but he was starting to realize this was their reality. This was Paris's reality. Trauma didn't get better just because he made him a blanket fort and took him on a toy store shopping spree.

There was no amount of Red Rope licorice and snow cones that would erase the scars of what had been done to him since he was a small child. And the truth was, Ben needed to decide if he had the patience and the strength to stay with Paris while he continued to work on himself.

It was a tough decision, but it was a realistic one.

"Do you feed these fuckers?"

Ben looked up to see Andrew standing a few feet away from the larger iguana that was perched on the bow, and he managed a dry laugh. "No. But I think they keep most of the really annoying pests from making a home on here, so I don't really discourage them."

"Do you think it would bite me if I tried to pet it?"

Callisto was on his feet immediately, drawing Andrew away while using his best dad voice on him. "We don't touch the nasty lizards, Andrew. Sit down and keep your hands to yourself."

"Yes, Dad," Andrew groused.

Callisto rolled his eyes as he dropped onto the bench near Ben and knocked their ankles together. "That's the first thing you've said in forty-five minutes. Is this helping at all?"

Ben let out a slow breath, then nodded. "Yeah. I think I was going to drive myself up the wall if I stayed inside all night and thought about all the what-ifs."

Callisto grimaced. "Yeah. Been there."

Ben picked at his cuticles. "Was it like that with your ex?"

Biting his cheek so hard it went a bit concave, Callisto's eyes moved a bit more frantically back and forth, which happened when he got stressed. "Yes and no. We tried to make it work for too long, so by the time he took off, I think losing our routine hurt more than losing him. But," Callisto added, "I remember when I realized I'd fallen out of love with him, and that felt really strange."

"I definitely haven't fallen out of love," Ben said. "I just don't know if I can do this again."

"Do what?" Callisto asked.

Ben glanced at Andrew, who was typing furiously on his phone, then looked back over at Callisto. "I know this won't be the first time something like this goes down. He's fragile, and I'm inexperienced. I don't want to be chasing him across the fucking islands every time he gets the wrong idea."

"You need to tell him that. My worst mistake with Kye was not telling him when things started to get bad."

"Do you think it would have made a difference?" Ben asked.

Callisto smiled softly and shook his head. "No. He wanted to have a kid because he thought he could gay-parent baby-trap me. I didn't realize it at the time, but I should have when he absolutely refused to donate his sperm or when he missed all the donor selection appointments. He was happy to write checks to our surrogate, but he never looked at the ultrasound photos and never wanted to go baby shopping."

"Shit," Ben said.

Callisto let out a slightly bitter laugh. "Yeah. Eva had just moved in next door, and when I told her about the baby, she threw us a baby shower. Kye said he was excited about it, but two days before, he disappeared on me. Literally. He didn't answer his phone, and no one knew where the fuck he was. I went to the damn thing thinking he was lying in a ditch somewhere. Then he comes back a day and a half later, telling me he ran into an old friend and lost track of time."

"Jesus," Ben breathed out.

Callisto's smile softened. "I got Lila out of it, so I don't really regret what happened, but I should have ended it then. I should have just told him how I felt. We would have fought, and he would have left me, and it would have saved me two years of being married to a person who only wanted me because he saw me as a possession."

Ben wanted to put his arms around his friend and hold him, but he wasn't sure how Callisto felt about that, and honestly, he'd already been in a compromising position because of his need to make everyone else around him feel better. He remembered Levi once warning him that one day his martyr shit was going to bite him in the ass, and he had to wonder if this was it.

"Hey, Ben?"

His thoughts were interrupted by Andrew, who was standing up by the railing, looking a little nervous. 'What's up?' Ben asked, flicking his fingers up his chest.

Andrew bit his lip, then let out a short breath. "Max is here. He just texted me asking me if he could come out."

Dread crawled up Ben's spine. "Shit. What does he want?"

"To talk to you," Andrew said with a shrug. "I told him if he even thinks about being a dick, I will deck him in his fucking face and throw him into the canal. I've been here a long goddamn time, and if he thinks he can come here and fuck with you, I will turn the entire island against him."

Ben felt a sudden rush of warmth because Andrew had always felt a bit like a fair-weather sort of friend. He wasn't sure how to feel realizing that Andrew actually cared about him. He stood up and hugged his middle. "I'll talk to him. But maybe you two can hang out for a bit longer?"

"We'll wait inside. Just yell if you need us," Callisto said. He dropped his hand to Ben's arm just as Max appeared along the walkway to the dock. "But we can stay closer if you want."

"I'm not here to cause a scene," Max said, obviously hearing Callisto.

Ben hesitated, but eventually, he waved his two friends off. "Go. I'll come inside in a bit." He watched them walk off, hyperaware of Max in his periphery as his maybe-ex's little brother came closer. His entire body was tense, and his head was starting to hurt from it.

"Are we okay to talk?" Max asked.

Ben snorted. "You didn't exactly give me a choice."

"No, I mean," Max said, then lifted his hands. 'Do you want me to sign?'

"Can you sign well enough to say what you need to say?" Ben challenged.

Max's hands fell to his sides. "Touché. I'm working on it, but yeah. No." He rubbed the back of his neck the way Ben had seen him do several times before, and he wondered if it was a nervous tic. "Can I come up?"

"Yes. But I have a vicious iguana that will literally bite your dick off if you try to come at me," Ben warned.

"Jesus. Why does everyone think I'm the kind of guy who'd hurt you?"

Ben raised a brow. "Because everyone knows you'd do anything to protect your brother."

Max's mouth dropped open, and then it snapped shut. "Okay, that's fair." He sighed as he stepped onto the boat and took a second to get his bearings. Once he was steady, he folded his arms over his chest. "Are you cheating on him?"

"No," Ben said tiredly.

Max studied his face. "Were you making out with Theo?"

"*No*. He was hurting, and I gave him comfort. And frankly, I needed it too. We got bad news tonight."

Max's face fell, but he didn't look surprised. "Fuck. That's what everyone else said. I'm obviously going to take my brother's side in everything, but I also know he's impulsive. And that he's scared shitless of you."

Ben's eyes widened. "He's *scared* of me?"

"Not in a bad way. Not, like..." Max trailed off with a frustrated grunt. "He's not afraid you're a bad guy. He's afraid you're a good one who will hurt him when you realize he's a sorry waste of space."

Ben felt a rush of rage hit him directly in the center of his chest, and he took a threatening step closer to Max. "You know what? *Fuck* you. He's not a waste of space. I can't believe you'd say that shit—"

"No," Max said in a rush, holding out his hands. "Oh my God. *No*. I don't think that about him. He thinks that about himself. I've been trying to tell him that there are good people out there who will love him for the man he is, but he's spent his whole life being hurt by the people who were supposed to protect him."

"I do get that," Ben said, deflating slightly. "It's why I let him go tonight. He wasn't going to hear what I had to say, so there was no point in trying to go after him."

"Yeah," Max said slowly, ruffling his hair, "I don't know if that's exactly true. I'm not gonna pretend like I know how Paris is going to react to anything right now because this shit has never happened before. He has never, ever let someone care about him before."

Ben winced. "I kind of got that too."

Max tried for a smile, and Ben could see him almost manage it. "I think he wanted you to go after him. I think he wants to know someone thinks he's worth it."

Ben's chest started to ache again. "I..." He squeezed his eyes shut and forced himself to speak. "I don't know if I can handle those mind games, Max. I can't resign myself to being tested every time he's insecure."

Max looked sad, but he nodded anyway. "I get that, and I'm not saying you should play them. And that's something he probably needs to hear. I don't think my brother will be like this forever, but he might need someone who's willing to call him out on his bullshit whenever he's acting like a toddler. And he needs it from someone who..."

"Loves him?" Ben chanced when Max hesitated.

Max grinned and shrugged, looking young and a little sheepish. "Yeah."

Ben laughed softly and stared down at his feet. "Well, I do. I'm so fucking in love with him I don't know what to do with myself. But the shit that went down tonight..."

"I don't want to know," Max said, then went quiet until Ben looked back up at him. "You need to hash that out with him. I'm just here to ask—no, fuck, I'm here to *beg* you to give him another chance."

Ben blinked, startled because he'd been pretty sure everyone expected him to do all the begging and apologizing. But maybe he had all these people totally wrong.

"I'm not giving up on him, Max," Ben said after a beat. "But I am taking tonight to get my head on straight."

Max sagged in relief. "Thank you. I know it's probably a giant red flag that your boyfriend's brother is out here asking you all of this, but—"

"I know life is a lot more complicated than that," Ben interrupted. He was exhausted, and now that he'd gotten a little buzzed and hashed things out, he wanted time to just decompress. "Do you mind if I—" He gestured toward the house.

Max quickly shook his head. "Of course. Uh. And I hope to see you around."

Ben nodded and turned on his heel, jumping off the boat and not looking behind to see if Max followed. He went in through his back door, then met Callisto and Andrew in the living room. "I need you both to go."

"Did he say something?" Andrew asked, his voice a low rumble.

"He said a lot of things, and I need to think. Please."

Andrew opened his mouth to argue, but Callisto was immediately on his feet, taking their friend's arm. "Come on. We'll talk to you tomorrow."

Ben gave them a tired smile, then locked the door after them. When he was finally alone, he pulled his processors off again, flopping on his bed, and he pulled his phone close. After a beat, he opened his contacts, and his finger hovered over Paris's name before he moved one message down to Theo's.

Ben: I didn't think tonight could get any worse, but somehow, it did. What do I do?

19

Paris felt like he was walking through quicksand as he made his way to the bike. He hadn't slept for shit and felt a little nervous about riding the damn thing, but he needed to get it to the shop so he could give the keys back to Max. His phone had blown up by the time he made it to the hotel, so after he checked in, he sent a text to his brother saying he was fine, and then he shut the damn thing off.

He knew he had to face the music at the shop, but he also knew the guys would give him whatever space he needed to process. It was the only comfort in the chaos of not actually knowing what had happened and what he wanted to do about it.

Ben had let him go. He'd denied anything happening between him and Theo, but then he'd just let him leave like he meant nothing. Paris didn't want to believe it was an admission of guilt, but if it wasn't that, then it was simply Ben not giving enough of a shit about him to try and make it better.

A still, small voice told him that wasn't exactly true, though. It told him that he was being absolutely irrational about the whole thing, reminding him he hadn't even given Ben a chance to speak. And that little whisper only got louder as he got closer to the shop.

By the time he rolled into the parking lot, it was screaming that he was the one being a moron. He was the one who had walked away without giving Ben the chance he absolutely deserved.

Paris was the one acting like a child.

"Fuck my life," he muttered to himself. He couldn't bring himself to believe that Ben was the sort of person who would hurt Paris so casually and deliberately. He was still just struggling to believe that a man like Ben wanted someone like him—mess and all. It made logical sense to him that Ben would seek comfort in the arms of his former lover to take the edge off how tiring it must be to fall for a man like Paris.

But that wasn't fair to Ben, who had done nothing but be amazing.

God, he needed to fix it. He needed to grovel. Hard.

He glanced at the back door to the shop and didn't know if he had the strength to go in. He had appointments, though, and he couldn't just cancel, so he'd have to check his baggage like a damn adult and get through the day.

Pulling out his phone, he stared at the blank screen, hoping it was going to hold all the secrets to the universe. Instead, it sat quiet in his palm, mocking him.

Just before he pushed the button to turn it on, he heard a deep rumbling voice. "Hey!"

Paris's head whipped to the side, and his eyes widened when he saw him—Theo—walking toward him. His heart began to hammer like it was lodged in his throat, and he braced himself for what was coming.

Theo was unfairly attractive, with wind-swept hair and dark mirrored glasses, and his full lips were pulled into something like a sneer. He came to a stop in front of Paris and took a breath before he began to sign deliberately slowly, 'I need to talk to you.' He made a pinching motion near his throat like he was turning off a switch, and Paris vaguely recalled that from his class as voice-off.

Right. Theo only signed.

'Okay. I'm slow,' Paris offered.

'I know.' To his credit, Theo didn't look offended or upset by it. He just jerked his head to the side of the building where there was an awning that would get them out of the sun.

Paris followed, not sure what the fuck was about to happen. Was Theo about to threaten him? Tell him to back off? Tell him that he was in love with Ben and wanted him back?

He did his best to breathe through his racing heart, but it wasn't helping. He wanted to run. Or scream. Or maybe punch a wall.

He also kind of wanted to cry, which hadn't happened to him in more years than he could count.

He cleared his throat as he took a stand a few feet away from the other man. 'What's up?' He was amazed that his fingers weren't shaking.

Theo let out a small snort. 'Understand me okay?'

Paris nodded.

Theo squared his shoulders, and when he signed, he mouthed the words like Paris was two years old, but it helped him follow along. 'Don't blame Ben. Last night was my fault.'

'How?' Paris couldn't help but ask.

'Bad news. Very bad news,' Theo answered. 'He wants to talk to you about it.'

'You and Ben...'

'No,' Theo signed very quickly, snapping his fingers in the air and making a frustrated sound. 'I love Ben. As a friend. Only friend. Understand?'

Paris did—and he didn't. He understood the concept, but he also couldn't understand how anyone who had been allowed to have Ben in their arms wouldn't be head over fucking heels in love with him. How could Theo let a man like Ben walk away to be taken by some mess like Paris?

'You understand?' Theo repeated.

Paris took a breath, then nodded. 'I understand. I'll see him later. After work.'

Theo looked somewhat mollified by it, and he gave Paris a slow up-and-down look. 'I want to like you.'

Paris let out a sharp laugh, unable to help it. 'Why?'

'Because I love Ben, and he deserves to be happy with you.'

Paris sure as shit wasn't about to try and argue that. He didn't want to give Ben up. He wanted to believe they had a future. 'Will he forgive me?'

'If you have a good apology,' Theo signed with a tiny smirk. 'He likes Better Than Sex cake from Midnight Snack.'

Paris mouthed the letters as Theo signed them, then grinned. 'Okay.'

'Text him. Don't make him suffer all afternoon,' Theo signed. He had to repeat that line a couple of times before Paris got it, but he did with all the patience Paris didn't deserve. Then he reached forward and clapped his shoulder before pulling away. 'You're learning sign for him.'

Paris frowned. 'Yes.'

'No one learns sign for him. It's important.' Theo startled, and Paris realized why a second later when he pulled his phone out of his pocket and frowned at the screen. 'I need to go.'

Paris had a wild need to ask Theo if that was Ben on the other end of that text, but he kept his mouth shut and just watched as Theo walked around the corner and disappeared from view. It took him a moment to get his body to move, but eventually, Paris turned and pulled on the side door, heading into the shop.

There was already music on, and he could hear the low murmur of voices, which immediately stopped when he walked in, and all eyes turned to him. His face felt hot, the tips of his ears burning as he glanced around. Not everyone was there, but the shop was pretty full.

"Um."

Before he could say anything else, Amelia had jumped up from her desk and was quickly hustling him back through the door. "The hell are you doing here?"

Paris stared at her. “I have appointments. I mean, as far as I know, I still work here.” He started to feel a rush of panic. Jesus, had he fucked up that bad? Had Tony messaged him to tell him he was fired?

Amelia sighed and gave him another shove. “Dude, I rescheduled all of them. I thought you’d be kissing and making up with your boyfriend.”

Paris groaned softly and turned, dropping his forehead to the wall. “Everyone knows?”

“No one knows anything. It’s hot gossip, dude. But Andrew told me about last night,” she added very softly. “He hung out at the motel for a while after the party.”

Paris’s head snapped up. “What did he say?”

“That Ben and Theo got some bad news and shit hit the fan. He didn’t give me details since he and Ben are pretty close. But you need to go fix this.”

“I can’t compromise my job,” he started, but she smacked him on the arm.

“Go fix this. Tony all but threatened anyone who let you work today before you and Ben had a talk. It’s fine. All your clients are fine.”

Paris hesitated, but he realized the only thing he wanted to do was find Ben, drop to his knees, and beg him to forgive him for being such a fucking dipshit. “Okay.”

Amelia breathed out a relieved sigh. “Good. Max said he’ll be by with your truck later.”

Paris was half-tempted to go back in and swap with Max now, but he hadn’t seen his brother in his stall, and he didn’t want to wait. This felt like a gift from the universe, and he didn’t get those very often. Racing to the bike, he hopped on and revved the engine, hoping against hope he still had time to fix everything.

Paris rolled to a stop in front of his room, jumping off the bike and taking only a second to make sure it was stable before rushing to the office. He flung the door open and came to a skidding halt in front of a thin guy with dark hair and thick-rimmed, red-tinted glasses.

The guy stared at him, and then his eyes widened behind his lenses. “You aren’t Paris, are you?”

Fantastic. Everyone knew. “Uh. Yeah. Is Ben here?”

“He’s out on the paddleboat, cleaning up trash near the mangroves,” the guy said. “If you want to wait—”

Paris didn’t give him a chance to finish his sentence. He bolted back out the door and ran under the covered parking spots, coming to a halt near the kayaks and paddleboards. Off in the distance, he could see the little paddleboat awning, and then he turned to see that the boards were all unlocked.

“Fuck my fucking life,” he muttered. But he knew what he had to do. Dropping to the ground, he peeled off his boots and socks, tossing them near the kayaks before he grabbed a board and a long paddle.

He was seconds away from dropping it in the water when he heard someone call out, and he turned to see Andrew running toward him.

“Bro. What the fuck?”

Paris dropped the board. “I have to talk to him.”

“You don’t think it can wait?” Andrew asked.

Paris shook his head. “I really don’t think it can wait. Look, charge my room for this or whatever, okay? I...I need to do this now. I’m in love with him, and I need to fix this.”

Andrew’s face instantly softened. “Okay. But be careful, alright? There’s been a bunch of jellyfish sightings here, and a couple people were stung earlier.”

Paris felt fear creeping up his spine, but he decided he cared a lot less about the painful sting than he did about getting to Ben. He set his feet on the board, then wobbled a few times as he looked down.

He couldn't be certain, but he was pretty sure he saw a few globs floating around with their little dick-stinging death tentacles.

But Ben was worth it. He was worth all of it.

Spreading his legs gently the way Ben had shown him, he shoved the paddle into the water, then pushed off from the dock. The board cut through the water easily, and though his arms started to burn after a minute, he could see the boat getting closer.

"Ben!" he called, but there was no response, which meant he was either too far or Ben had taken off his processors.

Paris dug the paddle into the water and pushed harder. Five strokes and he was close enough to see Ben's face. Three more and the tip of his board hit the boat.

Ben let out a startled cry and turned, and his eyes went wide. "What the fuck? *Paris*?"

Paris spread his hands, then wobbled and fell.

Water rushed around him, and he coughed, choking as his feet slid through sand and plant life. He braced himself for the sting as he struggled to break the surface, but nothing happened except a firm hand grabbing his wrist.

He was dragged to a small ladder and managed to make it up onto the back of the paddleboat, coughing half an ocean out of his lungs. That same hand gave his back a couple of firm pats, and when he could see through burning eyes, he met Ben's furious gaze.

"What the fuck are you doing?" Ben demanded.

Paris's shaking hand formed a fist and circled his chest. 'I'm sorry. I'm sorry.'

Ben scoffed and tugged on Paris, pulling him over the seat, then digging into the little console. He came out with a towel and shoved it in Paris's face. "Dry off, asshole."

Paris obeyed, rubbing his face and hair. He felt waterlogged and heavy in his jeans and a little terrified because Ben didn't seem thrilled that he was there, and he wasn't sure if maybe he was making the biggest mistake of his life.

Wiping his face, he chanced a look over, and he saw Ben slipping his processors on.

"You don't have to," Paris said in a rush.

"No," Ben said sharply. "I need to understand you."

Paris nodded, feeling both miserable and more determined than ever to get better at Ben's language. "Okay. Um." He sat up a little straighter and shifted uncomfortably in his wet seat. "Theo came to the shop this morning."

At that, Ben looked murderous. His voice was low and dangerous. "He did *what*?"

Paris held up a hand in surrender. "It was fine."

"You just took a fucking nosedive into the water you swore you'd never touch again," Ben said, throwing up his hands, "so it was definitely not fine."

"It was," Paris said. "Trust me, he didn't say anything I didn't need to hear."

Ben looked dubious, but after a beat, he sagged back and let out a breath. "Yeah, well, I guess I can't be too mad about people putting their noses in our business. Your brother came to see me last night."

Paris sat up straighter. "Please tell me he didn't make you feel like shit."

Ben laughed. "No. He came begging me not to give up on you. Like I needed someone to ask me that."

A dangerous spark of hope lit up under Paris's skin. "Yeah. Uh." He passed a hand down his face and grimaced at how badly his eyes were still stinging from the salt water. "I'm sorry. I'm so fucking sorry for taking off. You deserved better than that."

"Yes, I did," Ben said. His voice was tight with emotion, and Paris hated himself for being the man to cause it.

"You've done nothing but be amazing this entire time, and you deserved the benefit of the doubt." Paris hesitated because everything he wanted to say sounded like he was making excuses or was self-serving bullshit. "I don't know what to say. I've never had to do anything like this before."

After a second, Ben let out the smallest laugh. "Yeah. Me either." He leaned forward between his spread knees, his hands twisting together with his nerves. "There's...fuck. I want to talk this out, but there's something you need to know."

"Wait," Paris said. "I just...I need to know that we're okay. That you can forgive me. I swear I will do everything in my power not to pull something like that again. I can't...fuck. I don't want to lose you. I lo—"

"Don't," Ben interrupted, and Paris's heart threatened to crack because he didn't have to fall in love to know what that look on Ben's face meant.

"Please," Paris whispered.

Ben shook his head. "You can't say it until you hear me first."

Paris took in a fortifying breath. "Okay. Okay, just...please know I do."

Ben squeezed his eyes shut, and the smallest sob escaped his chest. "Yeah. Yeah, I figured. Um." He cleared his throat, then scrubbed both hands over his face before looking over at Paris. "Theo asked to meet me last night because he just tested positive."

"Positi—oh," Paris said. His heart began to hammer against his chest. "Are you...?"

"I don't know. There's a clinic that offers free testing, so I'm going to head over there this afternoon." Ben's voice trembled, and he took another long breath. "I was always careful when we were together. We always used condoms, and I'm on PrEP, but...you know..."

"Yeah," Paris breathed out. He felt a small tremor of fear racing through him because while things were tough now, that could disrupt everything. And then he realized why Ben was so afraid to hear the words he'd wanted to say. Paris quickly met his gaze. "Ben, that doesn't change anything. I love you."

For a second, it felt like the whole world stopped. There wasn't a single noise, a single movement, a single breath.

Then Ben shifted in his seat. "Paris..."

"I love you," he said again. He could count on two hands how many times he'd said those three words since his mom died. "I'm falling in love with you. I know it's only been a couple of weeks, and I know I majorly fucked up last night. And I know you're scared because this is a fucking terrifying thing, but it doesn't change how I feel."

Ben dropped his head, and after a second, Paris realized he was crying. He panicked for a second because he could barely handle his own emotions, and he had no idea what Ben needed. Comfort? Or to be left alone? Was it all too much for him?

Ben looked over after a second and gave a watery laugh. "I'm sorry."

Paris blinked at him. "What the hell for?"

"Falling apart," Ben offered.

Paris groaned, then reached out, and in spite of the console between them, he managed to get his hands cupped around Ben's face, holding him as tenderly as he could. "Don't you fucking dare. This was my mistake—my mess. I should have been there for you last night, and instead, I acted like a goddamn toddler." Ben started to shake his head, but Paris's grip prevented him from doing it. "Baby. My love," he murmured.

Ben let out another choked noise, and one fat tear rolled down his cheek.

"I'm gonna make up for it. Can we go back now, or do you need to finish up here?"

Ben's laugh was thready and weak, but he bit his lip and nodded. "We can go back. Let me tether the paddleboard first."

Paris didn't bother offering to help since he knew he'd just make the situation worse, and instead, he sat, soggy and uncomfortable in his seat while Ben chased down the board and paddle, then got them attached to the little boat.

The ride back to the dock was a little tense, but Paris was grateful there wasn't an audience hanging around to watch. Ben docked next to the stairs, then offered Paris a hand up as they both set foot on dry land.

"You should rinse off while I check on stuff in the office," Ben told him quietly. "Want me to meet you at your place?"

"Yes," Paris said. He took a step closer, then hesitated. "Can I—"

The unspoken part of his question was answered as Ben surged forward and met Paris's lips with his own. The kiss was chaste, salty, and cold, but it was also healing. It was a promise of more to come, no matter what happened down the line.

As they broke away, Paris felt the warmth in his chest burrow deeper, surrounding his heart. He made a promise right there to himself that no matter what happened, he would always make sure he was never the reason Ben was in pain. Ever again.

20

Ben was grateful that no one asked any questions when he popped into the office, though it was obvious from the expression on Andrew's face that he knew Paris had come back. He didn't have anything to do, but he needed a second to himself before he faced reality with Paris.

He'd told himself the night before he wasn't going to just jump in and forgive Paris the second he saw him, but the moment his eyes fell on the man who immediately toppled into the water, it was over.

Paris had won.

Ben was too deeply in love with him to pretend otherwise.

And it might have felt worse if Paris hadn't opened himself up the way he had, taking accountability for everything he'd done wrong. Ben had his own apology to make because Max was right—Ben could have gone after him. And maybe if it hadn't been for Theo's news, he would have. But Ben resolved to make sure that Paris knew he would fight for him—for them—if something like this happened in the future.

He wasn't going to give up because Paris got it wrong once or twice. Hell, he wouldn't give up even if Paris got it wrong a dozen more times after this. Yes, he wouldn't allow himself to become a doormat. He was done with that bullshit. But that didn't mean Paris didn't deserve his patience as he worked to become the man he wanted to be.

And Ben got a tiny thrill that he got to be the one to see it. To be the one who was loved by him.

Sitting at his desk, he felt the weight of his appointment coming —and the knowledge that things might change. But he also felt lighter because Paris knew, and he hadn't run. He hadn't panicked or gotten angry. He'd just held Ben while he fell apart, then promised to be there for him as he needed.

He felt a bit like crying again, but he bit the inside of his cheek until the feeling passed, and then he stood up from his desk and pretended like he'd been doing actual work instead of getting lost in his feelings. Pushing the door open, he swiped the master key from the desk, not looking at either Aya or Andrew as he exited the lobby as fast as his legs would carry him.

He took a few seconds at Paris's door before swiping the key, then let himself in and heard the faint sound of the shower running. Ben hesitated before walking to the bathroom door and managed to kick his shoes off before stepping in.

"Ben?" Paris asked, sticking his head out of the fogged glass door.

Ben bit his lip as he watched water slide down like tiny rivers over Paris's inked skin. "Um. Do you want some company?" He knew what he was asking—the weight of it. Now with Theo's news between them, there was more to consider.

But Paris didn't hesitate. "Please."

Ben's hands trembled as he pulled off his clothes, and he set everything neatly on the counter before taking off his processors. The world faded into immediate silence, and all he was left with was the tendril of steam wafting over his skin and the vibration of the water as it hit the tiles. Paris's warm, wet hand curled around his wrist as he tugged, and Ben came to a stop in front of him as the shower stream cascaded over his shoulders.

Paris said nothing for a long while. He just stared, his gaze moving over Ben's skin like he was taking him in. Then he shuffled close and hooked a finger under his chin, lifting his face for a kiss. It was heavy—full of unspoken emotions that they still needed to deal with. Ben couldn't quite shake the fear of what was coming that afternoon, but he could breathe a little easier with Paris's hands on him.

When he was backed against the wall and kissed, Ben let himself open to it. He let himself feel the tongue moving against his own, and the way Paris's thumb and finger pinched his chin to keep his lips parted, and the way Paris's other hand gripped his waist almost bruisingly tight, like he was afraid if he let go, Ben would disappear.

Ben lost himself to Paris's body pressing against his, basking in just being there as the water kept them warm, and Paris's arms kept him safe. He wasn't hard, and when he shifted and felt Paris's cock, he realized his lover wasn't either.

This was just a moment to exist with each other and let the dark clouds that had been hovering over them since the night before start to drift away.

When Ben could think straight, he eased Paris back, then lifted his hand between them, curling his middle and ring finger toward his palm. 'I love you.'

Paris looked down, and Ben could see his chest hitch before he curled a touch around Ben's wrist and lifted the sign to his lips. He pressed a kiss to the tip of each finger, then to the back of his hand, then to the inside of his wrist before he signed the words back.

'I love you.'

Ben swallowed heavily, then nodded and reached for the knob to turn the water off. They parted long enough to get dried and dressed, and then Paris took Ben's hand and pulled him to the sofa. He left his processors on the counter, but he didn't have the energy to go get them, and Paris didn't seem to expect him to.

He just curled his feet up on the coffee table and twisted his body to face Ben. 'Are you okay?'

Ben made a seesaw gesture with his hand. 'Sort of. I'm afraid.' He watched Paris mouth along with the signs. 'I'm tired.'

'Me too.' Paris's shoulders shook with a gentle laugh as he moved his hand between them. 'Appointment,' he spelled. 'When?'

Ben shrugged. 'Whenever. It's open all day.'

Paris bit his bottom lip, then nodded. 'Now?'

He did and didn't want to get it over with. There was some small comfort in not knowing, because once the test was done, he couldn't take it back. His current ignorance had no bliss, but there was something to be said about being ignorant for a little while.

All the same, he owed it to himself. And to Theo. And to Paris.

Standing up, he went back to the bathroom and put his processors on, then walked back out to find Paris slipping into his boots. He cleared his throat as he adjusted back to sound, then asked, "What if it's positive?"

"Then we figure it out," Paris said, looking up at him. He had his hands clasped between his parted knees, and his eyes were heavy-lidded and sincere. "I meant what I said on the boat, baby. I'm in love with you, and I'm in this. We talk to a doctor, and we figure out how to have everything we want and stay as safe as we can."

"But the risk," Ben started, then went quiet when Paris stood up and grabbed him by the waist.

"We talk to a doctor and figure out how to have everything we want and stay as safe as we can," Paris repeated, lower and slower. "My heart hurts for Theo, and my heart hurts that you're scared. But I'm with you, okay? I'm here. I fucked up last night, and I'm going to be working on that, but a future with you—whatever the fuck it looks like—I want it. I'm not running."

Ben closed his eyes, then surged in for a kiss and let the warm feeling in his chest carry him through the next long moment.

Ben was not a huge fan of motorcycles, but it was all Paris had, and he didn't think he could concentrate well enough to drive. The appointment itself hadn't taken long, and the nurse said his results would be emailed to him as soon as they were in. He and Paris took both tests to be safe, and now he had to play the waiting game.

His nerves were shot, and he didn't realize they'd passed the turn for the motel until Paris turned into the parking lot for Midnight Snack. Ben frowned as they rolled to a stop, and he tapped Paris on the shoulder when he turned the bike off.

'Why?'

'Theo,' Paris spelled, 'said you like chocolate cake.'

Ben rolled his eyes with a groan as he fished his processor box out of his pocket and palmed it. Of fucking course Theo would spill all of his secrets. Ben wasn't exactly in the mood to be social with the small population of Key Largo, but the idea of Jeremiah's Better Than Sex cake was more than appealing.

He wanted to curl up and eat his feelings and hide under his blanket until he and Paris got their results in. Paris would have to retest in a month, the nurse told him, but while Ben thought that might finally set Paris off, he just took the news with a calm nod, and he squeezed Ben's hand during the blood draw.

'Come on,' Paris signed when Ben hesitated at the door.

Ben debated about asking to get their food to go, but he decided he could do this with Paris. He slipped his processors on as they walked in, and he was relieved to see the place mostly dead. He spotted Jeremiah at the host stand, and he smiled as they approached.

"Hey, man."

Jeremiah looked up, squinted, then smiled. "Yo. I don't usually see you on weekdays."

Ben shrugged. "Yeah, well. It's been kind of a messy one. We're here for cake."

Jeremiah offered a small grin as he waved his hand toward the dining room. "Sit wherever. Preferably by the window so I can find you," he added with a grin.

Ben was one of the few people who knew that Jeremiah was losing his sight, and he only knew because he'd run into Jeremiah a few months ago eating cake behind his shop, crying into his to-go box. Ben couldn't exactly relate because he'd been deaf as long as he could really remember, but he could be a decent friend who was happy to sit and share cake while Jeremiah poured his heart out.

They weren't exactly besties who had sleepovers now, but Ben liked him.

"Let's sit there," Ben said, pointing to the corner table that was half-in and half-out of the sun. "Which seat do you want?"

Paris leaned in, dropping a kiss to his neck. "You choose," he rumbled.

Heat traveled up Ben's spine, and he sank backward against Paris for a long second before choosing the seat in the shade and sitting down. He glanced up at Paris's small grin as his lover took a seat, and for a moment, he forgot everything except how in love he was.

"So," Paris said when he got settled, "you know the owner?"

Ben rolled his eyes. "Please tell me you're not jealous."

Paris grinned. "I don't understand any single, available person who isn't fucking obsessed with you, but no. I'm more excited for cake."

Ben laughed, covering his mouth to hide how loud it sounded. "You're unreal."

"But you love me," Paris fired back, then froze like he was realizing just then that it was true. "You love me," he repeated.

Ben lifted his hand and signed it to him, and Paris licked his lips, looking vaguely terrified and also a bit hopeful. "Anyway, Jeremiah and I don't know each other that well, but we do have a bond over cake. And he is single, and I'm pretty sure he's bi, but it's never been like that."

Paris rested his elbow on the table and lifted one hand. 'Not worried.'

'Liar,' Ben fired back, and when Paris gave a confused frown, Ben spelled it for him. For that, he earned himself a middle finger, and he laughed. "I don't mind if you're possessive. Just as long as you trust me."

Paris's face fell a bit, and he nodded. "I do. And I'm—"

"Don't say sorry."

"But I am," Paris argued. "It's going to take me a while to stop feeling like I need to say it. I'm so goddamn mortified about how I acted."

Ben didn't really know what to say. It had been hell on earth watching Paris fall apart under his jealousy and suspicion when Ben needed him, but he also didn't want it to define their future. "Can we make a rule?"

Paris nodded. "Anything."

"Can we agree that you can have one apology a day—and only if you feel like you need to say it—for two weeks. After that, you have to wean yourself off."

Paris groaned, but he was clearly trying to fight a smile. "Fine."

"And I get to remind you every time you say sorry that I forgive you, that I accept your apology, and that I believe in all the work you've put into yourself since you moved here."

"I," Paris started, then stopped. "That's a lot."

"I know," Ben told him. "But it's true."

Before Paris could say anything back, Jeremiah appeared with a monster-sized piece of cake. He gave Ben a wink as he set it between them with two forks. "Drinks? Do you need something boozy?"

"I'm driving," Paris said, "but if you want something, babe, go for it."

Jeremiah's grin widened. "Babe?"

"He's my boyfriend," Ben said, then jolted in his seat because as ridiculous as it was, they hadn't had the talk. Maybe it was fair to assume since they'd said I love you, but...

"I could come up with something sappier and grosser," Paris said as he picked up his fork, "but I feel like you might have a monopoly on clever names."

Jeremiah laughed loudly and smacked the side of Paris's arm with the back of his hand. "I like you. I mean, I like your whole crew, and not because they're going to put all my future kids through college."

Paris snorted around a bite of the cake, then trailed off with a groan that was frankly obscene. "Is this why they call it Better Than Sex?"

"It's why they call my version that," Jeremiah told him. "Anyway, I'll let you two lovebirds enjoy."

"Not clever enough," Paris called after him.

Jeremiah took two steps away. "Give me a couple of days and I'll thoroughly humiliate you both."

Ben started to smile as he reached for his fork, but his phone buzzed. He glanced down at it absently, and then his heart jolted in his chest when he saw the clinic name on the screen. Fuck. Fucking... fuck. The nurses weren't kidding about the rapid part of rapid results.

"Babe?"

Ben swallowed heavily and looked up. "It's the clinic."

"Breathe," Paris said. He stood up and dragged his chair to the side of the table, reaching for Ben and cupping his cheeks as he sat back down. "Another breath."

Ben tried to obey, but his lungs felt like they were filled with ocean water.

"Do you want me to look?"

Ben tried to speak, but he couldn't, so he nodded his fist and pushed the phone over toward his boyfriend.

Paris picked it up, and Ben pretended not to see that his fingers were shaking a bit as he tapped the email twice. His eyes moved across the screen, and Ben felt like he was going to lose his mind. "Fucking say something. Please."

"I..." Paris swallowed. "Negative."

Ben felt like he was going to pass out. "Negative?"

Paris nodded and set the phone down carefully and deliberately. "Take a drink of water, Ben."

Ben did, though it was difficult to do it with the way he was trembling. He wanted to laugh, then cry, then scream, then run and dive straight into the damn ocean.

He did none of those things.

"I still have to wait for the second test."

Paris reached for him again, cupping his cheek with one hand and dragging a touch over his lower lip. "I know."

"And I have to go back in a month with you to be sure," Ben added.

Paris's lips formed a small smile. "I know. But right now, this is celebration cake, okay?"

Ben nodded, and he let Paris dig his fork into the soft chocolate, then press the bite to his lips. It went down a little thick and almost too rich, but then Paris kissed the taste of it out of his mouth, and it became absolutely fucking perfect.

21

Paris glanced up at Miguel, who spritzed some witch hazel over his new ink, then gently wiped it down with the paper towel. It was fascinating from an almost clinical standpoint to watch Miguel work with his nondominant hand. It was clear he'd been working that way for a long time because although his work was abstract, it was still put together with a skill and talent very few people in the industry had.

"What do you think?" Miguel asked.

Paris sat up and ran his thumb around the edge of his hip. "Fucking amazing, bro. Thanks. It sucks that y'all have to go back."

Miguel pulled a face. "It's home, man. But trust me, when they see the fucking museum's worth of pictures Amit took, especially all that shit he got while we were snorkeling, you won't be able to keep the guys out of your shop."

"Well, when Ben and I start thinking about a mountain getaway, you know where we'll be headed," Paris told him.

Miguel's face softened, making him look a bit less murdery. "I fuckin' hope so. This shit better go both ways."

Paris felt those words hit him right in the sternum. People had said stuff like that to him before, but he never took them seriously. He never actually believed anyone wanted him around. The last month had changed nearly everything, and he wasn't quite sure how to process it yet.

Swinging his leg over the side, he let Miguel snap a couple of photos of the inkblot piece, and then he reached for the Saniderm and spread a layer over his skin.

"Your boy gonna let you give him his first ink?" Miguel asked as he poured some of the ink solidifier into his water cup.

Paris stood up, stretching his legs out before grabbing his sweats off the end of his bench. "He's kind of weird about needles." It was a half-truth. Although they'd gotten Ben's second set of negative results, he was still nervous about contamination, and Paris was going to indulge him for as long as he needed.

"Yeah, but fuck. A literal blank canvas," Miguel said. "Don't tell me you don't got ideas for it."

Paris laughed and rolled his eyes as he hopped on one leg, then the other, to get his pants on. "Probably better if you don't ask."

"I bet," Miguel said with a grin.

Max's head popped up over his partition. "Can you two shut the fuck up about my brother and clearly what's happening with his dick?"

"I vote keep going," came Harley's low rumble, and Paris could hear his client cackling.

"I vote all of you mind your fucking business and stop thinking about my dick or my boyfriend's body," Paris fired back.

Max's grin softened. "Your boyfriend," he said in a near whisper.

Paris wanted to punch him for it, but he understood why it made Max so damn happy. Hell, it made him happy. He was riding a small high now that things were calmer, and though they planned to keep testing every so often for the rest of the year, they were both breathing easier.

Ben was hurting for Theo, of course, and Paris had long since stopped panicking that there was anything between them anymore. In fact, he was starting to really like the guy now that Paris's signing was getting more fluid, and he could carry on a conversation when Theo visited.

Theo was struggling because while he was doing well on his medication, it was affecting his ability to fly, and he was struggling with what his future held. That was why Paris was getting a tattoo at the moment. Theo was having an off day, and Paris insisted Ben spend time with him to take his mind off it.

It felt good to feel secure. It wasn't all the time, and Paris still struggled, but he and Ben were getting ready to look at a house, and God, he was starting to see the picture of the future so damn clearly.

"You're so gross now that you've started smiling," Max said, flopping back down behind his wall.

Paris rolled his eyes and laughed when Miguel slung an arm around him. "I think he's a beautiful son of a bitch, and we should spend more time encouraging him."

"You're only saying that because you're leaving tomorrow and you don't have to help move all their shit," Harley pointed out.

Miguel spread his arms in a shrug. "What can I say. I'm just lucky."

Paris shoved him away and walked over to the counter to collect his keys and his phone. There was a message waiting for him on the screen from Ben, just a little less-than-three to remind him he was loved. He shoved his phone into his pocket and turned back to Miguel. "We'll talk soon, yeah? There's a fuckload of conventions out this way, so I hope you guys make plans."

"You know it," Miguel told him. "We're kind of like a bed bug infestation, and it'll only get worse the more people who keep showing up to visit."

"You're so fucking weird," Max called from his stall.

Miguel grinned again. "Just like Zeke. Fucker has his own shop but can't keep away from the mountains. Bet a hundred bucks we'll all end up trading one day."

Paris didn't actually hate the idea of living in the mountains one day. His heart belonged to the sea, but he also knew that Ben's long-term plan wasn't to run a small motel in the Keys. Ben was still dealing with grief, and still trying to find where he belonged, but Paris could sense the need to wander in him, and he was starting to feel it too.

There were years ahead of them to settle in here, but there was nothing standing in their way. Paris no longer stayed up all night worrying about his brother and what would happen to him if they were ever separated. And when that tiny voice in his head whispered that he was nothing more than a broken shell of a man, another voice in his head—one that sounded like Ben's rough rumble—told it to shut the fuck up.

He took that feeling with him as he got into his truck and headed back to the motel, and he went right for his room since Ben had all but moved in. He couldn't remember the last time they'd slept apart, and he was looking forward to making it official.

Tossing his keys on the table, Paris flicked the light switch, and Ben's face appeared around the kitchen corner. He grinned, wiping wet hands on his jeans. 'How was it?'

Paris smiled and jerked his head for Ben to come over. 'Want to take my pants off and find out?'

Ben rolled his eyes, but he did just that. His fingers hooked into Paris's waistband and tugged both the sweats and the boxers to his feet. Paris laughed as Ben ghosted a hand over his limp dick, then took a step back to admire the handiwork. It wasn't as clear as it had been in the shop, the ink already leaking a bit into the shield, but Ben still grinned.

'Beautiful.'

'Thank you,' Paris signed, then tugged Ben into a kiss. Their tongues tangled hotly, and after a second, Paris's exposed cock started to get interested. Ben glanced down, then laughed lowly as he sucked a bite against Paris's collarbone.

'Bed?' Ben's free hand asked.

Paris nodded, tripping over his pants and boxers as he tried to follow, and he shook them off, going for his shirt as Ben started to strip in the doorway as he made his way toward the bed. Paris hung back just long enough for Ben's jeans to hit the floor before he was on him, grabbing him by the back of the neck and urging him to grip the side of the mattress.

'Okay?' Paris asked him, moving his hand into Ben's periphery. Fucking like this—without voice and without sound—was part of the new language Paris was learning, but it was no hardship to train himself to read Ben's body.

He was finely tuned in to every twitch, every gasp, every frown, every time Ben parted his lips or arched for more touch. He had been afraid he would need to check in so often it would kill the mood, but his fears were unfounded.

Ben nodded, then tipped his head back, letting Paris hold him by the front of the throat so he could kiss him. He lingered that way for a long time, then pulled back and laid a sharp slap to the side of Ben's ass. 'Stay.'

Ben's chest flushed red as Paris walked over to the nightstand to get what they needed. He dropped the condom and lube on the duvet and held the plug in his hand. Ben braced himself on his elbows as Paris ran the toy along his spine, then circled his hole before quickly grabbing the small bottle and giving it a thick coating of slick.

Ben let out a sharp pant as Paris pushed the toy inside him, and when it was nestled inside, his firm hands twisted Ben around, then sat him down. He let out a groan, and Paris knew the thing had hit his prostate.

'Hold still, gorgeous,' Paris signed, then spread Ben's legs wide. He dragged the tips of his fingers up his thighs, then curled them around his balls. His own dick ached as he watched Ben rock himself on the plug, trying to regain that friction, and he stroked Ben from root to tip.

Precome dribbled from his slit, and Paris dragged his thumb through it, feeding it to Ben and getting harder with each thrum of his pulse as Ben's tongue swirled around his digit.

'Please,' Ben begged, his flat hand circling his chest. 'I want you.'

Paris grinned and stroked him—still too slow for Ben to reach any kind of conclusion but just enough to drive him wild. 'I know you do.' He shifted closer and urged Ben to lean back. 'I love you.'

The faint color rose from Ben's chest to his neck. It always drove him wild whenever Paris said it while they were fucking. He knew Ben had spent his entire adult life waiting for those words to mean something to him, and now they did.

They meant the world to both of them, and Paris would make sure Ben spent every day knowing he would not just die for him, but he would live for him.

His hand moved to the plug, and he began to fuck it in and out of Ben's hole, sharp and rough, just the way he liked it. It dragged desperate moans from Ben's chest as he squirmed and begged wordlessly with soft noises and babbling hands until Paris finally took pity on him and pulled it out.

He had the condom on in seconds, slicking himself up before tugging Ben back off the bed and spinning him. He gripped his lover's soft curls as Ben braced himself on his elbows and stuck his ass out, and Paris guided himself to the waiting hole. He tested the looseness with his thumb, making Ben groan before he pushed the head in, and then there was silence apart from their stuttered breath as Paris pushed home in a single slide.

A beat passed, then two, and then Ben fucked his hips backward, and Paris rumbled a half shout while pleasure coursed through him. His skin felt alight as Ben's ass squeezed him tightly, and he met Ben thrust for thrust, losing himself in the sight of his lover's hips and the sound of skin slapping against skin.

"Uhg," Ben said, dropping his head lower so he could arch his back deeper. He was searching for the right angle, and Paris knew how to give it to him. He gripped Ben by the hips, stepped in close, and thrust down. Hard.

Ben let out a noise like he was dying, and his knees began to tremble. Paris kept up the furious, hard thrusts as he wrapped his hand around Ben's middle and found his cock. Ben gave an even louder, wounded noise as Paris started to stroke him, and it wasn't long before he was clenching around Paris's dick and letting go.

Come spilled in short, hot ropes over Paris's fist, and as soon as he started to make a noise of protest, Paris let him go and chased his own climax. He dug fingers deep into Ben's hips as he lost control of his rhythm. His eyes slammed shut, and he focused on how tight Ben was, how warm, how perfect. How much he was fucking in love with him.

And then, he fell.

Paris came to on his side, wrapped tightly around Ben's back, his lover chuckling softly as he traced a soft touch over Paris's arm. When Paris shifted, Ben's palm moved against his, repeating shapes until Paris's fucked-out brain was able to put the letters together.

'I L O V E Y O U.'

Paris gently slipped out, gripping the condom and tying it off to prevent a mess, then threw it somewhere in the direction of the bin with one hand while the other tugged and pulled at Ben until he was able to roll over. Face-to-face, Paris locked a leg around Ben's hips, then traced a touch over his jawline, his nose, his lips. His skin was flushed and hot, soft near his cheeks, rough over his five-o'clock shadow.

He leaned in and took a slow, steady kiss that pulsed with their rapid heartbeats. When he pulled back, Ben took Paris's hand and pressed it against his chest so he could feel the in and out of his breath.

'You're my forever,' Ben's free hand signed in the shallow space between them.

Paris took that hand, kissing his palm, then the inside of his wrist before letting go to tell him in the same words, 'And you're mine.'

Click HERE to subscribe to EM Lindsey's newsletter and get a copy of Housekeeping, a hotter than hot Fine Line deleted chapter.

HEAVY HAND

Please enjoy this sneak peek of Heavy Hand, the next book in the Irons and Works: Key Largo series.
Order now!

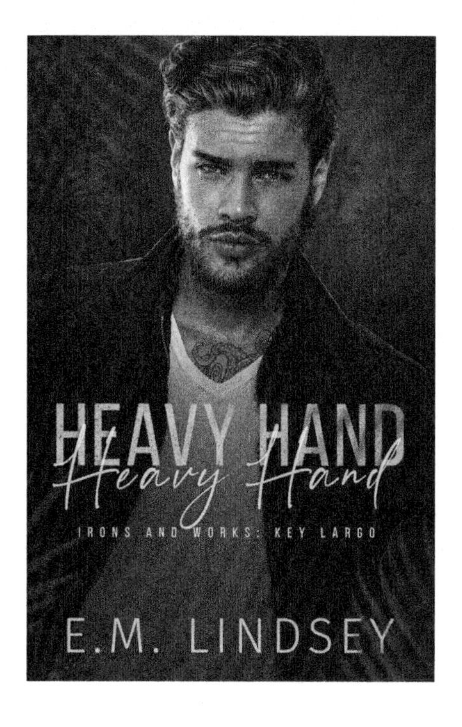

"So, can we talk about the storm chasing thing?"

Jeremiah sighed quietly. "Most people want to."

"Yikes. Okay. New topic."

"No, no," he said in a rush. "Sorry, I'm being a dick. It's just...it was a weird job, but I fucking loved it, and giving it up killed me."

Out of the corner of his eye, he could see Max frown. "Why did you? Like, I saw this Ted Talk with this astrophysicist who was totally blind, right? And she seemed like a science-nerd badass who worked at a university or something."

Jeremiah offered a wry grin. He knew who Max was talking about. "Yep. And she has a metric shitload of funding for her equipment. We could barely get an annual grant to keep us from going homeless every year. And honestly, I had no idea how bad my vision was going to get. The stress of not knowing was affecting my work." He fiddled with the edge of the box before setting it aside and grabbing another one. It popped open easier this time, and he ate one of the buns before he spoke again. "Plus, my ex was on my team and working with him every season just wasn't something I could keep doing."

"I get that. I mean...I don't get that," Max amended quickly. "I've never had a boyfriend, but I can't imagine what it would be like to go from loving someone to not loving them anymore and having to be around them all the time."

Jeremiah felt a rush of shock as he turned to face Max. "You've never had a boyfriend?"

Max shook his head. "No. Uh...remember how I casually mentioned childhood trauma?"

Jeremiah nodded, trying not to look like he pitied the guy because he didn't.

"It took me years to work through it, and I know I'll never really be done, you know...healing, or whatever. But I used to have a really hard time setting boundaries and saying no. I felt like I had to make everyone around me happy or they'd leave."

"Shit," Jeremiah said.

Max let out a slightly bitter laugh. "I know. A real catch, right?"

Unable to stop himself, Jeremiah set the box aside, then turned his body and reached for Max. He kept his touch light, his palms barely pressing against Max's warm, rough cheeks. His thumbs grazed his short, coarse hair growing along his jawline.

"You are."

Max swallowed so heavily, Jeremiah could hear it catch in his throat. "You're sweet."

"Just honest," he deflected. He shifted closer, trying not to knock everything over with his feet, but he felt a sudden desperation to be close to this man. He wanted to give Max at least one night where he felt important and beautiful.

Because he was.

"I didn't have any expectations when I suggested we come back here," he said softly.

"But?" Max pressed.

Jeremiah ducked his head to try and hide his grin. "But I hoped."

"Yeah?"

"Yes." He lifted his head again and turned his eyes to the side so he could see as much of Max as he could. His lips were full and pink and wet from where he'd licked them, his nose round at the tip, eyes a bright green under thick black brows.

He was maybe one of the most gorgeous men Jeremiah had ever seen.

And fuck, his skin was so warm.

"You can tell me to stop at any time, but I'd really like to fool around."

"Does that mean fuck?" Max asked, shifting closer and curling his fingers around one of Jeremiah's wrists. "Because I'd *really* like to fuck. I've been thinking about it non-stop since we were in line together."

"Jesus," Jeremiah breathed out. He nodded, then opened his mouth to say something, but he found it impossible as Max pressed their lips together. His short scruff tickled the bottom of Jeremiah's nose, but it was easy to ignore the sensation as he let Max's tongue slide past his lips—warm and velvet soft against his own. He tasted sweet like the barbeque sauce, and a little herby from the fresh sprigs of cilantro, and he felt like he could drown in that sensation forever.

ALSO BY E.M. LINDSEY

Broken Chains

The Carnal Tower

Hit and Run

Irons and Works

The Sin Bin: West Coast

Malicious Compliance

Collaborations with Other Authors

Foreign Translations

AudioBooks

ABOUT THE AUTHOR

E.M. Lindsey is a non-binary writer who lives in the southeast United States, close to the water where their heart lies.

Join EM Lindsey at their newsletter or join their Patreon and get access to ARCs, teasers, free short stories, and more.

Printed in Great Britain
by Amazon

37227030R00136